DIVINE DECEPTION
Blind Faith. False Prophets.

A JESSICA JANSEN THRILLER

SONNY HUDSON

ISBN 979-8-9931660-01 (eReader)
ISBN 979-8-9931660-1-8 (Hardback)
ISBN 979-8-9931660-2-5 (Paperback)

"The Bible is full of warnings about false prophets and false messiahs. These satanically inspired people have appeared in almost every generation of history."

Billy Graham

"Fear prophets and those prepared to die for the truth, for as a rule they make many others die with them, often before them, at times instead of them."

Umberto Eco

Prologue

Friday, October 10

It's hands down one of the most famous roads in America, if not the world, and arguably the most beautiful. The scenery is beyond breathtaking, and it passes through some of the most iconic cities and scenic small towns imaginable. While some people consider the Pacific Coast Highway, or as it's often referred to, PCH, to run the entire length of the West Coast from Washington to San Diego, most people feel that the 'real' PCH runs about 656 miles from Dana Point in Orange County to Eureka near the California/Oregon border. Thousands of people every year travel the PCH, especially between San Francisco and Los Angeles. And why not? With popular spots like Santa Cruz, Carmel/Monterey, Big Sur, Cambria, San Luis Obispo, Santa Barbara, Malibu, and so many others, it's little wonder that it's so popular.

It's probably no exaggeration to say that almost every American has seen many of the most famous scenic views of the PCH even if they've never set foot in California. One need only turn on their TV and view virtually any car commercial and chances are they filmed it near the Bixby Bridge in Big Sur or Point Mugu in Malibu. Bixby Bridge, especially, is majestic, standing 280 feet above the canyon floor and hard against the mountains on the east side and the beautiful blue Pacific on the west. And, like so much of the PCH, there is little room for daydreaming or inattention since the road drops off to the rocks and water below with very little in the way of guardrails to stop you. Of all the things that drivers have to be concerned about, inattention is probably at the top of the list, followed closely by the frequent marine layer fog that cuts visibility to near zero and the ever-present danger of falling rocks or, worse, landslides. One danger that most never feel the need to consider is other people, at least not beyond their concern for other drivers being reckless. Maybe we're just lulled into a sense of safety and security by the endless vistas that look like God himself painted them.

***

"Is it just me, or does this drive never get old?" Loren Bryant, PhD, asked as she gazed out at the azure waters of the Pacific and the waves crashing on the rocky coast a few miles north of Big Sur.

"Never," answered her husband, Keith Bryant, PhD, "at least if you're driving it for pleasure and able to take your time and enjoy the scenery. I can't imagine living way out here and having to use the PCH to commute to Carmel or south to Cambria or San Juan Capistrano every day. That would get old fast."

"True," she said, "but thankfully we're living in Carmel, basically heaven on earth, so we have all the civilization we need between there, Monterey, and Santa Cruz. If we need a big-city fix, it's only a few hours to San Jose or San Francisco."

"You won't hear me complaining. There are certainly days that I miss the bucolic life we had on the farm in Charlottesville, not to mention UVA. I'm just glad that we have such great caretakers for the place and are able to get back there every few months to enjoy it. Plus, I really want the kids to experience growing up around the horses and cattle and the wide-open spaces. Don't get me wrong. I love it here, too, but there's not quite as much room for kids to run and play and experience nature."

Almost two years before, they had moved from Virginia to Carmel after Keith's sister, Julia Bryant, was diagnosed with breast cancer. Even though Julia had a large circle of friends in the Carmel/Monterey area, Keith and Loren were determined to help her through what they knew would be a long and arduous journey. And it was. They were both professors at UVA, but because of the business that Keith had founded before they'd even met, Bryant International Consulting, they had substantial wealth that gave them the freedom to make the move. It was more challenging since they had kids in school, but that didn't turn out to be a major problem; there were plenty of top-flight private schools where they could enroll near their new home.

Even though money wasn't a major hurdle, which is often the case when people are trying to make the leap from most parts of the East Coast to California because of the high cost of housing, they still planned to continue teaching. Fortunately, Keith had several contacts from his work with multiple federal government branches, including the military, and secured positions for them both at the Naval Postgraduate School in Monterey. Because of their credentials and experience, the school happily accepted them as professors of political science and international relations.

"I'm glad that Julia is feeling well enough to take care of the kids for a few days. I just hope they don't wear her out."

"They can be a handful when they want to be, that's for sure," responded Keith with a smile. "But I think they're aware of how much she's been through and how they can't be their usual Tasmanian devil selves while we're gone. Plus, I think it will be great for Julia to feel like she has someone to take care of for a few days after she's had to depend on others for so long; that's not her style."

After more than 15 years together, they were completely comfortable with each other, whether they were gabbing like long-lost friends or passing time in silence and quiet reflection. Getting away for a few days from the rigors of teaching and raising two kids afforded them time to reconnect and remember the things that made them fall in love in the first place. It sounds cliché, but for them it was one of those fairytale, love at first sight, serendipitous moments that changed their lives forever. They'd heard dozens of 'meet cute' stories from others in the years since, but in their minds, nothing topped what they'd experienced and what they'd had ever since.

That is except, of course, the terror they'd lived through back in 2008, not too long after they'd first met and moved in together. At the time, Keith was a professor at UVA teaching a course called 'The Politics of Conspiracy' and Loren was a PhD candidate and graduate assistant. Keith's class studied several conspiracies throughout history and the role that the public and the media played in driving the conspiracy until it took on a life of its own. They studied the many conspiracies surrounding the assassinations of Abraham Lincoln and JFK and how they affected Americans and our role in the world. They also dug into the conspiracies around the attack on Pearl Harbor, especially the many people, even today, that still have the fervent belief that key leaders in the US administration knew about the attack in advance but turned a blind eye to it as part of the plan to get our country to enter WWII. Only when the class started studying and investigating the many conspiracies surrounding the events of 9/11 did their world turn upside down, nearly tearing this country apart in the end.

"I love this view." Loren never tired of the vistas as they rounded the curve and saw the iconic Bixby Bridge stretched out before them, barely a mile further down the road. "It never gets old."

"It's one of my favorites, too. And with this view of the winding road leading down to it, it's tempting as hell to punch this thing up to 100 plus and enjoy those long, sweeping curves."

Loren giggled. "Oh God, not again. You say that, or at least you think that every time we get on this road. I don't know where this wannabe race car driver thing comes from."

"Just the ramblings of a little boy that never fully grew up, I guess. Pretty much like every other man walking this earth." Just to make his point, he accelerated as they entered a sweeping left bend in the road.

As Keith reached out to take Loren's hand, the left front tire blew and practically ripped the wheel out of his hand. Loren screamed as he fought to get the car back under control, but with the narrow road and the car's momentum he couldn't keep it from crashing into the mountainside. The impact was nearly head-on, crushing the front end of the Mercedes and causing both airbags to deploy. The car spun several times and came to rest in the southbound lanes, only a few yards from the edge of the cliff.

Less than a minute later, two vehicles approached the crash site from the south and were the first on the scene. Both were large Escalade SUVs, and several people exited each vehicle to survey the damage. Neither called 911 despite seeing that the car's occupants were injured but alive. Keith and Loren were both barely conscious and cried out for help, but their pleas were ignored.

The lead SUV, which was equipped with a heavy push bar in the front, immediately pulled up tight against the Mercedes. Being much larger and heavier, the Escalade easily pushed the damaged car towards the edge of the cliff, and then, getting the 'all clear' signal from the other SUV, pushed it right over the edge.

The car bounced off the cliffs all the way down, with parts of the car flying in all directions. Miraculously, the seatbelts and crushed interior kept their bodies inside the car as it fell and came to rest on the rocks at the water's edge nearly 200 feet below. Keith and Loren had been fortunate to survive the initial crash, but no one could possibly survive this fall. Or to call it what it was — this *murder*.

1

Thursday, October 16

It was a picture-perfect October day in Santa Monica. The morning was cool with a moderately heavy marine layer, but by 11am it had mostly burned off and the temperature climbed into the mid-70s. Even on a weekday, when most Americans are working their dismal 9 to 5 existence, people still filled the streets and beaches while living their California dream.

Jessica 'JJ' Jansen and her business and life partner, Kristyn Reynolds, were working outside on the terrace of their luxurious rental home just off Ocean Avenue, less than a typical Tiger Woods 5-iron shot from the beach. They'd been living here since moving to California almost two years before, courtesy of the executive leadership at Highline Studios. Highline had wined and dined them and convinced them to move from Dallas to help develop a movie based on the infamous Murder Game case that they had cracked. Their agent and accountant advised them to buy the home they loved to help with their tax situation and to ease their guilt should they ever want to pursue opportunities with other movie studios.

"If someone had ever told me that I, a lowly ex-FBI Special Agent, would consider the purchase of an $8 million oceanfront home, I would have said they were crazy." JJ was still in disbelief at how well things had worked out since taking the leap into the movie business.

"Well, it's not exactly like I was pulling down millions as a lowly investigative reporter for the Dallas Morning News, either. I mean, let's get serious: if the two of us had combined our savings and incomes, we still wouldn't have been able to afford an offer on the guest house, much less the entire property." Considering that the house was 6500 square feet with 4 bedrooms, 5.5 bathrooms, a wine cellar, two offices, a beautiful pool, and a 3-bedroom guest house, her assessment was spot-on.

JJ and Kristyn first met in Dallas when JJ was the lead FBI Special Agent assigned to the Murder Game case, and when her superiors refused to provide the requested additional resources, she refused to back down or move the investigation in the direction they were advocating. Never considered a team player and always only one small fuckup from being kicked out of the Bureau, she nonetheless went outside of the agency and the chain of command and brought Kristyn into the investigation. While a seasoned and award-winning investigative reporter, she was still a civilian. Even though they broke the case and stopped one of the biggest serial killing sprees in American history, and even though the FBI gave JJ almost every service award possible for their field agents, they forced her out because she'd broken one too many rules — way too many — in defiance of her leadership.

The one bright spot, other than taking down some terrible people and surviving multiple attempts on their own lives, was the realization that their friendship and partnership had grown into full-blown, butterflies-in-the-stomach, giddy-as-schoolgirls love. At first, they weren't sure if it was just lust, or infatuation, or maybe just a short fling that resulted from the stress and fear they'd struggled with, not to mention the near-death experience. After two years, there was no longer any question: this was pure, once-in-a-lifetime love.

Their time in California had been anything but mundane. They'd made the move west to become co-producers and screenwriters for the Oscar-nominated movie based on the Murder Game, and while it didn't win the award for Best Picture it did garner Best Screenplay and captured more than $175 million at the global box office. Even getting the movie completed was a major undertaking. Ultimately, they delayed the release date several months, resulting in a multimillion-dollar cost overrun because of the vandalism, arson, and murders committed by Brookes Williamson and his vendetta against JJ and Kristyn. Working with a task force of FBI, CHP, and local police, they helped take Williamson down and get the movie back on track.

Their new production company, Supersleuth Productions, was gathering momentum and being sought after by an ever-growing number of screenwriters and studios. Besides producing movies, they'd also added, somewhat under the radar, Supersleuth Investigations to their portfolio. Both now had their private investigator licenses and their concealed carry permits, but so far, they'd resisted focusing on the PI business, instead relying solely on referral and word of mouth.

"Is it just me, or is this screenplay a lot tougher than the one we worked on for *The Murder Game*?" JJ struggled constantly with writer's block, and Kristyn found she was not immune, either, despite her years of writing professionally.

"No, it's not just you. I think it's the fact that we're creating the story this time instead of just regurgitating our experiences and spinning it into a screenplay like we did on our first effort. Also, the writing team is counting on us to contribute more this time, instead of just adding details from the Murder Game case and providing color commentary."

"That's true. Thank goodness we have such a great writing team to work with; we were really lucky to get so much of our old group together for this production."

Kristyn nodded. "Yes, and don't forget that we have firsthand knowledge of at least a portion of this story since we were part of the investigation into Alyssa LaCroix's killing spree from the beginning."

"Not to mention that we have Shelly onboard to help develop some ideas based on her experience." JJ was referring to Napa PD Chief

Shelly Blackburn, who they had worked closely with when bringing down one of the country's worst ever female serial killers. The three of them had grown incredibly close since being thrown together in a desperate attempt to save lives, including their own, and bring a serial killer to justice.

"We should reconnect with her this evening, get her thoughts on these last few scenes we've been struggling with. Maybe we can invite her down for the weekend, too."

"That would be great if she's able to make it. I'm so glad that she agreed to be involved in this production. I don't want to jinx things, but I'm feeling incredibly excited about *Blood & Vengeance*. It could be a major hit."

2

Friday, October 17

Sometimes the best-laid plans and intentions go astray, and this morning was no different. JJ and Kristyn had planned to get up early, go for a run on the beach, eat a healthy breakfast, and still be out the door and heading to Highline Studios by 8:30am. When the alarm went off at 6:00, they found themselves hungrier for each other than for exercise and eggs and bacon, and it wasn't long before they had practically destroyed the bed with their passion. Rather than allowing more time to slip away they made a beeline for the shower, but they should have known from dozens of past experiences that this was a bad idea. Pretty soon they were in the middle of Round 2 and, besides running out of hot water, fell even further behind schedule.

JJ was just finishing getting dressed when her phone rang. If it had been almost anyone else, she would have let it go to voicemail since they were already running late, but since it was her friend and former boss, SAC Ken Isaksen from the Dallas field office, she picked up. "Good morning, sir. It's been a while. How are things in your world?"

"First off, haven't we gotten to the point in our relationship where you can call me 'Ken' instead of 'sir'? I haven't been your boss for over two years."

JJ laughed. "Sorry, but you'll always be 'sir' to me. It's a hard habit to break, but more than that, I think you've earned it."

"Whatever. I actually called to see if you and Kristyn could join me on a video call this morning. I know that you two are working on your next motion picture project, but a case has come up that's very personal to me, and I can't think of anyone I would trust to handle this investigation more than you two."

"Give us 15 minutes to finish getting ready and rearrange our morning schedule, and we'll meet you on the video bridge."

***

"Did you guys hear about the recent fatal car accident on the PCH near Big Sur? The one where the car went off the cliff and ended up on the rocks almost 200' below?"

Kristyn looked at JJ, and they both shook their heads. "No, sir. It sounds terrible, but if it made the news down here in L.A., we must have missed it."

"Understandable. Two people died in that crash: Dr. Keith Bryant and his wife, Dr. Loren Bryant."

"Names don't ring a bell...." said JJ.

"They were longtime friends of mine and people I worked closely with when I was still in DC. We've been close friends since; in fact, I'm godfather to both of their children."

"It sounds like you were really close with them," Kristyn said. "We're really sorry for your loss."

"Thanks. They lived in Charlottesville, VA and were professors at UVA until about two years ago when they moved to Carmel to help take care of Keith's sister, Julia, who was going through some serious medical issues. It was Julia who reached out to ask for my help."

"Help with what, sir? From what you said, it sounds like just another car accident on PCH, which, as you know, is all too common. People get distracted with the scenery and, next thing you know, they run off the road and lose control." JJ tried to convey empathy but wasn't sure she was doing very well.

"Julia doesn't believe this was an accident. She's convinced that it was murder."

3

Friday, October 17

"You said that they were professors at the Naval Postgraduate School in Monterey. That's not usually a profession that makes you a target for murder. I'm guessing there's more to this?" asked JJ.

Isaksen spent the next 15 minutes giving them the backstory on how back in 2008, just prior to the election that brought Barack Obama to office, the Bryant's had been instrumental in taking down a clandestine government group that was planning 'the next 9/11' to reawaken America to the threat posed by our enemies. The group had been covering up the truth behind 9/11 since it happened, even going to the extreme of putting out their own 'false flag' conspiracies to keep people confused and make the conspiracy theorists look like they're part of the tinfoil hat crowd. Keith and Loren worked closely with a group of academics and conspiracy researchers called Let the Truth Be Told (LTBT), and as they closed in on the truth, they were all in harm's way and fighting to stay alive.

President Obama and the congressional leadership team asked Keith and Loren to lead the investigation into the renegades who were plotting this next horrific terrorist event. At first, the country came together in a scene reminiscent of the days following 9/11. Unfortunately, the *kumbaya* didn't last long. Republicans started vilifying them and the entire process because they thought it was a smear against their party. Democrats vilified them because they wanted to place the blame squarely on former President Bush and have him tried for high crimes and misdemeanors. The Bryants and their team had too much integrity to be pushed around by either side. In fact, they were the first to stand up and state publicly that President Bush was *not* part of the conspiracy. Though members of his administration were behind the plot, Bush was not aware of it, nor did he take part in it. As we've seen repeatedly throughout history, some people with a misguided sense of loyalty, duty, and patriotism took it upon themselves to do whatever they thought needed to be done to keep their people, their party, in power.

"Are you implying that their deaths, if determined to be murder, relate to these events from 2008?" JJ couldn't fathom how that could be the case.

"No, I don't think that's likely, but I'd like to ask you to take on Julia as a client—she's prepared to pay you whatever it takes—and meet with her to better understand what they were working on since coming to California. I won't try to sway you either way, but I think when you hear what she has to say you'll agree that there's at least enough unanswered questions to warrant a deeper investigation than the one performed by CHP and Monterey County PD."

4

Saturday, October 18

It was early afternoon when JJ and Kristyn pulled into Carmel-by-the-Sea, and while they always looked forward to spending time in this incredibly beautiful, incredibly charming village, they knew that the present circumstances weren't conducive to rest and relaxation. They followed Google Maps to Julia's street, San Antonio, and turned left off Ocean Drive. Unfortunately, from that point they had to rely on the directions that Julia provided because houses in the village didn't have traditional house numbers or mailboxes; in fact, there wasn't even mail delivery in the village, the people instead traipsing to the post office to pick up their mail.

"I'm glad that Julia provided us with the exact directions to her house. I'm familiar with the addressing scheme in the village since I've been here quite a few times, but it still requires me to sit and think it through." Kristyn looked down at the address. "So, she said her house is San Antonio 4SW of 8th, so that means we stay on San Antonio until we cross 8th Avenue, and then her house will be the 4th one on the southwest side, which will be on our right."

"Because the 'west' part of southwest means it's the side of the street closest to the ocean, right?"

"Exactly. She's only one block away from the ocean and smack dab in the middle of what locals refer to as the 'Golden Rectangle'. Definitely prime real estate."

JJ laughed. "Find me a house, no matter how old, how small, or how close to its neighbors, that isn't prime real estate in this town. It makes Santa Monica look like a bargain."

When they reached Julia's house, they pulled into her driveway, thankful to have a place to park their car off the narrow street that sees a constant flow of traffic from tourists and looky-loos. All they need to get this job off to a roaring start is someone sideswiping JJ's new Mercedes AMG GLS 63 SUV, her pride and joy.

Stepping out of the car, Kristyn stretched and took a deep, cleansing breath. "God, I love the sound and smell of the ocean, not to mention all the beautiful flowers and trees that are blooming. It's just so soothing here, much more so than SoCal."

"You're so right. It's like life is in slow motion compared to L.A."

Before they could even ring the doorbell, the door opened, and Julia stepped out onto the porch to greet them. She was strikingly attractive, especially for a woman in her mid-50s. She was about 5'7" and looked to be in great shape with not an ounce of fat evident on her solid and toned frame. Seeing her, one would never have guessed that she'd recently gone through months of absolutely hellish medical treatment. Impeccably dressed, with deep blue eyes and perfect hair and makeup so well done she could have just stepped away from a Vogue photo shoot. This was one of those rare instances where JJ and Kristyn felt underdressed and, compared to their host, somewhat slovenly. Fortunately, Julia couldn't have been more open and engaging.

"Let's move out to the back deck. I know that you guys had a long drive today and probably didn't have time to stop for lunch, so I threw a little something together. If you guys can grab the pitchers of iced tea and lemonade, that would be great."

They followed her through the house and to the kitchen, and then out the sliding doors to the back deck. To say that the house, as well as the entire property, was a stunningly beautiful oasis worthy of *Architectural Digest* was an understatement. As with most houses in Carmel, it wasn't very large, but every square inch was perfect and sported nothing but the best in terms of materials and taste. JJ gasped and stared in awe when she saw the kitchen, with its beautiful gray custom cabinets, quartzite countertops, 60" Wolf range, huge Sub-Zero refrigerator, and two built-in Sub-Zero wine coolers.

Whispering to Kristyn, she said, "I know I don't have the cooking skills to really do this kitchen justice, and I'm sure I never will, but so help me God, I covet it."

Kristyn giggled, and then, nuzzling her ear whispered, "I don't know why, but the kitchen vibe, hell, the entire house's vibe, is making me kinda hot. Makes me want to use that large quartzite-topped island to make you the main course."

Hearing Julia coming up behind them, they suppressed their schoolgirl giggles and headed outside. Julia followed with a large tray that held platters of gnocchi, ravioli, tortellini, and an assortment of sauces and cheeses.

"Oh my gosh, this is a feast fit for a king! You shouldn't have gone to so much trouble. We would have been fine just getting a pizza delivered, I swear," said JJ.

"Thanks, but as much as I love to cook, I can't take credit for this. I called one of my favorite local restaurants on Ocean Avenue and had them throw this together for me. They were even kind enough to drop it off just a few minutes before you arrived."

"We noticed that you have an amazing kitchen, the kind any chef or chef wannabe would die for. Do you cook a lot?" JJ realized that perhaps 'would die for' was not the most appropriate choice of words even as they were coming out of her mouth. *Whoops.*

"I do, or at least I did, until recently. Since the accident and all the resultant upheaval, it's been a struggle just to keep everyone and everything together. I guess you guys know that my niece and nephew, Keith's kids, are now living with me? I assume that Ken Isaksen told you."

"He did. I know that must be a major change for you." Kristyn was choosing her words carefully.

"It is. Don't get me wrong, I absolutely love these kids and have every intention of moving forward with the formal adoption process. Keith and Loren did an incredible job of raising bright, curious, and compassionate kids; I don't think anyone could have done any better. It breaks my heart that they won't be here to see the kids grow up and graduate school, get married, maybe have kids of their own."

"Not to get too personal, but Isaksen shared with us the health struggles you've been through the past couple of years. Any concerns that it will slow you down when trying to keep up with young kids?" JJ tried to be delicate with her questions but wasn't sure she was saying the right things.

"Well, the good news is that the latest scans and doctor reports show that I'm cancer free, but I won't kid you: I'm not back to 100% yet, but I'm slowly getting there. I won't be running any marathons anytime soon, but I feel a bit more myself every day. And now, because of these hellish circumstances, I've got more reason than ever to push myself to get better and stronger. I've *got* to be here for these kids."

"How are the kids holding up?" Kristyn asked.

"All things considered, amazingly well. I guess it's true what they say; kids are pretty resilient. They have their sad moments, and they've shed a lot of tears, but they've been a lot stronger than I probably could have been at their age." Julia's smile brightened.

"How old are they?" asked Kristyn.

"Patrick is twelve and just started seventh grade, and Karen is ten and in fifth grade. Would you like to meet them?"

"Oh, absolutely. So long as you think it's OK, we'd love to." Kristyn felt comfortable answering for them both.

5

Saturday, October 18

Julia led the kids out to the deck and introduced them to Kristyn and JJ. They both could have passed for child models that, were they a few years older, just stepped out of an Abercrombie and Fitch catalog. Or, maybe more accurately, a UVA catalog, which wasn't hard to believe since they'd grown up just a few miles away.

"Ladies, this is Patrick, and this is Karen. Guys, please say hello to Ms. Jansen and Ms. Reynolds, though I'm sure they'd be okay with you calling them JJ and Kristyn."

"Definitely," said JJ. "It's very nice to meet you both."

Before JJ could speak again, Karen practically blurted out, "Are you here because someone killed our mom and dad?"

That shocked everyone into momentary silence. Finally, Kristyn responded. "That's part of the reason, sweetie. We're going to speak with your Aunt Julia to find out how we can help her and ensure you get the best care."

Patrick had an almost panicked look on his face. "You mean you're going to take us away from Aunt Julia?"

"Oh, no. Never, and I'm so sorry if you think that's what I meant." Kristyn realized that the simplest statements, no matter how innocent the intent, still had the power to tear open the fresh wounds they had recently suffered.

"You don't ever, ever have to worry," Julia said, addressing the kids. "No one will ever take you away from me. I promise."

* * *

With the kids back in the house and camped out in front of the TV, Julia could finally talk about the supposed accident and the help she was hoping JJ and Kristyn could provide. "I'm glad you had the chance to meet Patrick and Karen. They're wonderful kids, just a joy to be around."

"Isaksen told us he's godfather to both. I've gotta tell you, that one caught us by surprise. We've never had the chance to see too much of the 'human' side of the man, as much as we love him," smiled JJ.

"It's true. And I'm their godmother. I'm not sure if Ken told you, but Patrick was named after Patrick Rockwell, the leader of the conspiracy research group Let the Truth Be Told that Keith and Loren connected with back in 2008. It's no exaggeration to say that between them they probably saved the country, hell, maybe the world, from a terrorist attack that would have made 9/11 look like a warmup act. It's also no exaggeration to say that the LTBT team saved Keith and Loren on multiple occasions. If not for them, the hit teams that were hot on their trail would have surely caught and killed them."

"Sounds like those were scary times," offered JJ.

"It was beyond scary. It was absolutely terrifying, and that's even with me being relatively safe here, 3,000 miles from the thick of the action. But the people trying to stop Keith and Loren had the resources, both people and technology, that they could have taken me out whenever they wanted to. And they threatened to do that repeatedly."

"What about Karen? Any significance to her name?" asked Kristyn.

"She's named after Karen Richardson, the only other female member of LTBT and one of Loren's closest friends. We're so blessed that she's continued to be a part of the kids' lives, too. Nothing would please me more than to see Karen grow up to be the same brilliant, curious, and compassionate woman that Karen Richardson is. She's one of the finest, most loving people I've ever met."

They spent the next two hours talking through the details of what Keith and Loren were working on besides their day-to-day teaching at the Naval Postgraduate School. Julia knew a lot, but she was the first to admit that she didn't know all the details of their investigation. She knew and shared enough, though, that JJ and Kristyn could understand everyone's concerns and doubts about the supposed 'accident'.

"So, to net this out, Keith and Loren were digging into the connections between all these right-wing groups, both in the US and abroad, including troublemakers like the Oath Keepers, QAnon, and an ever-growing number of Nazi sympathizers and so-called Christian Nationalists. So far so good?" Seeing Julia nod in agreement, JJ dove a bit deeper.

"Their investigation included delving into group memberships, especially overlapping memberships, common phrases and terminology used in social media posts, and similar public pronouncements and manifestos. As with many investigations into such organizations, many of which had long since crossed the line to criminal enterprises, a large part of the investigation focused on forensic accounting—a sure way to end up with a target on your back. Does that pretty well sum it up?"

"I'd say that sums it up perfectly, or at least as well as I know it. I'm sure there's a lot more that the two of you can uncover. Still, if I had to guess, based on your questions, your statements, even by the look on both your faces, you think there's enough here to warrant further investigation and to consider the possibility that their deaths were not the result of an accident. Am I right?"

Kristyn and JJ looked at each other and quickly nodded. Kristyn answered. "You're right. We don't know what we will find, if anything, but we certainly think a deeper dive is warranted.

Julia tried to hold back the tears. "Thank you, thank you so much. I can't tell you how much this means to me, to all of us."

"We're going to be staying tonight at the Cypress Inn, but maybe we can get together tomorrow to talk through some plans, figure out some logistics for how we're going to approach this." JJ was already slipping into agent mode with a bit of project manager mode thrown in.

"Perfect. Let's meet for brunch, say around 11:00? There's a great place just across the highway that you'll love. I'll text you the information."

"I'll never say 'no' to a great Sunday brunch!" Then again, JJ rarely says 'no' to any meal that involves good food, good friends, and a great outdoor location.

6

Sunday, October 19

Religion is a strange thing. While all espouse their own version of *the truth*, it's mind-boggling how many 'flavors' and interpretations there are. Christian. Muslim. Catholic. Hindu. Judaism. Wiccan. Even within Christianity, the world's largest religion, there are over 45,000 denominations, including 200 just within the US. People have fought more wars, and lost more lives, 'in the name of God' than any other cause. Religion has no rival in tearing families, nations, even the world, apart. And when religion stops being about the pursuit of God and the betterment of humanity and focuses instead on the almighty dollar, you know you're in America—most often in America's so-called heartland. How ironic.

No matter how you define it, Sacred Waters Church is the very embodiment of the word 'mega-church'. Founded in the 1980s near Fort Worth, Texas, they grew from a small, Southern Baptist community church into a 'Juggernaut for Jesus', as their crass and tasteless marketing shouts from hundreds of billboards and ads on TV, radio, and social media. The main campus, or as they call it, 'Ground Zero for God' is a former college basketball stadium that can seat nearly 17,500, and on any given Sunday, there's not an empty seat in the house.

Based on membership, attendance, and revenue at just the Fort Worth location, they would be one of the largest churches in America, but Sacred Waters had grown beyond that one site. *Way beyond.* They now have locations in nearly 30 cities across the US, not to mention several countries in Latin and South America, and their membership has grown beyond 100,000 self-professed 'Christians'. With a broadcast studio rivaling that of the major networks, they produce nearly a dozen daily TV shows that run on hundreds of stations, not to mention their own YouTube channel, multiple podcasts, and syndicated radio shows on AM/FM and satellite channels. Advertisers practically fall all over themselves to run ads for their products, regardless of how tenuous the tie-in to religion; so long as the ads reach the right demographics and the desired number of viewers and listeners, they continue to throw tens of millions of dollars per year into Sacred Waters' coffers. Not to mention directly into Reverend Jacob Bernard's pockets.

As the leader of Sacred Waters, Reverend Jacob Bernard (just call me 'Brother Jacob'), grew up in the church founded by his father, Reverend Ashford Bernard. It fell to him to take over the ministry in 2008 when his father died while piloting his single-engine Cessna to a tent revival in Houston. Brother Jacob helped drive rapid, even unprecedented, growth in membership and revenues. While his public proclamations of 'all glory to God' struck all the right notes with his flock, not to mention the general public, insiders knew that the growth had more to do with his flair for marketing and self-promotion. Of course, it didn't hurt that he spent millions hiring the best PR and advertising teams money could buy.

It was his dream team that encouraged him to soften his message by moving away from the usual fire & brimstone rhetoric of his father's era to draw in more young people and higher net worth parishioners. They launched focus groups in major US cities to test various messages, theologies, and delivery styles. The participants almost unanimously agreed that they would most likely become members of, and contribute their dollars to, a church that focused on what we now commonly refer to as 'prosperity gospel'.

***

"God *wants* you to be successful and prosperous! He *wants* to bestow blessings on you and your loved ones! Put your faith in Jesus, and he will *lift* you from poverty! Your faith and positive thoughts, along with your donations to enable us to keep spreading his gospel, will bring you material wealth beyond your wildest dreams!" Bernard's voice boomed from the speakers spread around the stadium, and even those sitting furthest from the stage felt like they could reach out and touch him because of the enormous video screens, especially the 70' screen behind the stage, that was managed by the Emmy-winning production staff sequestered in another section of the arena.

The message. The contemporary worship music. The celebrities from the world of sports, conservative politics, and country music waving to the crowd and relishing the congregation's cheers. It was theater, but on a much grander scale than anything Broadway had ever produced, and it brought in obscene amounts of money every week without fail. Even people who struggled to buy food had to tithe at least 10%, and those with more money felt pressured to donate even more. Bernard and the management team lived for Monday morning when they could see the receipts from across their fiefdom. They were rarely disappointed. On average, donations totaled almost $10 million each week, but even that paled compared to the money received from media sales, book sales, and online subscriptions.

Despite the riches, the love, and the respect from his congregation and many Americans, Brother Jacob's innate narcissism remained unsatisfied. His lust for power and influence on the world political stage knew no bounds. He fully intended to be the leader of the new world order, or at least the new American order, but he recognized that too many godless citizens would balk at a 'man of God' leading the change.

Enter: The Prophet.

7

Sunday, October 19

The twelve men assembled in the dilapidated warehouse just outside of Oakland were a rough and scraggly bunch, and that's being charitable. They were meeting at night, under cover of darkness, because anyone seeing this group together, whether police or civilian, would immediately sense trouble. And they wouldn't be wrong.

The Coalition, a moniker bestowed on them by The Prophet, is a rogues' gallery of influential leaders and enforcers for some of the most violent alt-right, Christian Nationalist, and conspiracy-spreading groups in America. Aryan Nation. Blood Tribe. American Nazi Party. QAnon. Patriot Front. America First.

The old saying, *the enemy of my enemy is my friend* perfectly describes this bunch. There's very little love, or even trust, among them. The only thing that binds them is their ultra-right wing, ultra-conservative-bordering-on-fascism philosophy. To a man, they hate anyone who's not a 'pure' white American of European descent, including blacks, Jews, and Latinos. They hate liberals (whatever *that* means on any given day), the government, and in at least some cases, their own mothers. And don't even get them started on the 'scourge' of gays and anyone identifying as anything other than cis/hetero (though several of them would go to their graves protecting the secrets of their own 'romantic' trysts while in prison).

At 9pm sharp, everyone grows quiet as the meeting begins. The video screen fills with the image of The Prophet, the man who rules this group with an iron fist and seemingly unlimited funds. No one, not even those who have been part of the Coalition since its inception, has any idea about The Prophet's identity. No one has ever seen his face, and because he uses virtual background images and different network connections for every video call, they are clueless about location; he could be anywhere in the world. On video calls and the rare occasions when he travels to California to meet with The Coalition in person, he relies on disguises and spy craft that would rival the world's top covert agencies: varying his departure and arrival cities, the locations for meetings, and running complex countersurveillance routes to ensure he's not being followed. The steps he uses to disguise his appearance would rival any Hollywood studio and, more importantly, would fool any facial recognition software used by law enforcement. State-of-the-art voice modulators disguise his incredibly distinctive and familiar voice to ensure anonymity.

The Prophet took control of the meeting. "Thank you all for assembling this evening. Since everyone is present and accounted for, I want to brief you on an important assignment that needs to be handled with precision and haste."

"Apologies for interrupting you, sir, but we're missing one member of the leadership team, Travis Ward. Since I assume that he's part of the planned operation, do we need to pause for a moment until he arrives? Maybe one of us should try to call or text him?" It was Andrew Tucker, an enforcer for one of the Christian Nationalist groups represented on the Coalition's leadership team and a man with a rap sheet that went back years. Not exactly a New Testament version of a 'Christian'.

The Prophet hesitated. Usually not one to abide any form of interruption, he was grateful that Tucker had interjected this time. It gave him the opportunity to make an important point. "Mr. Ward will no longer be a member of this esteemed group. It came to my attention, with confirmation from multiple sources, that he seems to have a predilection for running his mouth and bragging about his exploits in support of our cause. Like many people who lack discipline and self-control, he's most predisposed to running his mouth when he's had a bit too much to drink, which seems to be an everyday problem. Suffice it to say that he will no longer represent a threat to this group or our cause. And please let that be a lesson that we all take to heart. As the old saying goes, *loose lips sink ships.*"

The group was silent for a moment, all of them trying to imagine how The Prophet learned of Ward's indiscretions and pondering his fate. They knew instinctively that one of the leader's enforcers had killed him, and they were also certain that he would not hesitate, even for one second, to eliminate any of them that dared betray the group or their mission.

8

Sunday, October 19

"So, if I may return to the business at hand," added The Prophet, talking sternly and leaving no doubt that he expected no further interruptions, "I want to talk about our next mission. For a variety of reasons, it's imperative that this action take place no later than Tuesday night. That's admittedly a tight window for planning an operation of this magnitude, but I trust in your ability to make this happen; you already have the needed raw materials and access to the people possessing the requisite skills."

Seeing that everyone was rapt with attention, he continued. "Not that anyone in this group has ever shied away from killing innocent people or non-combatants, but this time there should be little or no collateral damage. Your job is to target the headquarters of Lofton Renewable Energy in San Jose. I want the place destroyed and reduced to rubble, and to ensure minimal casualties, I want this done in the middle of the night. The place should be empty since the second and final shift ends at midnight."

For the next 30 minutes, they discussed plans and logistics, including the materials and personnel required. There was a lot of focus on the timeline required to place the explosives since the building was strong, modern, and built with the latest earthquake-resistant technology, not to mention that the building covered over 400,000 square feet. Finally, they had the plans laid out and everyone briefed on their assigned tasks.

As the meeting was winding down, Steven Jorgensen, a leader in the American Nazi Party—no real surprise since he had a swastika tattooed on his forehead—addressed The Prophet. "I'm curious, as I'm sure others are, why we're targeting this particular company. We have no problem carrying out the orders and are 100% committed to the cause, but may we ask why?"

The Prophet's first inclination was to tell this piece of useless trash that 'why' was none of his concern, but he held his tongue and carefully offered an explanation. "Lofton Renewable Energy is a darling of the liberal left and the previous administration. They've taken hundreds of millions of dollars in American taxpayer grants and subsidies in the unending quest to reduce America's dependence on foreign oil and, not incidentally, ruin the lives and livelihoods of the tens of thousands of people that work for American oil and traditional energy companies. If that's all there were to it, we might give them a pass. My investigation, though, has uncovered the fact that Lofton has taken tens of millions of dollars from a joint China-North Korea cabal to share their technology with our enemies while slow-rolling the solution that the American people are paying them to develop. Bottom line, they are basically a front for the Chinese and North Koreans and are selling out the American people. Is that a good enough reason for you all?"

There was no dissension, not that The Prophet had expected any. Of course, if members of the Coalition knew the real reason for the action he'd ordered, there might be considerable dissension. Then again, he could say the same for *every* order he had ever given, which called on them to damage, destroy, or kill their supposed 'enemies'. In Lofton's case, he'd invested millions in their business but recently shorted their stock when most investors were buying up every share they could get their hands on. The stock had been on a great run for over six months and recently hit an all-time high of $425 per share and a market capitalization of nearly $600 billion. This action would drive the stock right off a cliff, and The Prophet would be right there, as he always seemed to be, to reap the rewards. God bless the free market, and God bless capitalism. But most of all, God bless the fact that most people lacked the sophistication or brains to succeed in the high-stakes world of international business, leaving it to elites like Brother Jacob to profit from our stupidity.

Sunday, October 19

JJ and Kristyn arrived just before 11:00 at the brunch spot Julia had chosen, a locally famous spot called 'From Scratch', in the Barnyard shopping center across Route 1 from the village. The place was packed, meaning a wait of nearly 20 minutes to be seated, but that gave the three of them time to talk about their plans for the investigation.

"Where are Patrick and Karen this morning?" asked Kristyn.

"They're spending the day with friends from school, another brother and sister who are the same ages and in the same grades. It works out well, especially since they live just a few blocks away on Lincoln Street. They need to have time to focus on just being kids."

"That makes sense. I'm sure this has been a traumatic experience for them. That's a lot for any kid to deal with." JJ couldn't help but feel sorry for what they were going through, not to mention Julia. Her entire world had been turned upside down.

As the hostess guided them to their table, Julia said, "I hope you don't mind, but I invited my friend Rebecca Stuart to join us. She should be here shortly; I told her about 11:30. Rebecca has been a godsend since this all happened. For that matter, she was one of the people who took great care of me during the whole cancer shitshow, bringing me food, taking me to doctor appointments, and just being a comfort. It was she, along with Keith and Loren, that got me through."

"Sounds like the type of friend we all need in our lives," offered Kristyn.

"Definitely. Rebecca is also a very talented and successful realtor, and I hope you won't think I'm sticking my nose too far into your business, but I asked her to look for a decent long-term rental here in Carmel so you guys would have a place of your own while you're conducting your investigation. Sorry if I've overstepped."

"Not at all. That should save us considerable time, and our time is much better served by diving into the investigation instead of scouring the Web for rental houses. I appreciate you reaching out to her." JJ was sincere; she was ready to jump into this investigation with both feet.

Moments later, the hostess approached their table with Rebecca in tow. The first thing they noticed was that she looked like the quintessential successful realtor: strikingly attractive, extremely well put together and stylishly dressed and accessorized, and obviously blessed with the most perfect anti-aging genes or the best plastic surgeon in the business. She was simply stunning, and every man, and many of the women, certainly took notice.

After everyone introduced themselves and placed their orders with the server, Rebecca opened her portfolio and shared the listings for a half-dozen rentals in the village. She explained that most of them were 'pocket listings' and weren't available through any realty company or rental site like Airbnb or VRBO. She also explained how the regulations regarding home rentals in Carmel required a minimum one-month stay, a regulation that was put in place years ago to keep out weekly and daily renters and keep the town from becoming more of a party destination.

"Wow, these are some nice properties," JJ said as she looked through the pictures and details of the houses, practically salivating. "I certainly wouldn't object to a house on Scenic Road or near Mission Beach. I'm guessing most of these homes belong to owners that only live here part time and have their primary homes in some other fabulous location?"

"You're right. In fact, that's the case for every listing that I showed you. Most of these places are owned by people who have multiple homes around the world."

"Maybe after we finish here, we can do a quick tour of the houses and hopefully pick one that will work for us? We can stay at the Cypress Inn until we're able to move in, but the sooner we can get settled into a place and really set up our operation, the better." Kristyn loved the Cypress, especially the evening happy hour when the bar had almost as many dogs as people, but she knew that the beautifully appointed but compact hotel room was less than ideal for their needs.

"We can do that," Rebecca responded, "and I can promise you that you'll be able to move into any of these places within 24 hours of signing the rental agreement. If you find a place you like that meets your needs, I can have our cleaning service there the next morning to ensure it's in perfect condition and ready for you to move in. And I'd be happy to have a local company that we use do the grocery shopping and stock the fridge and pantry for you so you can focus on your work."

After seeing all the houses that Rebecca had pulled together, they chose a beautiful home near 8th Avenue and Scenic Road with jaw-dropping views of the ocean, the beach, and a couple of holes of the venerable Pebble Beach golf course. At $15,000 per month, it was more than they'd hoped to pay, but they loved the house and location and overall vibe of the home. Warm, comfortable, with a well-appointed office and a large multi-level deck and beautifully landscaped backyard. While it was barely a third of the size of their house in Santa Monica, it more than met their needs.

JJ turned to Kristyn and asked, "Are you okay with spending $15,000 per month for this place, especially while we're trying to buy our place back in L.A.?"

Julia jumped in. "You don't need to worry about the cost. I have that covered, along with any other expenses you guys have while you're working on this case. And that's on top of whatever your daily rate is, or however you charge."

"Julia, no, that's way too much. We can't ask you to do that." The overly generous offer shocked Kristyn.

"Nonsense. I insist, plus, if I were being selfish—and I promise I'm not — it's much better to have you here working the case than flying back and forth every few days or weeks. And not to be gauche, but money isn't really a major concern. Besides my personal assets, Keith and Loren left me a sizable amount in their will and made me the trustee for the quite substantial assets they left for the kids."

JJ spoke up. "Just so we all have our cards on the table and there's no future misunderstanding, we're making this investigation our number one priority, but we also have commitments and deadlines for the movie production back home. Many people, both investors and the crew, are counting on us. We'll have to work on the millions of tasks involved with that production in parallel with this investigation, and we'll probably have to make at least a couple of trips back there over the next few weeks. Knowing all of that, are you still comfortable committing to your overly generous offer?"

"Absolutely," responded Julia. "I assumed all along that you'd have to juggle both things. Ken had warned me you were heads down on the movie project and, as principals and producers on the film, you couldn't just step away."

Seeing that everyone seemed to be aligned, Rebecca said, "Alright then, it sounds like we have a plan. You guys can plan to move in tomorrow. I'll call you when it's ready, but I'd say probably after about 1pm."

"Perfect. I think we're going to have a busy day tomorrow, and it's a relief knowing that we no longer have finding a place to live hanging over our heads. Thanks for making this so painless," said JJ.

"Hey, anything that I can do to help you and Julia, I'm all in. I'm glad I could at least do this one little thing for you."

10

Monday, October 20

The production team meets at 9am every Monday, Wednesday, and Friday to review progress, plans, and next steps. It's rare for everyone to make it into the office for every call; between the hellish L.A. traffic, traveling to different cities to scope out suitable locations for upcoming movie scenes, and the inevitable gotchas caused by Mr. Murphy, he of the dreaded Murphy's Law, it just wasn't realistic. Fortunately, JJ and Kristyn instilled in their teams that *work is something that you do, not a place that you go.* Meaning, simply, that if you can still be productive working from home, or on the road, or in the middle of the ocean, so long as you continue to meet your commitments and participate in these update and planning sessions, do what you gotta do. And in this case, that meant JJ and Kristyn working from the courtyard of the Cypress Inn and connecting to the video call remotely.

JJ took the lead in explaining to the assembled team that they were going to be away from L.A. most of the time over the next several weeks, maybe even as much as a month or more, but didn't go into a lot of detail about what they were working on. "Just to be clear, though, Kristyn and I will work on this movie every single day. *Every* day. And we also plan to be on all the scheduled update calls. We've asked Beth Hinshaw to take the lead in our absence, so anything you need involving production budgets, personnel, shooting schedules, whatever—start with Beth. We'll do our best to ensure that there are no delays in responding and will talk with her at least once each day, so hopefully it will be transparent that we're not at the studio."

Fortunately, the team had already bonded by this point, and Beth was a well-respected member of the group. In her early 50s, she had over 20 years of experience in the movie industry as a writer, producer, and director on dozens of films and TV shows. Her Hollywood profile may not have been quite A-list level, but it was certainly a lot higher than JJ's and Kristyn's at this point in their careers, even after the success of 'The Murder Game'. The fact that Beth was incredibly attractive, incredibly fit (courtesy of the multiple triathlons she entered every year), and had a constant stream of attractive younger guys squiring her about town, only added to her reputation and popularity.

JJ asked Beth to stay on the video bridge after everyone else dropped. "Are you OK with this, Beth? I know this got dropped on you with very little warning, but unfortunately, we had little advance notice, either."

"It's no problem, JJ. I've led production teams and even helmed movies enough times before that it's like riding a bike. Different movie, different teams and script, but basically the same mind-numbing exercise. Plus, I know how to reach you guys, and we've agreed to talk at least once each day, so I don't see it as any big deal."

"Thanks. You're really taking a load off our minds. Oh, and Kristyn and I have already talked about it, and we insist on paying you a bonus—a *significant* bonus — for taking this on and keeping the train on the tracks for us. I don't know what we'd do without you."

***

"Right this way, ladies, and watch your step. Lots of stuff on the ground around here for you to trip or slip on. Half the cars we bring in here have oil or gas or some other fluids leaking, not to mention glass from broken windows and shards of metal falling off." JJ and Kristyn were at the Monterey County impound lot to examine the car that Keith and Loren perished in. It had taken a few well-placed calls from SAC Isaksen and his San Francisco counterpart, SAC Michael Roberts, to get them access.

"So, Officer Beck, as I understand it, the car went over the cliff near the Bixby Bridge and had to be recovered from the rocks a couple hundred feet below? Was the car submerged at all, or was it completely out of the water?" Kristyn couldn't believe the amount of damage the car had sustained, including the roof being crushed down to the seats. No way anyone could have survived.

"Luckily, the car came to rest on the rocks. It was close enough to the water that it took a lot of spray before we could get it raised, but it never ended up in the ocean. That's lucky for us; if it had, there's a good chance we'd never be able to recover it. That's happened many times before."

"How'd you recover it from such a height?" JJ had been curious about that since she'd first heard about the accident.

"A few highly trained climbers rappelled down there with a heavy cable and hook from a large—*really* large—tow truck, and they simply hooked it up to the most solid part of the frame they could find. From what I understand, the toughest part was finding a piece of the frame that was still intact enough and strong enough to handle the weight of the car."

"You make it sound so simple, but I imagine it was incredibly dangerous and took hours. Especially for the climbers." Kristyn had been on that part of the PCH countless times and couldn't imagine climbing down those cliffs.

They spent nearly two hours examining and photographing every inch of the wrecked car, both inside and out. The interior was beyond disgusting: blood, clothes and other personal items from their destroyed luggage, and flies everywhere feasting on the tiny bits and pieces of what had been two living, breathing human beings just 10 days ago. As if the flies weren't bad enough, the smell of death still lingered even after all this time and with the car sitting outside exposed to the elements.

"I think I've found something," JJ announced as she examined the driver's side front and rear doors. Kristyn walked over to where JJ was bent down and sat on the ground beside her, a heavily padded moving blanket making the hard, dirty ground a little more tolerable. JJ pointed at the large dent and damaged panels. "What does that look like to you?"

Kristyn got close to the panel and saw what JJ was talking about. She snapped a couple of quick pictures then used her fingernail to scratch at the spot and came away with a bit of black material under her fingernail. "It's not paint, but it looks like something has rubbed against the panel; some kind of metal-to-metal contact would be my guess."

"That's what I was thinking, too. Like maybe a push bar of some type, like the push bars that police mount on the front of their cars. And see how the black marks show up against the white paint of the car? Seems pretty hard to miss, actually."

"True, but isn't it possible, maybe even likely, that this is just a mark from something that the car hit or rolled over as it tumbled a few hundred feet down to the rocks?"

"I don't think we can rule anything in or out yet, but I'm going to take a sample and send this to Quantico for analysis."

"Good idea." Kristyn looked back towards the gate and noticed that Officer Beck looked kind of antsy, probably because it was nearing time for him to lock up and go off-shift. "Let's give it another 10-15 minutes, and if we need to come back tomorrow, we can. Sound good?"

11

Monday, October 20

JJ moved past the driver's door and surveyed the front quarter panel and surrounding area, but she didn't find any further marks or paint transfer; it all seemed to be concentrated closer to the front and rear doors on that side. "If someone hit them, most likely someone driving a large SUV or pickup, it's almost like they were targeting right where Keith was sitting."

"When you say 'targeting', what exactly do you mean? If Keith's car collided with another moving vehicle, wouldn't the impact damage reflect more of a sideswipe, probably with a lot of paint transfer down the side of the car? This impact, at least to my untrained eye, looks like it was straight on."

"You're right. I'm just speculating at this point, but I think it's likely that Keith and Loren were sitting still when they were hit. And I think someone driving something big, heavy, and powerful, plowed into them."

"Like maybe they'd pulled over for the scenic view and while they were there, maybe getting ready to get out of the car to take some pictures, another vehicle hit them?" Kristyn thought about it for a second, a scarier scenario coming to mind. "Are you suggesting that someone plowed into them intending to push them off the cliff?"

"That's exactly what I'm thinking, and I'd venture a guess that they didn't pull over voluntarily, either. Keith and Loren have surely driven this section of the PCH countless times, so it's not like it's their first-time and they need to stop at every turnout for a picture. Plus, I didn't see any cameras inside the car, and there's none listed in the police evidence file, either. Obviously, if there was a camera, it could have flown out as the car was rolling down the hill, but per the investigators' notes, they scoured the hill and recovered a lot of stuff, but no camera."

"OK, putting aside the fact that they could have been using their phones to take pictures instead of a 'real' camera, I think your point about them having traveled this road a lot is even more compelling. There's only so many pictures you can take of the same scenery, despite how magnificent it is. So, if they didn't pull over on their own, how did they end up stopped on the side of the road within just a few feet of the drop-off?"

JJ didn't have a ready answer, but slowly and methodically continued her inspection. As she looked closely at the front wheel well, she slowly broke into a smile. "Kristyn, bring me that flashlight, please."

Kristyn walked forward and handed it to her. "What did you find?"

"Look down here." JJ focused the light on the flattened tire. "See right here? If I don't miss my guess, I'd say that looks like a bullet hole, probably from a large-caliber rifle. See how big that hole is, and there's no damage around that area to make it look like it happened as the car rolled down the cliff. Let's get a few pictures to share with the team."

Kristyn knelt and reached her hand around the back of the tire. "I think you're right. I can feel a hole on the other side of the tire, like it passed right through. And I'd echo your point about it being a large-caliber rifle; the exit hole on the other side is even bigger."

JJ shone the light around the inner wheel well and finally saw it. She had to use her hands to wipe away a lot of dirt and mud, but then it was visible. "Can you hand me that multi-tool, please? I think we may have finally hit pay dirt."

JJ had to try multiple positions and finally had to contort her body as if she were being stuffed into a FedEx box, but she finally managed to get the pliers on the object that had caught her eye. It took considerable effort, especially in her awkward position, but she finally got enough leverage to work it loose from the strut housing.

"I think we can now say with 100% confidence that this was no accident. Wouldn't you agree?" JJ held up the damaged remains of a large-caliber bullet for Kristyn to see.

"Definitely. It's pretty mangled, but hopefully our friends in Quantico can do their magic. Perhaps between the bullet and the damage to the driver's side from the ramming we'll have enough to really kick-start this investigation."

"We'll need to ask Isaksen to get a warrant to take this car out of here and let the local FBI team go through it with a fine-toothed comb."

12

Tuesday, October 21

They had planned on calling Isaksen first thing Tuesday morning to request his help in getting the wrecked car towed to a location where FBI forensic technicians could conduct a more thorough search, but before they were even fully awake, he was calling them. As it was barely 7am on the West Coast, they knew it must be something urgent.

"I'm sending you a link. I need you to join me on a video call in 10 minutes."

JJ knew Isaksen not to be the type of leader to panic or set meetings purely for the sake of hearing himself speak or exerting his authority. A request for a call at this early hour meant it had to be something important. "We'll be there, sir. And I'm sure you'll understand and appreciate that we won't be on camera."

Having moved into the rental house on Scenic Road late Monday night, they were happy to have room to spread out instead of dealing with the tight confines of their room at the Cypress Inn. The home office was much more conducive to a video call, especially early in the morning when they needed to be at the top of their game without the benefit of their first cup of coffee. They logged onto the call in less than the promised 10 minutes but were still the last to join. JJ and Kristyn were happy to see that it was a small group, so they didn't have to waste a lot of time on introductions.

Isaksen kicked things off. "JJ and Kristyn, let me introduce you to SAC Michael Roberts from the San Francisco office. He covers an area that spreads from Monterey County all the way to Sonoma. With him is his Assistant SAC, Evelyn Hurd, who heads the San Jose and Santa Clara County branches. Also, we have the San Jose County Chief of Police, Andrew Cook, on the call."

JJ jotted a quick note to Kristyn before responding. *This must be BIG!*

"Very nice to meet you all, and you'll excuse Kristyn and me for not being on camera. But trust me, you should be thankful. We're not exactly camera-ready this morning."

Isaksen took the lead. "I've explained to my FBI teammates and Chief Cook the scope of your investigation and how there is a strong likelihood that it's tied to the events of last night."

Kristyn looked at JJ, both acknowledging that they had no clue what he was referring to. "I'm sorry, sir, but I can't help but feel that we're missing something here. We went to bed last night around 10:30, so neither of us has any idea what you're referring to when you say, 'the events of last night.'"

"Then let us fill you in," interjected Chief Cook. "Last night around 2am there was a large—make that *massive*—explosion at a business here in San Jose. Fortunately, no one died or got injured, but the explosion completely obliterated the building that housed the HQ and production facilities for Lofton Renewable Energy. If you haven't heard of them, they're one of the largest, most successful US companies in the renewable energy field."

Kristyn looked at JJ for confirmation before speaking. "Neither of us has heard of them, but we know that renewable energy is a growing market right now, not to mention a hot topic of debate and growing division between the right and the left."

"True enough," said SAC Roberts. "Then again, nowadays it feels like every topic causes nothing but arguments and heated rhetoric between the right and the left. It's tearing this country apart."

"This sounds like a terrible blow to the renewable energy sector, at least that would be my guess, but I'm not sure how this connects to our investigation into the murders of Keith and Loren Bryant." JJ looked to Kristyn, who nodded in agreement.

"Then let me cut to the chase," answered Isaksen. "I think, and SAC Roberts agrees, that this bombing was likely carried out by the same group or groups that Keith and Loren were investigating. If that's true, then it's likely that these same people, or at least people they're aligned with, were involved in their murders."

That hit both JJ and Kristyn like a triple espresso mainlined straight into their veins. Kristyn responded. "We can be in San Jose in just a few hours, certainly no later than 12:30 or 1:00. Who should we rendezvous with, and where?"

SAC Roberts spoke. "Meet with Assistant SAC Hurd and Chief Cook. His office would probably be best since it's closest to the crime scene. And just to be clear, their job is to investigate this bombing and bring those responsible to justice. They're not part of the investigation into the Bryant's deaths, especially since *officially* it's still considered an accident. But, like SAC Isaksen, I have my doubts and concerns, so we will work as cooperatively as possible. We'll share information with you as we learn, and we expect you'll do the same."

13

Tuesday, October 21

JJ and Kristyn finally got on the road around 10:30, leaving them plenty of time to get to San Jose by 12:30. Or at least in theory; this being California, there were never any guarantees.

"I don't know about you, but I'm getting hungry. That muffin and cup of coffee didn't really fill me up, and once we're on scene, we probably won't have time to break for lunch."

Kristyn knew JJ well enough to know that she was hinting at something. "Let me guess: you're thinking about making a quick stop at In-N-Out to wolf down a Double-Double combo before we meet with Hurd and Cook?"

JJ giggled. "Damn, you know me too well."

"Actually, I could go for that, too, and I'm way ahead of you. I've already got the address for the In-N-Out in Gilroy pulled up on Google Maps, and it's only about another 10 miles up the 101."

After practically inhaling their meals—and amazingly, not getting a single crumb or drop of food on their clothes—they continued on to San Jose. They didn't bother to stop anywhere for dessert, but they dug into a tin of Altoids that Kristyn was carrying to cover up the severe case of 'burger breath' they both had. Or, as JJ so delicately put it, *'breath that could knock a buzzard off a shit wagon.'*

***

JJ said, "It's nice to meet you both in person," as an introduction when they led her and Kristyn into Chief Cook's office. Assistant SAC Hurd was already there and seated, and as they were getting acquainted she mentioned that she and Cook had a long history of working together on cases. Having someone you can trust and rely on, especially in a different branch of law enforcement, was rare. And invaluable.

"Thanks for making it up here so quickly. We can head on over to the site and talk on the way if you'd like. I'll be happy to drive." Cook stood up and grabbed his keys and led them down to his car.

As they were making the short drive to the site, Kristyn asked, "Since it's only been a couple of hours since we were on the video call, I'm guessing there's not much new information to share?"

"Not a lot," said Hurd, "but we have recovered some of the bomb components — actually, make that 'bombs' plural — and the preliminary conclusion is that it's the same signature we've seen at several other businesses around different parts of California and the western US."

"This is the first we're hearing about multiple bombings. I'm guessing that's because the FBI is trying to keep a lid on the fact that the attacks are likely related?" JJ knew from her experience that this is often the case.

"Exactly," Hurd responded. "There have been almost a dozen bombings in the last couple of years that we believe to be the work of the same group or groups. Last night's attack was probably the largest and most sophisticated, but I think that's just because of the massive size of the target rather than an escalation. Fortunately, there were no injuries or fatalities last night because the building was empty. That hasn't always been the case. We've got almost a dozen dead, and dozens more injured, since this started."

"At first blush, this bombing appears to be an attempt to disrupt the business, or maybe even the whole industry. Are there other instances where the attack appeared to be directed at a person or group, maybe someone that was an enemy of sorts to these people?"

"Great question, JJ, and I can tell you that the cases here in the Bay Area have run the gamut." Chief Cook signaled to turn towards the bombed building, which they could still see smoldering from several blocks away.

"He's right," said Hurd. "There have been bombings at other businesses that are connected, albeit loosely, to industries that are left-leaning, as with Lofton. A couple have been non-profits involved with the environment, like one in Oregon where they were working to remove some dams that had practically destroyed the river and the salmon population, not to mention the local Native American tribe and their way of life. Plus, there have been a couple of attacks directed at local and state Democratic offices, and those resulted in several deaths."

"And I'm guessing we can add the deaths of Keith and Loren Bryant to the list, though it's early in the investigation." JJ chose her words carefully, not wanting to misdirect or sway the case. "I'm sure that Isaksen and Roberts made you aware that the Bryants were investigating a bunch of far-right groups and their coordinated attacks—whether with words or weapons—on any person, group, or industry, that was aligned with the left."

"So, you don't believe that a simple car accident caused their deaths then?" This from Cook.

"We initially had some doubts but tried to keep an open mind, but we've uncovered some incontrovertible evidence that proves this was no accident. It was murder."

* * *

Detective Sergeant Dwayne Geddes was everything that the San Jose Police Department despised and wanted out of their ranks. To Geddes, his retirement couldn't come soon enough; he'd had it with their political correctness and 'woke' policies and blamed both for being passed over for promotion multiple times over the past 15 years in favor of cops that he considered 'less than'. Women. Blacks. Latinos. Even a detective who was openly gay. The situation sickened him, and he usually found solace at the bottom of a bottle. Or, increasingly, in the company of others that shared the same rage and hatred for anyone that didn't look or speak like 'real Americans'.

As the Coalition's inside man with the SJPD—he was never sure if he was their only source, and knew better than to ask—he sent a group chat via the Signal application from a burner phone that was reserved for Coalition business only:

Heads Up! Two private detectives, Jessica Jansen & Kristyn Reynolds, here in San Jose with SJPD Chief and FBI digging into recent action at Lofton Energy. Word has it they were retained by the FBI SAC from Dallas to investigate the deaths of Keith and Loren Bryant. They've been to the impound lot and snooped around the car, and per my sources, took some evidence with them, but no details re what it was. We should assume they sent the evidence to Quantico for analysis and are looking for a connection between the Bryants and the action taken at Lofton. Recommend immediate action to dissuade them from their investigation.

14

Wednesday, October 22

JJ swung the car into the parking lot of the Monterey Regional Airport. While far from a major hub, it was very convenient for travel into and out of the Carmel/Monterey area and saved travelers the long slog to larger airports in San Jose (60 miles) and San Francisco (90 miles).

As JJ and Kristyn walked towards the terminal, they heard the roar of an approaching regional jet. Looking up and seeing that it was a United Embraer jet, Kristyn said, "That's probably McLean's flight coming in now". The plane was so low, and the engine noise so loud that JJ could barely hear her despite being just a few feet away.

Yesterday, while on the way back to Carmel from San Jose, they reached out to Harold McLean, the FBI Hostage Rescue Team (HRT) leader from the L.A. office. They'd met McLean during the Brookes Williamson investigation, and in fact, it had been McLean that took the shot that disabled Williamson's trail bike and brought about the eventual end to the wild chase through the heavily wooded Topanga Canyon area. As a former Marine Recon specialist and sniper, he'd pulled off a shot from a moving helicopter, in the dark, that only a very select few could make. If not for him, Williamson likely would have escaped and continued his killing spree.

They met McLean at the baggage claim area and then walked with him to the United baggage office. "I dropped off a few big Pelican cases of equipment, not to mention one of my sniper rifles and ammunition. The airlines and the TSA both get kinda nervous every time I check them in for a flight." He smiled as he said this, though like most soldiers and people in his position, he didn't trust anyone else with his weapons. Fortunately, his badge and federal credentials allowed him to fly with his FBI-issued sidearm; otherwise, as he shared with them, he'd feel practically naked.

"There's a great place right next door—Tarpy's Roadhouse—where we can grab an early lunch and fill you in on the details of what we're working on," said JJ. "Then we can head down to Big Sur after that."

They sat out on the terrace since it was a nice day and, not coincidentally, so they could monitor their car and the highly valuable—and deadly—cargo in the back.

As they ate, JJ and Kristyn filled McLean in on their investigation into the deaths of Keith and Loren Bryant and how SAC Isaksen suspected there were ties to a larger conspiracy being led by neo-Nazis and Christian Nationalists. They also explained that they now shared Isaksen's belief that the accident was staged.

"It sounds to me like you guys are probably spot-on in your suspicions. It wouldn't be hard to conduct an operation on the PCH and make it look like just another run-of-the-mill car accident."

He took a sip of his iced tea and looked at them both. "So what can I do to help? I'm happy to dive in, and after Isaksen looped-in my boss, SAC Alexander, I've got the green light to get involved. I'm just not sure what I can contribute."

Kristyn spoke. "We wanted to take advantage of your expertise as a sniper and recon specialist to see if you can zero-in on the spot where the shooter set up, see if we can find anything there that might help in the investigation. While we know there's a lot of high ground where a shooter could set up for the kill, we don't have the expertise to identify the exact spot. We're hoping you can."

"Right," said JJ. "We know that even if we find the spot it may not yield any clues, especially since a couple of weeks have lapsed, but we feel it's a thread we have to pull."

***

It was just after 1:30pm when they pulled the car over just north of the Bixby Bridge, close to the exact spot where the Bryant's car had gone over the cliff. Kristyn volunteered to stay with the car while JJ and McLean hiked up the hillside, and they'd stay in communication via the comms that McLean had packed.

"We should get moving. Sunset isn't until after 6pm this evening, but if the fog moves in earlier, like it seems to do a lot this time of year, it could really cut our time short. You ready, JJ?"

"Yep, just need to lace up my hiking boots and I'm ready to go." JJ was in pretty good shape, but as she looked up at the steep hills here on the Big Sur coastline, she questioned her endurance, if not her sanity.

McLean saw the concern in her eyes and just smiled. "C'mon, JJ, you've got this. Just another leisurely walk on the beach in Santa Monica, right?"

"Smartass. You won't be laughing when you're stuck carrying my dead carcass back down that hill."

They'd been searching for a little over an hour when McLean held up his hand for JJ to stop. "I think this might be it." He stood and looked in every direction, then lifted the binoculars to his eyes and looked at the angle and distance to their car parked alongside the road.

JJ looked around but didn't understand why this was the spot versus the acres they'd already covered. Any location on that hillside had an unobstructed view down to the highway. "I don't get it. Why here? Why not closer? This seems pretty far to me."

"Not really. For anybody with even average skills, at least in the sniper world, this is just a chip shot." He measured the distance to the car through his scope. "It's only about 550 yards, so not a real challenge for a skilled shooter. The hardest part is accurately calculating the drop over that distance and accounting for the wind. The winds can be tricky here on the coast, but when I checked the reports from that day, they showed light winds, less than a few knots."

"So, we're talking about a shooter who is probably more skilled than your average hunter, but not necessarily someone of the caliber of a SEAL Team Six member then."

"Exactly. Probably some military training, maybe even some sniper training, but he's no rock star."

"Could a shooter have just as easily shot Keith, the driver, if they weren't trying to make this look like a simple traffic accident?"

"Without a doubt." McLean spoke into his comms. "Kristyn, get behind the wheel for a minute and let us see what it looks like from up here."

"Here, JJ, look through the scope. At this distance, her head is an easy target, and with the high-powered sniper rifle that this guy almost certainly used, the window wouldn't have impeded or deflected the shot at all. Even if Kristyn were driving the car right now and moving right to left—north to south—across our field of vision, I guarantee I could take her out 99 times out of 100. Honestly, I couldn't show my face in front of my team if I missed even once from that distance."

As JJ looked through the scope, she had to concede his point. "You're right. While I'm not even close to being in your league, I'm still pretty damn good. I could probably make that shot 75% of the time, if not more."

McLean pointed a few feet to his left. "One last point: here's the reason I'm certain this is the spot. See this flat area here? This is the perfect spot for the shooter to hide and really blend in with the terrain. And these marks here in the dirt? This looks to me like the imprint from a bipod, something any shooter would want when taking a shot from this height and distance."

"Guess we're lucky that it hasn't rained since this happened, otherwise that imprint would have washed away. Great catch."

They spent the next 30 minutes photographing the spot and searching for any potential clues, but no such luck. No cigarette butts, no candy wrappers, no litter or remnants of food or drink of any kind. JJ hadn't been too hopeful on that point, not just because she expected the perpetrators to be careful and experienced, but because of the many days that had passed since the day of the crash.

"Kristyn, we're headed down." JJ started making her way back down slowly and carefully.

"Any luck?" asked Kristyn.

"We found the sniper's lair, but that's about it. I didn't hold out much hope that the guy would be nice enough to leave us his business card or driver's license, but we didn't find so much as a piece of gum or a cigarette butt. Still, finding his hiding spot is something. At least now we can go back to Isaksen and the others with even more certainty that this was a hit."

15

Thursday, October 23

The weather forecast may have called for a beautiful fall day with lots of sunshine and temperatures in the low 60s, but the morning was anything but. The marine layer was heavy and damp, and with their rental house being a stone's throw from the ocean, visibility was only a few hundred yards. JJ and Kristyn had hoped to take their early morning call with the studio and production team from the back patio, but that idea was quickly pushed aside after less than five minutes outside.

At the very least, the news from the production team was positive. Everything was still on schedule and on budget, thankfully, and by all accounts, Beth Hinshaw was doing such a great job in their absence that the team hadn't missed a beat.

"I knew we made the right call by putting Beth in charge while we're gone. She's a real pro."

"True," said JJ. "Compared to us, especially, since we've only done one movie. She's probably forgotten more about the movie industry than we know."

Their next call was to Isaksen to see if the FBI forensics team had finished their analysis of the bullet that they'd pulled from the Bryant's car. JJ didn't expect miracles, assuming that the bullet was probably common, off-the-shelf ammunition available pretty much anywhere in the US.

"I got the preliminary report back from Quantico, for what it's worth," Isaksen said as he started off. "I'm surprised they got anything at all, considering how badly the bullet was mangled," he said.

They saw him reading through the report before continuing.

"So, no fingerprints, of course. Not that we expected to be that lucky. They confirmed that it was a 7.62x51mm NATO round, also known as a .308. Very common, available at pretty much every sporting goods store in America. Probably even at 7-11 and Buc-ee's here in Texas."

"When we were with McLean yesterday, I asked him if he had any guesses regarding the type of weapon used," JJ interjected. "He said that a lot of snipers prefer a Barrett 50 caliber model like the 107A1, but that would have been overkill for this shot. Not to mention that the rifle weighs over 30 pounds and is a lot to carry up the hill to the shooter's lair unless someone is in fantastic shape."

"Did he have any thoughts assuming that the shooter was using standard NATO rounds?"

"Yeah, he did. No guarantees, of course, since there are a lot of rifles on the market that shoot those rounds, but he said that the most likely weapon was a Remington M24 or one of its variants. Relatively inexpensive, readily available, and accurate at that distance. As he described it, this would have been an easy shot for a shooter with a modicum of experience. I'd have to agree. I'm pretty sure that even I could make that shot."

As they were wrapping up, Kristyn asked, "Any luck processing the evidence recovered at Lofton Renewable Energy yet?"

"Nothing that helps us put a name to the person responsible, but preliminary reports point to it being the same person who built the bombs used for other attacks attributed to the domestic terrorist groups we're investigating."

Before they dropped from the call, Isaksen added one more thing. "You guys watch your six. We don't know how many people are involved in this mess, but by all indications it's quite a few, and they're spread all over northern California and a few other states. There's also some indication that they've got eyes inside multiple city and county PDs and some of the federal buildings. Probably including ours."

16

Thursday, October 23

The temperature was almost 20 degrees warmer in Carmel Valley when they arrived at Bernardus Lodge and Spa for lunch. That wasn't unusual; the Valley was almost always significantly warmer than the Village, even though it was only a short distance away across Route 1.

"It's nice enough that maybe we can sit outside on the covered patio, don't you think?" asked Kristyn.

"Sounds perfect to me. This is a great idea, coming here. I've been wanting to try Lucia Restaurant and Bar for a while. Thanks for making the reservations; I know I could really use the break and change of scenery."

"I was a little surprised when I went online earlier this week to make the reservations. They had no availability at all for yesterday or tomorrow, and this was one of the few times available today. And dinner? Forget about it. The first available reservation is three weeks out."

The scenery was spectacular and reminiscent of Napa, as was the cuisine. "Oh my God," JJ said while taking a sip of her iced tea, "this might be the best Dungeness crab cake I've ever had. How's your Chicken Paillard?"

"Divine. The chicken is perfect, and the cous cous and braised vegetables are a real treat." She wiped her mouth before continuing. "Save some room. I just saw the server bring the couple at the next table the chocolate cake, and it's *huge*. It looks to die for."

"You know you never have to twist my arm when the subject is dessert, especially if it's chocolate. Count me in."

Despite their plans to relax and decompress to take their minds off the case, if only for a few hours, the conversation kept circling back to the murders of Keith and Loren and the probable ties to the bombings that the FBI was investigating. While they trusted that Isaksen's theory about the ties to the domestic terrorists was accurate, they'd yet to see anything that provided definitive proof or that would persuade a US Attorney to file charges.

After paying their tab, they waited while the valet pulled their car up to the entrance. Deciding to extend their relaxation time a couple of more hours, they headed east towards Carmel Valley Village to indulge in a little wine tasting and shopping. They counted on the fact that, being mid-afternoon on a Thursday, they wouldn't have to fight the maddening crowds that are typical of weekends.

They spent almost two hours exploring the town before heading back to their rental house in Carmel-by-the-Sea. It had been a nice, peaceful afternoon and exactly what they needed to clear their minds and bounce back refreshed. As JJ pulled out and headed west on Carmel Valley Road, Kristyn noticed JJ glancing at the rearview mirror every few seconds.

"What's wrong? Something going on behind us?"

"I'm not sure. There's a large Suburban or Escalade back there, and I'm sure it's the same one that I saw several times while we were shopping. Every time we came out of a store, I noticed them somewhere nearby. Like they were keeping tabs on us."

"Are you sure you're not just being paranoid and having flashbacks to your days at the FBI? It's possible they're just doing the tourist thing at Carmel Village, just like us. There aren't many other places they can go on this road."

"I guess that's possible, but you know I don't put a lot of faith in coincidences." The SUV was about a quarter mile behind them but seemed to match their speed and maintain their distance.

"I'm going to speed up and see what they do. Maybe it's nothing..."

JJ pushed it to 75 miles per hour, and seconds later any doubt about whether they were being followed was gone. The big SUV quickly gained on them and closed to within a car length of them.

"I guess that answers that question," said JJ. The tension in her voice and on her face was clear.

JJ floored it; the big Mercedes SUV roared with 600 horsepower and pulled away. Looking in the rear-view mirror, JJ saw someone reaching their arm out of the passenger window. "Gun! Get down!"

As they both ducked low in their seats, the rear windshield shattered. Other bullets slammed into the back tailgate but, luckily, didn't penetrate the cockpit.

"We need to get off this road! There's a right-hand turn about half a mile up, right beside Bernardus, called Laureles Grade. It goes over the mountain and dumps out onto the Monterey/Salinas highway about a mile from Monterey Airport. There are enough twists and turns that we might lose them or at least put some distance between us." Kristyn pointed to the road quickly approaching.

"Hang on!" JJ took the turn so fast that they almost went up on two wheels, but as soon as she got it under control, she jammed the accelerator back to the floor. The road was narrow and winding, and even though the road was only about 3.5 miles long between Carmel Valley Road and the Monterey/Salinas highway, over that short distance the road climbed over 1,000 feet and had dozens of tight turns and switchbacks.

"We need to keep them off our ass and create some space. You keep an eye out for them, and if you see them getting close, or you see someone getting ready to take a shot at us, you unload on them. Aim for their windshield." JJ looked at Kristyn to make sure she understood and was ready to do as she asked. Although Kristyn had trained hard and become quite proficient on the shooting range, she had only shot paper targets. Could she take a shot at another human being, especially one shooting back at her? *Or would she freeze?*

Kristyn nodded and retrieved her Glock from her purse, though the fear was evident on her face. Loosening her seatbelt, she turned in her seat and focused her attention on the road behind them. As the SUV rounded a curve and accelerated hard to catch up to them, she fired off three quick shots, two of which hit the windshield. As JJ had predicted, that forced them to back off as they had to fight to regain control.

"The GPS shows an intersection about another mile ahead called Sundance Road. If we can get there before they close the gap again, we can try to take them out as they pass by. Hold on!"

JJ was already running 65-70 mph on a road that can barely support the posted speed limit of 45mph, but soon she was hitting speeds as high as 85mph in the straighter sections. Not that there were many straight stretches on this mountain road.

Reaching Sundance Road, JJ slammed on the brakes and pulled just off the main road and behind some scrub bushes. Grabbing her pistol, she quickly yelled, "Use the car for cover and do whatever you can to take out the passenger. I'll try to take out the driver or at least disable the car."

JJ took off at a run before Kristyn could object. They could hear their pursuers closing quickly. Barely making it across the road and across the shoulder and into the culvert that paralleled the pavement before the SUV came around the curve, JJ raised her gun and fired at the driver's window and the tires until her gun was empty. Kristyn fired half a dozen shots from the other side.

Several of JJ's shots shattered the driver's side window and hit him in the head and shoulder, killing him almost instantly; several other bullets shredded both tires on that side. The now out-of-control SUV crashed into a house-sized boulder on the far side of the intersection but, surprisingly, remained upright.

"Kristyn, are you OK? Call 911, then call Isaksen!" Kristyn gave her a wave showing that she was OK.

JJ ran to the other side of the SUV while slapping in a fresh magazine, keeping her gun aimed at the passenger door. As she approached the car, she could see that the passenger was still alive but in need of immediate medical attention. She reached in and took his gun, then handcuffed both hands through the grab handle.

"Hang in there, MAGA boy. Don't die on me. We have a *lot* of people who want to talk to you."

"Are you okay?" Kristyn asked, coming around the car to take JJ's hand. "You scared the hell out of me!"

"I kind of scared me, too. But you've gotta admit, life with me is never boring."

17

Friday, October 24

Friday morning came much too early. Sleep hadn't come easily for either of them despite their exhaustion. The adrenaline had long since worn off, but even that crash hadn't helped. While they were lucky to have survived and sustained only minor injuries, the cuts and bumps and bruises that they suffered didn't make for a comfortable evening. JJ's new car was not so lucky; broken rear windows and bullet holes don't exactly buff out easily. They were both too keyed-up and anxious to even consider dinner Thursday evening; a glass of wine and a handful of Advil had to suffice.

JJ took some comfort in knowing that when she'd talked to Isaksen last night, he'd immediately reached out to his counterpart, SAC Roberts, to request that he post agents around their rental house on Scenic Road. Roberts took things a step further and looped in the Carmel PD and the Monterey County Sheriff's Office to add even more manpower. She didn't enjoy depending on others or feeling like she needed a babysitter, but recent events proved that this was a deep and wide-ranging conspiracy. She wasn't even sure who they could trust; all indications seemed to point to there being one or more sympathizers within law enforcement leaking information about their investigation.

Shortly after 10am, Kristyn's phone rang with an incoming call from Quantico. She was barely awake, and her brain was still foggy, but she forced herself to answer. "This is Kristyn. I hope you have something that makes waking up worthwhile. If not, I swear I'm going to hunt you down."

"Good morning, sunshine! It's Sue Vencill and Keith Hughes, your favorite Quantico forensic specialists. Wake up, wake up, wake up!" Vencill said in a singsong voice, fully intending to be comical and irritating at the same time.

"God, don't be so freaking cheerful this early in the morning, you sadist." Kristyn stretched and rolled over, slowly emerging from the bed and stumbling towards the kitchen.

"Early? It's after 1 o'clock here, and it's not exactly sunrise in California, either," added Hughes. "You guys have really gotten spoiled by your life of leisure and a work schedule that would make a banker jealous." He was rubbing it in hard, just to get another rise out of Kristyn.

"Oh yeah, a real life of leisure. We're working a case that may or may not have connections to domestic terrorism, trying to keep our movie production on track while we're hundreds of miles from home, and, to top it all off, having a bunch of nazis and other lowlifes trying to kill us. It's a laugh a minute."

"Ooohhh, we hadn't heard about someone trying to kill you guys. Come on, spill the tea! We want to hear the details." Vencill loved hearing about the danger and excitement that field agents often encountered, though she readily admitted her preference to experience it vicariously. The lab was her domain, and the scariest thing she usually experienced was testifying in court. Some of those attorneys were probably worse than the criminals that the field agents dealt with.

Kristyn gave them the quick and dirty version of yesterday's events and then brought it back to the reason for their call. "Now that we've gossiped enough, I hope you're going to share some good news based on the evidence we sent you for analysis."

Hughes took the lead. "A bit of good news, though certainly nothing earth-shattering. As you expected, the paint sample that you sent us shows that the Bryant's car had contact with another vehicle that likely pushed it over the cliff. Based on the photos that the Monterey County PD sent, along with the paint samples, we can see where the impact occurred. Based on the impact zone, especially the distance from the ground, there's no doubt that it was a large truck or SUV."

"No actual surprise there. That's what we expected all along."

"True," continued Hughes. "But testing shows that this impact was from a bar mounted on the front of the truck. Based on the damage shown in the pictures, we're confident that it was a heavy-duty 'bull bar' instead of the more popular, lighter-duty push bar. Lots of trucks and SUVs that are used for off-road travel have them, as do most law enforcement vehicles."

"What about the paint sample itself? Anything that will help us narrow down the make and model of the vehicle?"

"The paint sample you sent us is actually black powder coating. If you can find the vehicle, we can absolutely match it to the sample." Vencill showed a few pictures from the samples that were tested.

"I'm confused. Isn't powder coating just paint with a different type of application process?"

"Yes and no," offered Hughes. "Powder coating is a polyester-based coating that's made from polymer resins, pigments, and curing agents. It's applied to aluminum and other metals using a powder coating gun rather than a typical spray gun or brush."

"Bottom line, then, nothing particularly unique about the samples we sent you, but if we find the truck or SUV responsible, we can match the sample to the bull bar, which likely has some scratches on it from the impact."

Kristyn thanked the techs for their help and poured herself another cup of coffee. She saw JJ looking at her expectantly, hoping to hear some good news after the call. "Don't even ask."

18

Friday, October 24

After showering and getting dressed, JJ and Kristyn moved out to the patio and reached out to Isaksen to compare notes, not to mention they hoped that he'd have some news about the person arrested yesterday after the shootout.

"He's not a real chatty sort of guy," offered Isaksen. "We've tried buttering him up, threatening him, everything but slapping the hell out of him. And trust me, there are people standing in line for that option."

"Has he asked for a lawyer yet? I would've thought that he'd have demanded that the second you placed him under arrest." Kristyn looked at JJ, and she nodded in agreement.

"Not yet, surprisingly. He refuses to answer questions and just sits there as if he's mute, but he hasn't asked for a lawyer. I figured these guys would have a dozen scumbag lawyers on speed dial for just this kind of occasion."

JJ jumped in. "Even if he's not talking, you must have learned something about him by now. At least his name, where he's from, his criminal history..."

"Yeah, we got quite a bit. His name is Terry White—how appropriate—and he's originally from Texas. Again, not exactly a big surprise there. Last few years, he's been in Idaho and hanging out with the other inbred ne'er-do-wells that call that place home. As you'd expect, he's got a long and colorful rap sheet going back over 20 years, everything from car theft to assault, domestic abuse, robbery, and on and on. He's done three different stints in state prisons, which is basically like a PhD for criminals."

"To say nothing of finding kindred spirits that share your racist views and bloodlust." JJ had seen way too many people leave prison far worse than when they went in, and that's saying something since many were total wastes of space to start with.

"So, what's the plan moving forward? Offer the guy a deal if he provides evidence against other group members?"

"That's one possibility, Kristyn. First, we want to see if we can find evidence to tie him to the bombing in San Jose. We figure that will make our case against him even stronger. If that doesn't pan out, we're considering either putting the word out on the street that he's giving up the other groups as part of a plea deal or threatening to send him to the county jail awaiting trial while surrounded by a hundred black and Latino gang members. That might put the fear of God into him. He'd be Mr. Popular, but for all the wrong reasons."

***

Early afternoon found JJ and Kristyn picking up a rental car, a new Chevy Suburban, before searching Keith's and Loren's offices at the Naval Postgraduate School. Luckily, the offices had not been emptied and assigned to other instructors, but according to the person escorting them around the campus, that could soon change. The school was actively looking for replacement instructors to salvage the semester for the students.

The search of their offices revealed nothing relevant to their investigation, not that they expected it to after so many weeks. Next stop was a meeting with the IT staff, and that was considerably more interesting, if for all the wrong reasons. The tech gurus told them they'd discovered hackers had wiped every bit of data that Keith and Loren generated during their time teaching at the school from the servers, including the cloud accounts. Every document. Every web search. Every email and chat. Gone.

JJ dove into investigator mode. "Was this a system-wide loss impacting all users, or only the Bryants? And when was this deletion discovered?"

Harold Evans, the head of the IT department, responded. "Fortunately for the school, it only impacted those two accounts. If it had been the entire school, well, I don't know what would have happened. It would be a catastrophe, that's for sure."

"Have you been able to determine when this happened, and how?"

"We have. It happened last night just before midnight. We've done our own investigation and even brought in outside experts, and everyone agrees it was intentional, not some glitch in the system. And trust me, with the level of security that we have on our network, it had to be somebody with some serious skills. They left no trace or digital fingerprints, and while we expected to find other viruses, trojans, or malware infecting our systems, everything is clean. Whoever did this had their sights set on removing any trace of the Bryants, and that's what they did. It's like they were never even here."

"And I assume you filed some sort of police report? And maybe with NCIS or other Navy offices since this is a US government facility?"

"Yes, and yes. Their investigation is still ongoing, but everyone is breathing a small sigh of relief. It could easily have been so much worse."

19

Friday, October 24

"Let's call Julia and have her meet us at Keith's house and we'll go over it one more time. I know the police have already been through there with a fine-tooth comb, as has Julia after the police released the scene, but I'd like to give it one more look. Maybe between the three of us we'll find something they missed. Nothing against the cops that ran this investigation, but since they jumped right to the conclusion that their deaths were an accident, they probably didn't spend too much time and effort searching their house, much less their offices."

Kristyn nodded. "That's a good point. Not that I blame them; once they'd ruled that it was an accident, I'm sure they saw no reason to do any digging beyond a cursory look around."

After almost an hour of methodically searching the house and finding nothing out of the ordinary, JJ sat at the kitchen table trying to make sense of the situation. Someone had scrubbed their entire work lives from the onsite servers and Amazon Web Services (AWS) cloud associated with their school accounts, yet their offices appeared to be untouched. Similarly, there was no evidence that anyone had searched the house, but JJ knew that someone with the right skills could conduct a thorough, top-to-bottom search and not leave a trace. No prints, no DNA, no sign of forced entry.

"Hey Julia, now that you've been through the house a second time, are you noticing anything that appears to be out of place or missing? Anything that sets off alarms for you?"

"No, nothing jumps out at me. When I first came here with the police, I expected to find the place trashed like you see on all the cop shows, but nothing appears to be disturbed or out of place, at least to the best of my recollection."

"It still bugs me," Kristyn interjected, "that we haven't found their PCs here or at their office. That seems a little too coincidental for my jaded mind. Did the detectives speak to you at all about that?"

"Honestly, they didn't seem to put a lot of focus on that and discounted it pretty quickly. When they didn't locate them, they wrote it off as 'lost or destroyed' in the crash. Like they flew out of the car and ended up in the ocean."

"Would it be typical for them to take their computers with them on what was supposed to be a weekend away for just the two of them?" Kristyn knew some people find it hard to cut the cord from work and social media even for a single day, but since she never knew Keith and Loren personally, she was relying on Julia to help fill in the blanks.

"It's hard to say, to be honest. They almost always had their computers with them, but since they were both so looking forward to a weekend away from the stress and tension of their research, I'd like to think that they planned to disconnect for a few days."

JJ started pacing as she thought things through. "So, they might have left their PCs here, or maybe in their offices, and now both of them are missing. If someone broke in, it's not like they'd have to trash the place or make a mess to grab a couple of laptops. They'd be sitting right out in the open; they could take them, and no one would be the wiser."

"Right," offered Kristyn. "And Julia, while I didn't know either of them, I would bet with their background and experience, especially investigating conspiracies, they were meticulous and fanatical about backing up their research."

"Definitely. I know they both backed up to OneDrive religiously. They were both incredibly anal about that. I mean that in a good way, of course."

"When I looked at their desks, I didn't see any evidence of missing external hard drives, like cables still hanging there that someone left behind. Though I guess that someone could have taken that stuff, too." JJ's mind was running through the possibilities, trying to put herself in the shoes of whoever searched the house. Assuming that someone *had* searched the house.

Julia's eyes lit up as the realization that something was missing popped into her head. "I don't know why this didn't occur to me earlier: I didn't see a single USB flash drive anywhere on or in their desks. I don't know if they used them for backing up their research, but I know Keith used them for his work. He'd mentioned many times that he would have to save a presentation to a flash drive so that he could plug it into the dedicated computer and media system in each classroom and lecture hall."

JJ felt a surge of energy, realizing that Julia's epiphany might be a major piece of the puzzle. "You're right. I didn't see a single USB drive anywhere either. If Keith, and likely Loren too, for that matter, used flash drives, I'd expect to see a lot of them scattered about. The fact that there aren't any in either location makes me think that someone took them along with the PCs. They couldn't know what was on those drives without taking the time to search through them, so the logical thing to do is just take them all with you when you grab the PCs. You can look through them later."

"Would Keith and Loren leave backups for their valuable research just sitting out on their desks?"

"Absolutely not, JJ. They'd keep them somewhere safe."

Friday, October 24

"If they had a safe place to hide flash drives, it would make sense for it to be here at the house or at their office, right?" said Kristyn. "I can't imagine them storing it somewhere offsite, like a safe deposit box, because it would be impossible to back stuff up and then take it to the secret location every time they made a change."

"Makes perfect sense." Turning to Julia, JJ continued. "Do you know if Keith and Loren had a safe here in the house? Like maybe hidden under some floorboards or behind a false wall panel?"

"I know that there's a gun safe in Keith's office. The thing is massive; it must weigh like 1,000 pounds."

"I don't suppose there's any chance that you know the combination, do you?"

"Actually, yeah, I do. It's a combination of the kids' birthdates." As they walked towards Keith's office, Julia added, "I've been here a few times, and I've seen no indication that anyone has gotten into the safe. And unless they've got some serious safecracking skills, I can't believe they'd figure out the random string of numbers that Keith used. Even though the numbers are from the kids' birthdays, they're not in any type of order that would be obvious to someone trying to break in."

They all moved to Keith's office, and it took less than a minute for Julia to enter the code and have the door opened. Inside were six rifles of various types, including a Springfield 30.06 hunting rifle, a Mossberg 12-gauge pump-action shotgun, and several AR-15 types commonly lumped together as 'assault weapons'. There were also several handguns and more than a dozen boxes of ammunition of various sizes and calibers.

"Wow," Kristyn said, startled by what she was seeing. "Keith was serious about his guns! He's got some serious firepower here."

"I can't really blame him after all they lived through, especially back when they took down that clandestine agency that was trying to launch another 9/11 type of attack. There were multiple attempts on their lives, it's no exaggeration to say that they barely survived. Even now, more than 15 years later, they still receive a dozen or more threats every year directed against them, their kids, and even their business back in Charlottesville. Then those threats became even more frequent when they started their current research into these white supremacist groups."

"I don't see any thumb drives in here, unfortunately. Let's think about where else they might try to hide them. I agree with Kristyn's conclusion that they'd have to hide them either here or at the school, and my money is on here. I have to believe that they did the bulk of their research from home since they had a packed teaching schedule. Plus, it just makes sense that they'd want to keep the data close at hand and under their control."

JJ looked around the office for what seemed like the hundredth time, but still nothing clicked for her.

Kristyn had been quiet for a few minutes, deep in thought. The wheels were turning. "If we assume that someone broke in here and stole their laptops, then we can also assume they searched all the normal places for their storage devices, right? In dresser drawers, behind picture frames, under the mattress, whatever. Even though it appears the house was untouched, they must have looked around for hidden items."

"Makes sense. They couldn't have broken in here and torn the place apart looking for the files, whatever format they may be in, because that would have raised suspicion about their supposed accident. You may be on to something. Keep going."

"I'm not really sure where this is going... I'm just thinking that it needs to be something easily accessible, relatively speaking, but still hidden."

"So, maybe hidden in plain sight..." JJ got up from her chair and started walking around the office, looking for anything that didn't seem quite right.

Standing on her tiptoes, JJ felt along the top of doorway frames, including the closet. Nothing. She removed the grills from both HVAC vents, then looked beneath the sink in the attached bathroom to look for anything hidden there. Nothing. After 15 minutes, her frustration was turning into anger, and the anger turned into a string of four-letter words.

"Take it easy, sweetie. Maybe we're wrong about someone even breaking in here. If that's the case, we're looking for evidence of something that never even happened."

"I don't believe that..."

"Or maybe these guys are smarter, more organized, and a lot slicker than we give them credit for."

JJ had a 'light bulb moment', a smile slowly emerging to replace her scowl. "Oh my God, that's it!"

"What's it?" asked Julia.

"Kristyn just gave us the answer without even realizing it. Have either of you ever heard of a hiding place referred to as a 'slick'?"

Julia and Kristyn both shook their heads.

JJ jumped up and started looking around the office, paying particular attention to the doors to the bathroom and closet. "An old spy trick is to hide things like microfiche, SD cards, and USB drives where they're covered up by some kind of hardware, like a door hinge. They carve out a niche behind the hinge, literally digging into the wooden door frame, and hide things there."

"I gotta admit, that's pretty brilliant," said Kristyn.

"Yes! This has to be it." JJ pointed to the middle hinge on the closet door. "Look here. There's only one screw holding the hinge on the frame side. Can somebody get me a Phillips-head screwdriver, please."

Julia reached into the top drawer of Keith's desk and brought out a small screwdriver. "Hopefully, this will work if the screw isn't too tight."

"I'm guessing it won't be..." JJ backed out the screw and swung the hinge open. She couldn't contain her smile and excitement.

Using the screwdriver, she pulled the thumb drive from its hiding place and held it up for the others to see. Their excitement, not to mention their relief, was palpable.

"Let's get this USB back to our house and do a quick review of the data and then send copies to Isaksen and the Quantico lab specialists for analysis and safekeeping. Call me paranoid, but I don't feel safe having only one copy in case something happens to the USB drive, or us, for that matter."

"Makes sense," said Kristyn. "But after we're done, I think the next stop should be happy hour at the Cypress Inn. I'm feeling stressed to the breaking point, plus we've been so busy that we missed lunch. I could use something to eat and a glass or two of wine, and I'm guessing that you two could use the break, too."

Julia smiled. "You read my mind."

21

Monday, October 27

If there's one thing The Prophet, aka, Reverend Jacob Bernard, despised, it was leaving the sanctity of his home, his refuge, to travel around the world to meet with his followers and listen to their sniveling sob stories about their health, their financial predicaments, or any of the other thousand inane things that he couldn't care less about. His Fort Worth home was enormous, even by wealthy Texas landowner standards, at nearly 51,000 square feet and smack dab in the middle of 12,000 beautiful acres that included a large lake and his own private airstrip. Not a huge ranch when compared to some of the rich ranchers and land barons, but considering that he only owned a few dozen cattle and even fewer horses, all of which he kept just to fulfill his fantasy of being a simple 'gentleman rancher', it was still impressive.

It wasn't just the ranch that he hated to leave when traveling; he also hated leaving his wife, Karoline. It wasn't because he was a hopeless romantic or harbored any undying feelings of love; it was because he didn't trust her as far as he could throw her. Admittedly, she was the perfect Christian wife and mother to their two kids, Brett and Angela, for their TV and multimedia empire: former model, able to cry on demand as she feigned sympathy for others' suffering, and able to plead for contributions to the ministry that, even by TV evangelist

76

standards, was a master class in grifting. Only Brother Jacob himself was better at the grift. He'd known for years that she made a habit of sleeping around with many men, and quite a few women, whenever they were apart. Their marriage was more of a financial commitment than a genuine love affair, and he'd already promised himself that he'd put a plan in place to dissolve their partnership—*permanently*—soon. He didn't even care what happened to the kids, whom he disparagingly referred to as 'semen demons' in private, if Karoline was out of the picture. They were actually an impediment as he pursued his plans and had no place in the future he was envisioning. All Christian posing aside, he was not likely to be a finalist for Father of the Year.

***

The Prophet was in a foul mood while on his way to the exclusive Wing & Barrel Ranch in Sonoma, CA, where he was to be the headline speaker for a meeting of wealthy Republican movers and shakers. It's not that he wasn't looking forward to the beautiful facilities, the great food, wine, and activities, or the generous donors that would be in attendance; he was. It's just that he'd had to get up much earlier than normal and, to top it off, felt like he was traveling in squalor since he had to travel in his 'backup plane', a Gulfstream G500. While barely four years old, it wasn't nearly as impressive as his newer, faster, and more expensive G700. Because of the relatively short runway at Napa County Airport, roughing it in the G500, which most mere mortals would *kill* to own, was a necessity. How was he supposed to show off for the others if he couldn't fly in the ultimate rich man's toy? He took a bit of solace knowing that none of the attendees, all of whom would rather die than fly commercial, wouldn't be able to travel there in anything larger than his G500, either. He sincerely hoped they were as miserable and upset with the situation as he was. Misery loves company, even when the misery is caused by the very definition of 'first world problems'.

It was early afternoon when the chauffeured SUV pulled up to the entrance of the swank retreat. Brother Jacob had been here several times before and considered it one of his favorite destinations in the US, if not the world. He only regretted that his high profile, even within this group where everyone was a VIP or VIP-wannabe, kept him from bringing, or hiring, some much-needed female companion-ship. Then again, if not for the rampant gossip and prying eyes he'd often witnessed here, he might consider some companionship of the male persuasion. It certainly wouldn't be the first time. He had to fight hard to tamp down his urgent desires since he was painfully aware of the potential price he'd have to pay if word ever got out. In his experience, you can't trust people to remain silent, especially about something salacious. And the people at this event? Even more so. They would use any bit of gossip or overheard whispers to raise their own profiles and further their own agendas.

Brother Jacob had always known that people, especially those with little or no discretion, could be the downfall of the strongest leaders and the best-laid plans. That's why he wouldn't hesitate to have some-one eliminated if he suspected them of spreading rumors or plotting against him; for that matter, he wouldn't hesitate to have them dis-patched proactively to ensure they never had the chance.

22

Monday, October 27

"**I**'m honored to be here today among so many fine men and women, so many fine Americans." Brother Jacob's velvet-smooth tenor voice, amplified by the state-of-the-art sound equipment and professional production team, reached every person and had them enthralled. He was in his glory, in his element.

"I know that you and I have a lot in common: We're all Christians, or at least I know all of you profess to be." The audience laughed at that little dig, though Brother Jacob knew, with absolute certainty, that most of the people in the room harbored and espoused beliefs that were the very antithesis of the teachings of Jesus Christ. If needed, he could produce documentation and videos to prove that point. Then again, he could hardly deny that the same could be said about him, if he were honest, but he worked hard to keep such things hidden from his adoring flock. And the authorities, both state and federal.

"We're all also proud Americans. We *love* this country. Many in this room have served by proudly wearing the uniform; we all thank you for your selfless service and sacrifice. Some of you have served our nation by representing your fellow citizens in your respective state legislatures and in the US House and Senate. Still others have served on the bench as state and federal judges, safeguarding our liberties and protecting us from abuses from the very government that we love. Can I get an amen?"

"Amen" shouted every person in the room, their voices booming as one.

Brother Jacob smiled. It was hard not to. Barely two minutes into his talk and they're already eating out of his hand and hanging on his every word. He often said that people, including the so-called 'elites' and 'intelligentsia', were basically sheep in designer clothes. This lot proved the point.

He continued with a voice barely above a whisper to ensure that the audience was listening intently to every word. "But while people like you, true American patriots, work and sacrifice tirelessly to provide for your families and to make our country, and the world, a better place, there is a growing army of disaffected Americans—and I use the word with barely suppressed anger—that want to tear this country apart. They want to tear down everything that is good and holy about this country, all while embracing godless socialism, if not full-blown communism, and dissolving our democratic republic. They're determined to erase God from every part of our lives and make secular humanism, to use that old term, the norm in our society. Can you imagine? Can you imagine an America where believing in God or having God as our guide—our North Star, if you will—for how we live as a society and how we treat each other becomes a crime?"

His voice rising, "Is that the America that you want for yourselves, your families, your business?"

Shouts of 'hell no', along with a few other non-Christian swear words, erupted from the crowd. He let the shouts and the underlying talking and murmur go on for nearly a minute.

Putty in my hands. The crowd was so aroused that they resembled a Pentecostal tent revival in the deep South more than a group of rich, influential WASPs sitting in California wine country. He half expected someone to start speaking in tongues or handling snakes at any minute. *Religious idiots.*

For the next half hour Brother Jacob spoke about the fight that he was leading to save America's soul and how it was critical for our country's survival for him to have the support, not to mention the funding, of the very people in this room. They were the true elite, the leaders of business and government, and it was up to them to help fight the good fight and save America from the enemy within. They all recognized the enemy—enemies, actually—for who they were: Progressives. Immigrants. People who live or support the LGBTQ+ 'lifestyle'. DEI supporters. Pro-choice murderers. Simply put, anyone that wasn't, in their view, a 'real American'.

Brother Jacob closed with a plea. "I know you support me and the work we're doing, and I ask you to open your hearts, your minds, and yes, your wallets, to help us continue to spread the word and bring God back to his rightful place as the guiding light for our country."

It was a stellar performance, even for someone who's used to taking center stage every single week. The audience applauded. They surrounded him and kept him in conversation for more than an hour, not to mention over lunch. And they opened their wallets. They *really* opened their wallets.

***

Lavinia Newton, the Republican congresswoman from southwest Virginia, had been a fixture at these conferences for years and always contributed enormous sums of money and leveraged her considerable influence to support the far-right wing of her party. Born into considerable wealth—her family had been major players in the coal industry for nearly a hundred years—she considered herself worthy of all the good things that family money had provided, even while almost every one of her constituents struggled just to survive. She was also an ardent and huge financial supporter of Brother Jacob and his ministry. Though she professed to be a 'real' Christian, her true leanings tended towards both 'prosperity gospel' and the more strident vitriol associated with white nationalist groups. As she said on more than one occasion, including once on an ill-timed hot mic moment, '*God wants his children to be rich; the poor are simply a drain on society.*'

And therein lies her quandary. If she'd simply been a hypocritical politician, very few people would have taken notice; after all, the term 'hypocritical politician' is the very definition of redundancy. Lavinia, though, had crossed the line: it's one thing to claim to help the poor, but it's another thing to falsify your tax returns for almost 15 years to show that you've contributed hundreds of thousands of dollars when you haven't contributed a single dime.

The FBI, IRS, and other government agencies offered her a choice: work as a confidential informant to help uncover other high rollers engaged in the same behavior, especially those using the church to claim religious exemptions when their contributions are 100% political, or go to jail. It wasn't just Brother Jacob the feds were interested in, though he and other high-profile TV evangelists were certainly on their radar. They were also laser-focused on the big money contributors, and this conference room was full of them.

Unfortunately for Lavinia and her law enforcement handlers, they had no clue how deep the darkness was surrounding Brother Jacob. They would soon find out.

23

Tuesday, October 28

"Whoever accessed their cloud accounts, they certainly did a number on them. They wiped them clean." FBI forensic scientist Sue Vencill was sharing the findings that she and her partner, Keith Hughes, had found as they examined the OneDrive accounts belonging to Keith and Loren.

It was barely 9am in Carmel, but JJ and Kristyn had already been up and working for several hours. This was their third video call of the morning, the first being an update with SAC Isaksen about the Bryant investigation and the second being a call with SAC Roberts, Assistant SAC Hurd, and San Jose County Chief of Police Cook about the bombing at Lofton Renewable Energy. While they were admittedly miles away from making any arrests in either case, they had reached a consensus that the cases had to be connected. They put the probability at about 75%, which, if they were honest, was based more on their collective gut feelings than any hard evidence.

"Then I guess we're lucky we recovered the USB drive that they used for onsite backup. Since the last file saved was just a few hours before their deaths, I've got to believe that we have everything that would have been in the cloud." JJ counted her blessings, for probably the hundredth time, that they'd found the USB drive hidden at their house.

"Not to be a naysayer," started Hughes, "but that's not entirely accurate. The USB certainly appears to contain backups of every document that they created relative to their investigation, but we have no way of knowing if there were other files, perhaps in other formats, that they didn't save to this drive. Certainly, there were hundreds, if not thousands of other files on their PC's, we just don't know if they applied to this case versus something to do with their course work..."

"Or their favorite recipes, or pictures of their kids. We get it." Kristyn was hoping to get her point across without sounding overly snarky. "I don't think we'll ever know everything that was on their PC, but I think it's pretty safe to say Keith and Loren backed up their work diligently to multiple locations, so we probably have everything relevant to the investigation."

"Sorry, Kristyn, you're right, of course. I didn't mean to imply otherwise. We're lucky that they were so anal, which in my mind is a wonderful thing. I wish everyone practiced such great data and security hygiene." Hughes felt a bit chastened, despite Kristyn's efforts to temper her earlier response.

JJ tried to change the subject and move things forward. "Kristyn and I probably spent at least 18 hours looking through the data, and I feel like we've only scratched the surface. One thing we noticed, and presumably you guys have too, is that Keith and Loren never identified their sources, or most of the suspects, by name. They used code names in almost all instances, which was a smart move on their part but makes it tough for us since we don't have any way to identify the players."

Vencill nodded her head. "Yes, we noticed that, too. We've leveraged one of our AI programs to generate a list of characters, if you will, whether they're informants, suspects, or just general interview subjects. So far it doesn't look like it will help with actual names, but it has done a good job of relating statements, locations, dates, etc. to specific players."

"That's helpful, without a doubt, and probably a path that prosecutors will want to discuss and exploit if the case leads to arrests and trials. JJ and I will continue searching through the files, as well as doing another physical search of their home and offices, to see if we missed something, like maybe a 'key' that correlates code names to actual names and contact information."

"That would be the Holy Grail, for sure. We'll keep our fingers crossed."

"Agreed, Keith. One last question before we go. We've already noticed that there is a huge amount of money being talked about in these files. Millions of dollars, in fact, and it's quite clear that (a) a lot of that money is being used for bad things by some very bad people, and (b) there's somebody sitting at the top of this conspiracy that's siphoning off obscene amounts of cash, and dollars to donuts, most of his or her minions are clueless. I think we need to bring in someone like a forensic accountant who can follow the money."

"Funny you should say that," said Vencill as she smiled widely. "We had already planned to hook you up with our newest forensic accounting specialist, an absolute freaking goddess. Keith and I have already briefed her on the case, and she can't wait to meet you guys and get started."

24

Ⓢ

Tuesday, October 28

"I don't get it," said JJ. "I've reviewed everything I can find, from social media, to LinkedIn, to the FBI files Isaksen sent over, and I don't understand how this Diane Salter lady can be glorified as such a rock star in the forensic accounting world."

Kristyn took a bite of her sandwich while flipping through some of the same reports that JJ had already reviewed. "Why do you say that?"

"She's supposed to be God's gift to forensic accounting, but she's not even a CPA. In fact, unless I missed it, she never even graduated from college. Well, at least not with a four-year degree; she graduated from community college, but with an Associate of Applied Science degree in HVAC repair. Are you fucking kidding me?"

Kristyn could barely suppress her giggle. "That kind of education and background doesn't exactly scream 'Deloitte' or 'Ernst & Young', does it?"

***

Since they had an hour before their scheduled call with Salter, JJ suggested they do a quick video call with Isaksen to see what he knows about her and the range of cases she's worked during her tenure at the FBI.

No sooner had they gotten Isaksen on the call than he broke into a big smile and laughter, which was definitely out of character. "Oh, you guys are in for a treat!"

"I'm not sure whether you're saying that like it's a good thing or a bad thing. And truthfully, I don't think we have the time or the mental bandwidth for it to be a bad thing." Kristyn didn't mince words despite the deep respect she had for him.

"Trust me, you have nothing to worry about. I've worked with Diane on several cases and let me assure you she's brilliant and extremely capable. Scary brilliant, to tell you the truth. Think about a cross between Albert Einstein and the guys from *The Big Bang Theory*."

JJ sighed. "Let me guess: she's more 'Sheldon Cooper' than Einstein, right?"

"Well, yes, that's correct. You'll quickly realize that she's most definitely on the spectrum, but that's what makes her exceptional. You're probably aware that autism research has shown individuals on the spectrum have increased brain activity compared to neurotypicals. It's this brain activity that seems to be responsible for their superior ability to recognize patterns, and in complex forensic accounting, enhanced pattern recognition separates the great ones from the merely competent."

***

Salter didn't just impress them; she left them absolutely awestruck. They didn't really know what to expect, but it certainly wasn't this. Mid-40s. African American. Smoked like a chimney and cursed like a sailor. And the bawdiest, most ribald sense of humor they'd experienced in years that kept them in stitches. If forensic accounting didn't work out for her, she had a bright future as a standup comic. They loved her from the get-go.

"So as you can see, there's a clear pattern that shows thousands of money transfers since 2016 that have gone in and out of literally dozens of banks in countries that have, shall we say, weak banking laws and a reputation for turning a blind eye to criminal behavior and money laundering." Salter sat back with a satisfied smile and took a long drag from her cigarette, finally blowing the smoke towards the ceiling of her home office. The smoke hung thick in the air, a sign that she must go through a couple of packs a day, if not more. Then again, the overflowing ashtray on the side of her desk provided more than ample evidence of that fact.

JJ and Kristyn looked at each other, both feeling completely overwhelmed, like they'd just sat through a lecture on theoretical physics or quantum mechanics. It was JJ who spoke first.

"I think we both follow your logic and trust your findings, but to be honest, it's way over our heads. We don't see the patterns, but if you say they're there, that's good enough for us. I just hope that, should this case eventually make it to trial, it can be simplified enough for the DA and the judge and jury to understand it."

"Diane, if you had to net it out from what you've learned so far, what would you say? And where does that take us?" Kristyn felt certain that they were on the right path; she just wasn't sure where that path was leading at this point.

"I can say with certainty that the Bryants were on the right track, and while the data we have doesn't positively identify the players—*yet*—there is zero doubt that the money is being funneled through one or more religious organizations and then on to various Christian Nationalist groups. And maybe more importantly, I can confirm their suspicions that whoever is running this little enterprise—the head of the snake, if you will—is skimming a shitload right off the top. We're talking about tens of millions. I can't imagine that their merry band of misfits and white trash followers would be thrilled to learn that."

JJ couldn't help but smirk. "I'm glad that you can confirm that point; that could be an area of weakness that we can take advantage of down the line. We'll file that away under 'future leverage'. Keep us updated as you uncover more information, especially if you're able to identify any of the players. We'd like to ID the leaders, of course, but if we have to settle for the assholes contributing to the cause and work our way up from there, then that's what we'll do."

25

Wednesday, October 29

It was barely 8am when her phone rang. JJ was sleeping, cuddled up as the big spoon to Kristyn's little spoon, and was right in the middle of an erotic dream where they were lying on an island beach in the South Pacific after a night of passionate lovemaking. This was the first day she'd had the luxury of sleeping in beyond 6:30 or 7:00, and she was none too happy to be awakened by the obnoxious screeching from her iPhone. Her anger dissolved quickly when she saw the name displayed on the screen.

"I guess it's good that it's you, 'cause if it was anyone else that ruined the incredibly sexy dream I was having, I'd probably tear them a new one."

"So sorry to ruin your erotic adventures, but I've got something that might be even more important. But I'll let you decide." Shelly Blackburn, chief of police for Napa, California, was one of JJ's and Kristyn's best friends and the inspiration for the hero character in the movie they were currently producing. The three of them had met the year prior when JJ and Kristyn had gotten pulled into a murder investigation while they were vacationing in wine country, only to find out that this murder was just one in a string of them over the past few years in California's far-flung wine-growing regions. Shelly had been instrumental in the investigation and bringing down the demented serial killer Alyssa LaCroix, and now because they served and survived the traumatic events together, they had a bond that would last a lifetime.

"Let me put you on speaker. It sounds like this is something Kristyn needs to hear, too, if I can rouse her. I swear, this girl could sleep through an atomic bomb." JJ started shaking Kristyn and calling her name, but she was doing her best to ignore the interruption.

"Noooo, let me sleep, damn you. I'm tired, and you woke me from the sexiest dream ever. If you let me go back to sleep, I promise I'll tell you all about it later. I'll even role-play the dream with you if you'll just leave me alone until nine."

JJ and Shelly laughed. "Well, as fun as that sounds, I'm afraid that something even more important than your dirty dreams and fantasy role-playing needs our attention. I'll let Shelly fill us in now that she's heard all your erotic plans for the day."

Kristyn blushed crimson, not realizing that Shelly was on the phone and had heard her erotic musing. "Oh my God, I'm so embarrassed. I didn't realize that you were on the phone, much less with someone who could overhear my side of the conversation. Sorry, Shelly! I swear I'm not always this graphic and crazy, especially not this early in the morning."

Shelly giggled. "You don't have to apologize, and you certainly don't have to play innocent with me. Remember, I've stayed in your guest room on lots of occasions, and I've overheard the two of you getting busy more times than I can count."

"You said that you had something that would interest us. What's up?" asked JJ.

"You guys told me recently about the case you're working regarding the Bryant murders and the probable links to the spate of business bombings, including the one last week in San Jose. There was an explosion last night in Napa, and I think there's a likelihood they're related."

Kristyn was now wide awake. "Oh, my gosh. What kind of business did they bomb? And was anybody hurt?"

"It was a custom crush facility that makes and stores wines for a couple dozen smaller vineyards that don't have their own manufacturing facilities. The explosion completely destroyed the place, killing three people and injuring almost a dozen.

"Did this happen overnight? I wouldn't think there'd be anybody in that kind of facility late at night, or certainly few." JJ knew little about wine production, but she assumed she was on the right track.

"No, it was earlier in the evening, around 7:30. To your point, during most of the year there wouldn't be many people onsite after 5:30 or 6:00, but since harvest is just wrapping up, there's a lot more activity. It's not exactly around the clock, but it definitely goes late into the evening."

"I think we should head up there and see if it does, in fact, connect to our investigation. We can be up there by noon, right JJ?"

"Absolutely. And we'll reach out to the FBI team that is investigating the San Jose bombing, too, and ask them to join us. Unless you've already taken that step?"

Shelly responded. "No, I haven't, but only because I was waiting for the preliminary report from our on-scene investigators to make sure that it wasn't some kind of industrial accident. Since we've determined with 100% certainty that this was a bomb, we'll want to involve the FBI and the ATF for sure."

"We'll leave here within the hour. And maybe while we're driving up there you can perform some of your 'concierge magic' and get us a room at the Villagio."

Kristyn jumped in. "And I wouldn't say no to the three of us having a nice dinner somewhere in or around Yountville. Maybe you can reach out to your contacts at Bottega or one of your other favorite restaurants that's willing to accommodate us on short notice. Although I've yet to see any restaurant or hotel in the Valley that wouldn't bend over backwards for you regardless of the circumstances." Kristyn was always thinking ahead, especially when it involved good food and accommodations.

"I'm sure I can arrange something, both the hotel and the dinner reservations. You guys just concentrate on getting up here ASAP. I'd prefer it if you were onsite before the Feds come storming in here to take over and muck things up."

"So true, unfortunately. Text us the company name and address so we can pop it into the GPS, and we'll call or text you when we're getting close."

26

Wednesday, October 29

It was just before noon when JJ and Kristyn pulled into the lot across the street from the burned-out remains of Napa Custom Crush. Police tape surrounded the building and kept everyone back as far as possible. Traffic was being forced into a single lane on north-bound Route 29, and Oakville Crossing, the road that the facility fronted, was closed to all traffic.

Shelly greeted them as they climbed out of the car, wrapping them both in big hugs. "Thanks so much for rushing up here. I hope you didn't hit too many delays with the traffic backups this is causing."

"I'm sure we would have if not for you giving us a heads-up and pulling some strings with your team. If we hadn't crossed over to Silverado Trail and gotten your blessing to sneak in the back way on Oakville Crossing, it probably would have taken at least another 30 minutes. Thanks for clearing the way for us; I could get used to this kind of VIP treatment." Kristyn was happy to see Shelly, and even happier not to be stuck in traffic. JJ's lack of patience and road rage tendencies were rubbing off on her.

"Have the FBI and ATF shown up yet?" asked JJ.

"No, but the ATF is on their way. They told me they were sending agents from San Francisco and Sacramento."

"We called our FBI contacts, the ones that are leading the investigation at Lofton Renewable Energy. SAC Roberts' area of responsibility includes a good swath of wine country, and he has assigned Assistant SAC Evelyn Hurd, who handles the San Jose region, to run point on the investigation into these bombings. They'll both be here within the next couple of hours."

They spent the next ninety minutes walking through the remains of the building, at least those sections that the fire chief had deemed safe. All three donned Tyvek protective suits and latex gloves and booties since it was still an active crime scene, though truth be told, they were happy to wear them to keep from ruining their clothes. As far as the smell that would permeate everything they were wearing, there was no getting around that.

Lieutenant Maury Rogow, Shelly's lead investigator, approached and guided them to a table where they bagged and tagged all the collected evidence. "There's not much evidence left because of the force of the explosion and the resultant fire, but we did find a few bomb components and what we assume is the trigger device."

JJ inspected it. "I'm no expert, and I'll obviously defer to the ATF and FBI, but based on what I saw at the San Jose bombing, I believe this could be the same signature. The trigger device and the colors of the wires on the circuit board, what's left of it, strike me as the same. Let's wait for a formal determination before any information gets shared with the media. For that matter, it's probably best if it's kept under wraps as long as possible during the investigation."

Kristyn's phone rang, and she stepped away to take the call in a quieter spot. Walking back up to JJ and Shelly a few minutes later, she said, "That was Vencill and Hughes circling back with me. I texted them a while ago to see if they found any online chatter for groups taking credit for this bombing or any other talk that may point us in the right direction."

"That was smart," said JJ. "Do they have anything?"

"They said there's been no public statement from any of the groups that are suspected of being involved in the earlier bombings, or from anyone for that matter. But there are already hundreds of posts and videos being shared by miscreants all over the country, not just here in California, praising whoever did this. Many people commented that those who were killed, injured, or suffered a huge financial loss deserved it because they were '*a bunch of rich, liberal elites that are destroying our country.*'"

Shelly just shook her head. "Every day I feel like this country is one step closer to out and out civil war."

"And every day I feel like we have more and more people trying to make sure that's exactly what happens." JJ couldn't even begin to hide her disgust.

27

Thursday, October 30

Back at his Texas ranch, Brother Jacob was angry, highly agitated, and practically wearing a path in his expensive hardwood floors as he paced back and forth, grumbling and cursing under his breath. The bombing at Napa Custom Crush had gone off without a hitch, not that he doubted that outcome for a second. With the money he spends financing these groups, not to mention the high-tech weapons and tools he equips them with, he expects and demands perfection. He also hadn't lost a second of sleep worrying about the people killed or injured, much less the loss of millions of dollars of lost production equipment and stored wine. *Fuck them.*

What he was stressing about was how to craft and manipulate a story for the media that he could spin to his advantage, or more accurately, to the advantage of the Christian Nationalist movement that he reigned over. He was the puppet master, and they were the puppets. While the earlier bombings were nothing more than smoke screens to allow him to make millions of dollars while framing it as real American 'patriots' fighting back against the godless left-leaning, limp-dick liberals that were ruining this country, this action wasn't so clear cut.

In truth, this bombing wasn't about money at all; it was about retribution. He didn't stand to make a dime. As he always did when planning these actions, he had created a backstory for his followers to rationalize the terror they were about to unleash. It's just that in this case there wasn't an ounce of truth behind it. Not that the stories he'd spun for earlier actions weren't fairy tales, but this time he'd taken it to new heights. He claimed that the company hired dozens of Mexican drug cartel members as 'employees' and allowed them to use old wine barrels as storage vessels for the hundreds of millions of dollars' worth of drugs that they shipped in from Mexico each month.

The reality was altogether different. There were no Mexican cartel members, and there were no drug shipments. He knew that rolling out those tired tropes would resonate with his followers; one could hardly turn on the news—or what passes for 'news' these days—without hearing these lies being constantly parroted by the current administration. This action was strictly business: Napa Custom Crush had canceled all contracts with Beckett Estates Winery when they uncovered massive fraud. While Beckett claimed to be a 100% organic and biodynamic winery—every advertisement, every wall poster, even every one of their servers in their St. Helena tasting room espoused their 'clean' bona fides—lab testing found that to be anything but true. Their wines had enough chemical additives to rival many of the processed foods and drinks found on grocery store shelves. Even worse, while they claimed to source their grapes from some of the premier vineyards in Napa and Sonoma, an investigation discovered that they were importing virtually 100% of their fruit from outside California.

Not only was this fraudulent for consumers who paid a much higher price for supposed 'premium' wines, but it was criminally fraudulent labeling and money laundering that under-reported tax revenues to the US and the states from which they sourced the grapes. Potential fines ran into millions of dollars.

The Prophet wouldn't normally have involved himself in such mundane dealings, but this one was personal: he was the owner of Beckett Estates Winery, or at least one of the many LLCs that he owned via a labyrinth of shell companies, was the owner. He took it as a personal affront that he was being shut down and, even worse, referred to the state and federal authorities that have their fingers in every aspect of alcohol production, sales, and taxation. He felt certain, as smug narcissists often do, that the authorities would find it impossible to trace the ownership back to him. His team had created so many cutouts and shell companies, mostly in countries renowned for their banking privacy laws, that it would be next to impossible to unravel.

Still, Beckett had provided a steady income stream that was a godsend for laundering money from several less-than-legal sources, to say nothing of serving as an operational slush fund for certain undertakings where it was especially critical that he remained anonymous.

* * *

"Have you noticed that almost everybody in here is talking about yesterday's bombing?" asked Shelly. She, JJ, and Kristyn were having lunch at Mustards Grill where there was the usual mix of locals and tourists, and since the bombing was still fresh on everyone's mind—and the restaurant was less than a mile from the site—it was a frequent, almost constant, topic of conversation.

"I certainly have. I even overheard a couple of tables talking about it as I made my way to the restroom," said Kristyn.

JJ absently stirred her iced tea while speaking. "Since the preliminary report from the FBI and ATF confirms that the bombing appears to be the same signature as the other recent ones, I think we should work with Roberts and Hurd to find some kind of paper trail that may point to a particular person or winery that was the target."

Kristyn nodded. "I was thinking the same thing. We should ask them to pull Diane Salter in on this and have her work her magic. Look for companies or individuals that may be deeply in debt and trying to collect insurance dollars, or companies that may have had dealings with our domestic terrorist friends that may have gone a bit off the rails."

"Shelly, do you think the owners of Napa Custom Crush will cooperate with the investigation and open up their records to us without delaying things waiting for a warrant?" JJ had yet to see a situation that Shelly couldn't finesse with the locals, but she had to ask.

"Without a doubt. They're good people, and they've lost something that they've worked decades to build. I know they're devastated; they lost long-time friends and employees, people that were like family to them. Not to mention that most of their customers had been with them for years, even built their businesses together."

"Let's dig in then. I don't want to get ahead of myself, but something about this one feels different. With Lofton Renewable Energy and the earlier bombings, it was easy to see a serious disconnect between the targeted company's politics—or at least their *perceived* political leanings—and those of the domestic terrorist groups. But here? It doesn't seem so clear to me." The growing awareness that this bombing was different made JJ uneasy.

"I agree," added Shelly. "Especially because no person or group has claimed responsibility yet, and it's been over 24 hours. If I'm not mistaken, in the other cases someone made a public proclamation within 1-2 hours."

"If there's one bright spot," said Kristyn, "it's that we can probably rule out a copycat bomber since the preliminary report points to this being the same bomb maker. Hopefully, that helps us focus the investigation more narrowly."

"True, unless it turns out that we have a bomber who's willing to freelance and sell his wares to whoever can pay for them." JJ didn't even want to consider that possibility.

"Well, thanks for that, Little Miss Sunshine. You just opened the list of suspects to include every person with access to the Dark Web, if not the entire internet." Shelly intended this as a joke, but all three of them barely cracked a smile.

Fortunately, the lemon-lime tart with the mile-high brown sugar meringue that they split helped brighten the mood. It was just the antidote to the heavy conversation and stress they were feeling.

28

Friday, October 31

In all his years with the FBI, Isaksen could count on one hand the number of times that he'd been on a call with the FBI director. He'd served under five directors during his career, the days of one imperious, long-serving leader like J. Edgar Hoover having been long since relegated to the past. Not that anyone wanted to see a return to the Hoover days, but things are vastly different in today's world. In this crazy political environment, the director often changes with each new administration, for better or for worse. Fortunately for the dedicated men and women of the FBI, and for all Americans, FBI Director Carl Ferguson was one of the rare holdovers from the previous administration. At least he was, for the time being. It was a well-known fact that he had a giant target on his back. The president had made clear his personal animosity towards him and complete dissatisfaction with his politics. Because Ferguson was widely respected by most members of Congress and the thousands of agents and specialists under his command, he was a major thorn in the president's side.

Isaksen and his San Francisco-based counterpart, SAC Roberts, were summoned to this video call by Director Ferguson. The only other person on the call caught him totally by surprise: Attorney General Pam Honig. If meeting with the FBI director was a rare occurrence, it was nothing compared to the rarity of meeting with the

Attorney General. Isaksen and Roberts didn't even have to communicate their surprise, or their distaste, for Honig. She was the polar opposite of Ferguson, someone for whom the Constitution and laws of the land were merely annoyances to be circumvented in furtherance of the president's agenda. As one would expect, there was no love lost between Ferguson and Honig, and everyone knew it was just a matter of time before she persuaded the president to fire him and replace him with someone that would toe the party line and pledge loyalty to the administration instead of that 'annoying' thing called the Constitution.

Honig didn't engage in any pleasantries or even any introductions, but rather just jumped right into the matter at hand. She had little respect for anyone in the FBI and knew that the rank and file viewed her with barely veiled contempt. *Fuck 'em.*

"Gentlemen, let me get right to the point. I've read the reports on the bombings that you've been investigating, including the two most recent incidents in California, and I don't like the direction of this investigation. To be clear, I think you're barking up the wrong tree by focusing on these so-called domestic terrorist groups. From everything I've seen, I think we should focus on foreign powers, whether state-sponsored or rogue terrorist groups."

Isaksen took a breath to calm himself before responding. He knew she didn't even buy her own bullshit, just using her position to intimidate them and guide the investigation in a direction that suited the administration. "May I ask what information you've seen that would warrant moving the investigation in that direction? I ask simply because everything that we've seen so far, every bit of evidence, points to domestic white supremacist groups."

"For starters, Mr. Isaksen"—not even giving him the respect of using his earned title—"there is no such thing as 'white supremacist groups' in this country, and I'm determined to strike that term from any and all references in government and media. I never want to hear or see that word again, because to me it has the same ugly connotations as the n-word. Anyone I hear using that term will face disciplinary action, up to and including termination."

Honig sat back with a self-satisfied smirk on her face, loving the shock and dismay she was witnessing from these men that were powerless to challenge her or even craft a response.

SAC Roberts finally spoke. "Do you have any suspicions about which foreign actors might be involved in these bombings? Maybe the Russians or the Chinese?" He knew she was full of shit and trying to derail their investigation. He also knew that she'd do everything possible to keep any mention of Russian involvement out of the investigation and any media reports. Like others in the current administration, she showed more loyalty and fealty to Russia than to her own country.

"I'm certain that it's not the Russians. The president and I have had conversations with Putin, and he assured us of that fact, and we take him at his word. While I am less certain about the Chinese or North Koreans, I don't see how these events benefit either of them. Still, I wouldn't completely discount them. My money is on the Ukrainians, probably as their way of paying us back for drastically reducing the funding we provide them to continue their illegal war."

29

Friday, October 31

Isaksen, Roberts, and Ferguson sat in stunned silence for several moments after Attorney General Honig dropped from the call without so much as a goodbye. Just one of her patented smirks.

FBI Director Ferguson was the first to speak. "I know what you're both thinking, and I'm right there with you: she'll do everything she can to spin this in a way that's favorable to the administration and easy to sell to their cult followers. What's worse, she's fucking stupid enough to think she's convincing everyone else of her brilliance."

Isaksen nodded. "No doubt, sir, but how do we continue following this investigation where it leads with her trying to cockblock us at every turn?" Isaksen rarely cursed, and for him to use language like that was a sign that he'd reached his limit.

Ferguson was not so buttoned-up with his language, especially when someone was stifling investigations in favor of politics. "Fuck her. We go around her. I've already started putting plans in place to accomplish that."

"How do you plan to do that, sir? She's the Attorney General, so basically the highest law enforcement person in the land. Not to mention that she's your boss. Aren't you afraid that she'll fire you and try to ruin you in the process?" Roberts was genuine in his concern.

"Look, let's face it: as far as my career is concerned, I'm already a dead man walking. I shouldn't have survived this long in this shit-for-brains administration, and it's just a matter of time before I'm forced out. Luckily, I've got 30-plus years of government service, so I can retire at any time. And maybe I'm kidding myself, but I think I have a lot of options if I head out to the private sector. Bottom line, I'm not worried about her or the president or any of these other assholes. I've got my pension, my wife is a managing partner at one of the top DC law firms, and we're fortunate enough to have done well over the years, financially speaking. I can walk away tomorrow if necessary."

"Good to know," responded Isaksen. "So, tell us: what's your plan for pursuing this investigation with the Wicked Witch of the West looking over our shoulders?"

"Simple. You're going to report directly to me, and I'll ensure that the information is 'sanitized' as needed. I want you guys to double-down on these white supremacist and Christofacist groups. Increase surveillance; pull in more agents if you need them. As far as warrants go, anything you need, let me know. I'll go directly to friendly judges, up to and including the judges at the Ninth Circuit. They fucking hate Honig and this administration as much as I do."

Isaksen and Robert both nodded in agreement. It was obvious how much respect they had for their leader and his willingness to stand up for what's right, even in the face of career suicide.

"One more thing that you gentlemen should know and follow-up on. We have a confidential informant who's part of the rich oligarch-wannabes that are sympathetic to these groups, if not outright funding them. She's been working with us for almost six months, and as I'm sure you'll appreciate, her cooperation is not exactly voluntary. She's anything but cooperative, but we have some heavy charges hanging over her head that help to keep her in line."

"How do we contact her, or is she deep cover?" Roberts asked.

"You can contact her directly, but the conversations need to be private and off the books. I'll let her know to expect your call."

"Is she a member of one of the neo-Nazi groups in California?" asked Isaksen.

"No, she's actually part of a group here in DC. That group is the US House of Representatives. You may have heard of her; she's a card-carrying piece of shit that should have lost her seat years ago, but apparently her constituents are dumb enough to keep electing her even though she couldn't give two shits about them."

"That sounds like half the people in Congress, off the top of my head, but if I had to pick one that fits the bill perfectly, I'd have to guess you're referring to Lavinia Newton." Isaksen hoped he was mistaken.

Ferguson just smiled. "Bingo."

30

Monday, November 3rd

"I feel like we're spinning our goddamn wheels here," griped JJ. Kristyn's expression showed she felt the same frustration.

The weekend had brought no new useful leads or information despite the many hours of research and investigation they invested. No recent developments on the bombings at Lofton Renewable Energy or Napa Custom Crush, the murders of Keith and Loren Bryant, or any of the other instances of domestic terrorism that they were sure were the work of the same groups. Then, to top it off, they'd heard from SACs Isaksen and Roberts about their meeting with Attorney General Honig and her orders to focus the investigation on foreign actors, both state sponsored and rogue factions, instead of homegrown terrorists.

The only bright spot was FBI Director Ferguson's orders to stay focused on the domestic angle and essentially ignore Honig's demands. They expressed admiration for his determination and integrity, as well as his plans to circumvent the attorney general and go straight to the federal courts to get the warrants necessary to put these assholes under a microscope. JJ had probably summed it up best by saying, *'You gotta love this guy—he's got balls the size of church bells'*. Political correctness was never her strong suit, but they all agreed with her.

Kristyn was reviewing her Outlook calendar and planning their next steps. "After we have our movie production update call with Beth Hinshaw at 10am, which shouldn't take more than an hour, let's focus on putting together a list of targets for those search warrants. I say we start with the cell phones and social media of those miscreants who tried to kill us over in Carmel Valley."

"I like that. Last time I checked with Isaksen, he said that the passenger, Terry White, had still barely uttered a word but, surprisingly, hadn't lawyered up. He's just cooling his jets sitting in the county jail."

"Since the Monterey PD considered the attack on us an open and shut case, there wasn't much follow-up. Maybe we start with those two—White and the driver, Travis Wilke—and as we identify the people that they talked to or collaborated with on social media, we'll have Isaksen and Roberts apply for additional warrants. Basically, cast a wider net and see what we catch."

JJ smiled. "It's definitely a fishing expedition, but right now we've got nothing better to go on. Let's dive in."

True to his word, once Ferguson received the request that she escalated through Isaksen, he reached out to members of the Ninth Circuit court and had warrants for White's and Wilke's Verizon mobile account and their various social media accounts within a couple of hours.

"How long do you think it will take before we see the data from Verizon and the social media companies?" asked Kristyn.

JJ gave a wry smile. "In my experience, it's like night and day. Verizon will probably have their information to us within 12-24 hours; they're used to this kinda stuff and they're usually pretty cooperative with law enforcement. Social media companies are anything but cooperative and usually complete dicks about it. They'll often go to court to block the warrants, especially asshole companies like Signal, Telegram, and Twitter..."

"You mean X..."

"Fuck them. I hated them then, and I hate them even more now. They'll always be Twitter to me."

"Will they be able to quash the warrants?"

"No, but what they're always counting on is that the government will get so tired and frustrated with the delays that they eventually find other avenues for the investigation or settle charges with the defendant. They just want to stand up and say that they protected their user's right to privacy, regardless of what criminal acts, including terrorism, they may have committed."

"And then they wrap themselves in the flag and crow about their so-called 'patriotism', right?"

"You got it. But between you and me, I think it goes well beyond that. I could never prove it, but I'll go to my grave believing it: they not only fight the release of the user data covered by the warrants, but they've gone so far as to tip off the suspects to give them time to cover their tracks. I think sometimes they've even taken proactive measures to help erase the information from their databases to protect the person or group being investigated."

"Let me guess: the person or group they try to cover for are usually members of the alt-right that try to curry favor with the current administration, right?"

JJ smiled. "See? You're so much more than just another pretty face."

31

◈

Tuesday, November 4th

It was late afternoon, Pacific Time, when Isaksen pulled everyone together on a video call to get an update and plan next steps. Although it was getting late on the east coast, Vencill and Hughes were there, too, as was Diane Salter.

"I understand Verizon provided you the data for White's and Wilke's phones this morning, correct?" Roberts was jumping right in.

"That's correct, sir," answered Hughes. "They maybe would have gotten it to us today, or tomorrow at the latest, but we pulled a few strings with some of our contacts there."

"Excellent. Anything jump out yet?" Roberts was all business.

"A lot of what we've uncovered so far still needs a deeper look, but we've found where both phones have made and received dozens of calls from the same numbers. When we've searched those numbers, mostly from California but quite a few from Idaho, Texas, and a few other states, we found they belong to a veritable rogue's gallery of bad actors." Hughes knew he was sugarcoating the findings, but he preferred not to interject his opinions unless requested.

"How so?" asked Assistant SAC Hurd.

Vencill responded. "A quick search of the FBI's criminal database provided the basic information like arrest records, etc. but then we went a step further and looked these people up on their public-facing social media pages...."

"Ahhh, so no warrant required..." interjected Kristyn.

"Exactly," continued Vencill. "Obviously, we haven't had a lot of time yet, so we've barely scratched the surface, but just let me say, these characters are none too shy about spouting their racist and white supremacist opinions. Every single one of them has Nazi symbols and flags and quotes all over their pages. I also noted something that could help identify suspects from crime scene photos or videos: every one of them has multiple tattoos that are as identifiable as fingerprints or DNA.

"Good work, you two, and if you need additional eyes on this, let me know and I'll work with your boss to get more people assigned. In the interim, we'll continue working on the warrants for the social media companies so we can go deeper and uncover their past and deleted posts, plus we need any text messages that aren't tied to their Verizon accounts. Every day, criminals are growing more savvy about hiding their communications by leveraging Signal or Telegram." Isaksen, like most people in law enforcement, had grown increasingly frustrated by the ease with which some criminals evaded detection, often with the aid of the app companies themselves.

Roberts asked Diane Salter to provide an update on her line of research. "One thing is for certain: whoever is behind this has built an incredibly complex and diverse web of offshore companies, accounts, and false fronts that rivals any of the multinational criminal and terrorist organizations I've investigated over the years. The foot soldiers may be a bunch of inbred bubbas from the reddest shithole depths of the country, but it's obvious that whoever is pulling the strings is no dummy."

Everyone couldn't help but chuckle at Salter's unique sense of humor, even if it wasn't the usual buttoned-up approach of the typical FBI call. If asked, they'd all have to admit that she was a breath of fresh air and exactly what they needed to lighten the mood.

"Have you reached any conclusions, or at least best guesses, at this point? Anything that is solid enough to focus in on a particular person or group as a suspect?" Isaksen was eager to show progress, not just to advance the investigation but to provide much-needed cover for Ferguson if it should become necessary. He knew that day would come, probably sooner than later. He had serious doubts, though, if there was anything he could do that would help if the administration set its sights on him.

"I can't name names yet, but I can say with a high degree of certainty that money is being funneled to these domestic terrorist groups through one or more religious organizations. I'm closing in on them for sure. With the huge amount of money involved here, my focus is twofold: mega-churches, and the parent organizations or orders that rule the multitudes of so-called 'Christian' denominations."

"I take it you're not particularly a fan of what passes for Christianity in America today," quipped Roberts with a smile.

Salter's voice got serious, and the anger and hatred on her face and in her voice were clear. "These motherfuckers have taken the message of love taught by my Lord and Savior Jesus Christ and shit all over it in the name of hate and greed. I have nothing but contempt for those who have turned Christianity into a nationalistic, authoritarian movement and replaced Christian Jesus with 'Republican Jesus'. And to top it off, these motherfuckers don't pay a penny in taxes, and you can bet your ass that instead of feeding the hungry and housing the homeless, they're doing everything they can to destroy democratic, secular America and replace it with what's essentially the Christian Taliban."

Nobody on the call disagreed with her sentiment or argued the point.

32

Tuesday, November 4th

J "J, can you and Kristyn please remain on the call with SAC Roberts, Assistant SAC Hurd, and me, please," Isaksen said as the call was winding down.

Once it was just the five of them, Isaksen continued. "We've arranged for a call tomorrow morning with Congresswoman Lavinia Newton, and we'd like the two of you to join us. We scheduled the call for 8am Pacific.

"I'm surprised that she agreed to the call. I would have expected her to find a million and one excuses to put you off." JJ had never met Newton, but she'd seen and heard enough from her over the years to know that she was one of the most reviled legislators in Washington, and that was saying something.

"She tried, but we not-so-casually reminded her of the arrangements the FBI had negotiated with her and her attorneys. Basically, any attempt to delay or obfuscate an investigation would render her deal moot and send her straight to prison. She didn't like it, but she finally saw the writing on the wall and agreed to meet." Roberts clearly had no love or respect for Newton whatsoever.

"What do you hope to question her about, assuming she even shows up?" asked Kristyn.

"As you're aware, Newton has done everything possible to push an ultra-conservative agenda for years, and now she has her head so far up the ass of the current administration it's absurd." Roberts didn't shy away from sharing his opinion of her.

He cleared his throat, then continued. "She's also what I've always called a 'Christian of convenience', meaning, whenever she needs to whip out the Jesus card to play to her base, she'll do it. Otherwise, she's about as much of a true believer and follower of Jesus as the local Wiccan group. Anyway, Newton always shows up at all the big-money circle jerks where the mega-rich conservatives gather to talk about God and country and wave the flag..."

"While figuring out how to take food and shelter away from the poor," Hurd interjected.

"Right," continued Roberts. "Last week she attended one of these gatherings at a super upscale resort in Sonoma, and from what we could piece together, there were hundreds of people with a lot of money and influence there. It was apparently part 'rah-rah USA' and part old-fashioned tent revival rolled into one, albeit at a $1,000 per night resort with enough food and alcohol to support a Roman bac-chanalia."

"Has anyone from the FBI or DOJ debriefed her since?" asked JJ.

"No, at least not beyond the very basics of how many attended, any notable attendees or speakers, etc. Not to lay blame on the agency people involved, but since they're not that up to speed or involved in the bombing case, they didn't really see the connection or the urgency. Luckily, we do, so we're going to have some very pointed questions and discussions with the Congresswoman." Isaksen's demeanor over the past few days had grown more agitated and anxious. He wouldn't be showing Newton any grace, that was for sure. He was spoiling for a fight.

33

Wednesday, November 5th

"Just so we're clear, you understand how this works, correct, Congresswoman Newton? We're going to ask you some questions and try to have a civil conversation on a few topics, all of which are covered under your agreement with the DOJ, and we will record the audio and video from this call to ensure accuracy for all parties. And further, we will provide you and your legal team with a copy of the Webex recording and the transcript along with all shared documents. Are we clear?" Isaksen was taking no chances and covering all bases. He didn't trust that Newton, despite the supposed leverage that the government had on her, wouldn't try to wiggle out of her commitment to cooperate at every opportunity. Criminals always did.

"Yes, Mr. Isaksen, crystal. And though I appreciate you showing me the respect of addressing me as 'Congresswoman', let's make it easier and more like friends chatting and have everyone in attendance just address me as Lavinia. It seems so much more personal."

"If you're comfortable with that, agreed. And since you don't care to stand on the formality of titles, which you made pointedly clear by not addressing me as Special Agent in Charge Isaksen, then from this point forward you can address me as Mr. Isaksen and SAC Roberts as Mr. Roberts." There wasn't a trace of humor or warmth in his voice, making it obvious that he didn't intend to let her drive this agenda or control the tone in any way, shape, or form.

The loathing she felt for Isaksen and the entire team was obvious. Her eyes practically shot daggers, and her body coiled tightly like a snake ready to strike. When she saw Isaksen and the others smirk at her discomfort, she almost came out of her seat in a rage but fought hard to keep it under control. *Never let them see you sweat.*

For the next 90 minutes, the team questioned the congresswoman about her involvement with the wealthy conservative groups she was a part of, as well as the so-called political action committees (PACs) that funneled money to political campaigns. While constantly trying to dance around the topic, offering half-truths, and claiming not to remember details, the team kept pushing and, when needed, calling her on her bullshit. Kristyn was especially effective at this, since she 'brought the receipts' after doing a deep dive into LexisNexis and Newton's own congressional financial filings.

"So, Lavinia, if I understand correctly, you donate heavily to these assorted groups and regularly attend events like the one in Sonoma. How much did you donate at that event, and to whom exactly was the donation made?" Kristyn was clear and direct in her questioning; her investigative reporter background served her well. To anyone watching, she could have easily passed for a seasoned prosecutor.

"I donated $250,000 at that event, which, to my understanding, was about average for most of the attendees. I made the check out to the group that sponsored the event, SOB."

"SOB?" queried JJ.

"It stands for 'Seal Our Borders', quite clever if you ask me. It's one of the key touchstones of these conservative groups, as I'm sure you're well aware."

Isaksen shared a document on the screen. "This is a list of every attendee, to the best of our knowledge, who was at the Sonoma event. Does anyone stand out as especially vocal in their talk or actions? Anyone that you can think of who was there but not on this list?"

Lavinia took her time looking through the list. "Honestly, none of these people stand out in my mind. Yes, they're all rich, white, and conservative, but none strikes me as especially strident. Certainly not violent. I can't guarantee that they're not hiding their affiliation or support for some less-than-desirable groups, but I have no direct knowledge or evidence of that."

34

Wednesday, November 5th

"Tell us about the keynote speaker, this Brother Jacob, or whatever he calls himself. Some famous mega-church preacher, probably from the '*Our Lady of the Perpetual Pedophiles*' brand of religion, am I right? The kind that claims to preach the gospel of Jesus Christ while living in a multimillion-dollar mansion, the less fortunate be damned. And claims to be a man of God while flying to his private island in the Caribbean where he can diddle underage kids without the prying eyes of the US authorities looking over his shoulder. Basically, nothing more than a fake gospel-spouting version of Jeffrey Epstein reincarnated." JJ had zero respect for men like him but was more concerned with goading Lavinia and drawing out her true feelings for him.

"Well, he is a pompous ass, that's for sure. And yes, he has the requisite trappings of a TV preacher, especially one that preaches the so-called prosperity gospel. He has the mansion, a fleet of exotic cars, and not one but two private jets. You can't really overstate his power and influence in the conservative Christian community; he has literally millions of followers. And contributors."

"Is he politically active?" asked Hurd. "And are you close to him on a personal level? I'm not insinuating on a romantic level, just if you have more than a passing acquaintance with him."

"Yes, he's extremely politically active and outspoken. So much so, in fact, that I can't believe the IRS hasn't smacked him down and moved to revoke his tax-exempt status; he steps way over the line for mixing politics and religion and has been doing so for years. Maybe he's got something on some powerful people in the IRS, or threatens them with harassment, or worse, the way the Church of Scientology is reportedly fond of. Of course, losing tax-exempt status is usually the death knell for any church. I say good riddance."

"And personally?" prompted Hurd.

"He pretends to be this upstanding, God-fearing man that's only interested in saving the world from sin. The reality though is he's just a flawed little man with a lot of skeletons in his closet. It's a known fact, at least among those who run in these circles, that he's had multiple extramarital affairs over the years. And though he goes on and on about the 'sin' of homosexuality and gay marriage, I have it on good authority that he's had affairs with several men over the years, as well. And if you can believe the rumors, which I do, even calling them 'men' may be stretching things a bit."

"You're suggesting that some of these partners were underage? As in Brother Jacob may be a pedophile?" Roberts had a disgusted look on his face.

"I can't say with 100% certainty, but the rumors have persisted for years. There may be someone out there who can prove those allegations, but I don't know who it would be. Maybe the victims themselves, if they're still around. At the very least, someone probably paid them off and forced them to sign ironclad NDAs."

Lavinia noticed the looks of shock and disgust on their faces. "What? You're shocked? Spare me; you can't be that dense or out of touch. Do you think this is something that only happens in the Catholic Church? Don't be so naïve."

"Last question," Isaksen said, looking directly into Lavinia's eyes, almost daring her to look away. "Setting aside the disturbing information you just shared about Brother Jacob's, shall we say, *proclivities*, do you think he could have a deeper involvement in these domestic terrorist groups? Maybe subsidizing them financially? Maybe even spiritually, for lack of a better term?"

"It never occurred to me to consider that possibility, but since you mentioned it, I can't deny that it raises some concerns in my mind. As I mentioned earlier, he's got a lot of followers, and his church, his TV stations, his books, and the rest of his multimedia empire bring in literally millions of dollars per week. He could certainly afford it, and it's in his best interest to keep stirring the pot and keep the left and the right at each other's throats. That helps drive his vision of a new Christian-led America that erases what he demonizes as our current godless, secular America."

"He sounds like the quintessential narcissist. Could you see him taking it ever further? Actually instigating such action?" JJ was eager to hear the answer, but also more than a little nervous.

"I don't think he'd hesitate, not for one second, to start a civil war to achieve that end. Worse, I think thousands, maybe tens of thousands, of his followers would gladly sign up as foot soldiers in that conflict. You know that many of these nut jobs, the ones who fancy themselves as 'true believers', would gladly start World War III if they thought it would bring about the Second Coming and the Rapture. Fucking morons."

35

Wednesday, November 5th

It was early evening, and Brother Jacob was relaxing in front of the TV with a glass of Cabernet from one of his favorite Napa wineries, savoring both the wine and the fact that his wife was out of town. He loved his time alone. A time to relax, to unwind from the stress of his hectic life and all the trappings that went with it. A time to be alone with his thoughts. And eventually, after a couple of glasses of wine, time to roam the online hookup sites in search of a partner, maybe two, for an anonymous, under the radar romp.

It was nearly 8pm when his burner phone, hidden in a lower desk drawer, started ringing. Very few people have that number, and those who have it know better than to call him for anything that isn't urgent. He considered not answering it, as the caller would probably ruin his evening, but he didn't fully trust anyone else to make the right decisions for this mission. The number on the display was from one of his top government assets, who was using the burner phone he'd supplied when first recruiting her.

"Attorney General Honig. I have to say that this is quite a surprise. I hope you're not calling me with bad news. I assure you I'm far from in the mood for that this evening."

"I'm sorry to be calling you at all, Brother Jacob, especially this time of evening. Trust me, though, you'll want to hear this and put together a plan of action to nip it in the bud."

"I'll take that under consideration. Now why don't you tell me what is so urgent, and more importantly, why isn't it something that you have taken care of personally without involving me?"

Honig was a bundle of nerves, and she felt the underlying threat in Brother Jacob's words. "I'm sure you recall being informed that the DOJ had ensnared Congresswoman Lavinia Newton in a sting operation, somewhat by accident, and we've forced her to act as a confidential informant."

"Yes, and as I recall, you assured me she'd be kept at a distance from any critical investigations, especially where our operations are concerned. Am I correct?"

"Of course, and as the leader of the DOJ, I've been able to make that happen. So far, we've had her in for just a few high-level briefings where she's had absolutely nothing of value to contribute. Still, it helped to keep up appearances."

"Now I sense that something has changed?"

Honig hesitated, wanting to convey the seriousness of the situation while covering her own ass, if that were even possible. "Yes, it has, unfortunately. Two of our regional SAC leaders, Isaksen and Roberts, have been leading the investigation into the recent string of bombings. I gave them direct orders to shift the focus of their investigation from domestic groups to foreign state and non-state actors, but they have defied those orders and continued to focus their investigation on groups that could eventually lead back to us. Today they dragged the congresswoman onto a call with their investigative team and interrogated her for almost two hours."

"Do you know what they're investigating?"

"Better than that. My IT team has accessed the Webex recording and transcript, so I've seen and heard every word. I can send you a copy if you're interested."

"I'm beyond interested, but in the meantime give me the highlights. And let me be clear: don't even think about leaving out anything important or attempt to minimize your role in this mess. Do I make myself clear?"

"Yes sir. Completely clear."

The longer she talked, and the more she detailed the direction that the conversation had gone with Newton, the more Brother Jacob raged. She'd always known that he had a barely concealed, near-psychotic temper hidden just below that faux man-of-God exterior. Few people had witnessed it, but she had. In fact, when he'd first 'recruited' her—his polite term for blackmail—and presented the evidence of both her marital infidelity and the embezzlement from her New York law firm, she acted defiant and threatened to have him arrested. His response was swift and brutal, beating her unconscious and leaving her bruised and bloody on the floor of her hotel room. Dozens of stitches and multiple days and nights in the hospital followed. To this day, she still maintains to anyone that asks that she was the victim of a mugging.

"So to net this out, this clueless excuse for a congresswoman, without even knowing anything about what's going on, ends up pointing the FBI in my direction and puts our entire plan, our destiny, in jeopardy."

"Unfortunately, I'd say that's accurate. We need to derail and redirect this investigation ASAP."

"No shit, though we see how fucking effective you were at redirecting things! You should fire those two SACs, not to mention your goddamn FBI Director. You need to get rid of them all immediately." He was seething.

"I can't do that, at least not quickly. And I'm not sure how that solves our problem. Anybody who assumes their positions are going to be following the same leads and investigation, and trying to steer them away may only lead to our exposure."

"One thing is for certain: the congresswoman needs to be taken off the board, and I mean immediately. She's already compromised us, and it's for certain that they'll continue to pressure and leverage her to get close to anyone and everyone that's supported our cause. The last thing we need is her running her mouth to the other rich, racist, polite-society assholes that she knows."

"You can't be serious. You're talking about taking out a sitting member of Congress? Are you crazy?"

"Let me assure you I'm deadly serious. And one more thing for you to keep in mind, and please, *please* take this to heart: I have zero compunction about taking out a sitting member of Congress. And further, if at any time I believe the situation warrants it, I will also have zero compunction about taking out the Attorney General of the United States. Are we clear?"

Honig felt the blood drain from her face and her stomach churn. It was all she could do to fight down the bitter bile rising in her throat. The fear was obvious on her face, and as she disconnected from the call, the now rising vomit had her scrambling, unsuccessfully, to the nearest toilet. She threw up for what seemed and felt like forever, her entire body aching and shaking. *So, this is what it's going to feel like to die. Or at least how it feels when you wish you were dead.*

36

Thursday, November 6th

The large, midnight-black Ford F250 pickup was barely visible in the fading daylight and heavy shadows of the neighborhoods surrounding American University. Situated near the intersection of Massachusetts Avenue NW and Nebraska Avenue NW, it was a respectable and well-established area of the nation's capital. The university itself sat on 90 prime acres, a highly desirable area that real estate developers would trade their firstborn to own. As Mark Twain once quipped, '*Buy land, they're not making it anymore*'. And in high-dollar cities like Washington, DC, where commercial buildings sit cheek to jowl with Federal government buildings and upscale residential neighborhoods, finding any sizeable parcel of land was almost impossible.

Steven Williams had zero interest in the land, the buildings, or even the area's history. He hated DC and everything it stood for with a passion, though he was quick to admit that he supported everything that the current administration was doing. Deporting people without due process? Absolutely. Snatching mothers and children off the street, even dragging them out of school? Oh yeah. Arresting people or rejecting their entry into the US for being critical of the president or his policies? Damn right. *This is America, asshole. Fucking love it or leave it.* And if you're not a white, cis-gendered Republican, get the fuck out anyway.

Williams told all that would listen, and even those who wouldn't, that his 'privilege' in life was not because he was born white but because his ancestors had come over on the Mayflower. That claim, as was so often the case with people who considered themselves better than the working class, couldn't have been further from the truth. His father's side of the family were slave owners from rural Georgia and fought for the Confederacy. His mother's side was from Mississippi, and while not rich slave owners themselves, they fought for what they believed was their divine right to have dominion over 'lesser men'. When the war was over and the slaves freed by President Lincoln, both families did everything in their power to keep their tenuous grip on power and privilege. Whatever their twisted logic and rationale, the bottom line was a deep hatred and mistrust of the black race and the Yankees that had freed them. Eventually they, along with thousands of other Southerners, took matters into their own hands by forming local chapters of the KKK throughout the former Confederate states. Williams' great-great-grandfather on his mother's side was, in fact, the first Imperial Wizard of the KKK in Mississippi, and people considered them one of the most violent groups in the US. While no records exist verifying the actual numbers, most historians agree that there were several hundred lynchings, burnings, and other crimes attributed to them, and Williams was proud to carry on with their cause.

That's why when he received the call from Jason Thompson, one of his former prison cellmates, offering him a job, he was more than happy to take it. While he couldn't be certain, he thought it likely that Thompson, the founder of the Aryan Brotherhood chapter in northern Idaho, was probably up to his ass in the recent events in California. He didn't dare ask; better, and safer, not to know. Someone offered him $10,000 for a night's work, so he quickly dismissed any lingering doubts about taking the job or any disappointment in learning his target was white instead of black. This was four times as much as he usually got for a job, and Thompson had already wired half to one of his offshore accounts. He would receive the remaining $5,000 when the job was complete.

The only instructions from Thompson were to get the job done no later than the end of the day Friday and to make it look like an accident. No firearms, no home invasion, nothing that would cause an extensive police investigation. He was to do the job and then get clear of DC; where he went and how he got there was totally up to him.

When told the target's name, it didn't register at all, but he was certain that the target must be someone important or high-profile for him to be offered four times his usual rate. Once he received the target's job, home address, and other information like her daily habits, her route to and from work, etc. he understood. He didn't know what the target had done to come onto Thompson's radar—or who Thompson answered to—nor did he really care. *Ours is not to reason why...isn't that how the quote goes?*

Knowing that the target usually got home around 5:30pm, he repositioned the truck a few houses away. It was almost dark, but he was counting on the target following their usual evening routine of jogging the two well-lit blocks to the American University campus and then running several miles on the lighted track before heading home.

Just before 6:00, he saw her step out onto the porch, dressed for her run. She wore black leggings and a light blue windbreaker, and to maximize her visibility, she wore a neon-green vest with safety lights front and back and reflective strips on her shoes. Smart. Steven appreciated the extra visibility; it made it easier to keep her in sight as the daylight quickly faded.

By the time she'd run a block and started across the intersection, the deed was done. Though the big truck was only going about 25mph so as not to attract undue attention, the sheer size and weight of the vehicle threw her nearly 20 feet, landing in a crumpled heap. He wasn't sure if the impact was fatal, but he wasn't about to take any chances. He backed up a few feet so he could see her clearly with the bright halogen headlights, then rolled slowly forward until his right front tire literally crushed her torso. Had anyone been close enough to see or hear the resulting splatter, it would not have been a sight or sound they would likely ever forget.

The news reported it as a hit and run, one of the most gruesome ever seen in the District. Even though she was far from universally loved or respected, the obligatory thoughts and prayers came from people across the political spectrum. Congresswoman Lavinia Newton wouldn't be missed by many, but that wouldn't stop people from going through the motions if it meant getting their 15 minutes of fame in front of the cameras or getting quoted in the papers.

37

Friday, November 7th

"The DC police found the suspect vehicle last night around 10 down in Anacostia behind some abandoned warehouses. I'm sure it comes as no big surprise that someone torched the vehicle, but DC Metro was able to pull the VIN number and found that it was reported stolen yesterday morning in Morgantown, WV.

"Did any cameras in the area pick up anything useful, like maybe a usable picture of the driver?" asked Hurd.

"That would make our jobs much too easy," responded Isaksen.

"Right," interjected Roberts, "but DC Metro recovered about a half-dozen shots of the truck in and around the Massachusetts Avenue and American University corridor, but they really weren't of any use. Between the heavily tinted windows and the driver appearing to be wearing a dark hoodie, we got nothing. The driver appears to be male, but that's all we have at this point."

"Anyone here naïve enough to think this was an accident, like a simple hit and run?" JJ asked already knowing the answer.

"Or anyone here naïve enough to believe that it's purely coincidental that we interviewed Newton on Wednesday and someone killed her on Thursday?" After working with JJ and others to solve several high-profile crimes over the past few years, she was no longer a big believer in coincidence. Some might say that she'd become jaded, but she preferred to think of it as experienced.

JJ hesitated to broach the next statement, but only for a moment. Somebody had to throw it out there. "Outside of the handful of people on this video bridge, did anyone else know that we were interviewing the congresswoman, or did anyone else have access to the information she shared?"

"Are you suggesting a leak, JJ?" Isaksen asked gently.

"I am, sir, but I'm not suggesting it was anyone here. I guess it's possible that Newton blabbed to someone in her office about the interview, but that's hard to believe. She's working as a CI for the DOJ, and I'm sure she'd take that to her grave—no pun intended — before letting that get out and jeopardizing her standing in the social and business circles she ran in."

"I can't say that I disagree," said Roberts.

"And as I understand things," Kristyn interjected, "it was no big secret that she was acting as a CI, at least among the prosecutors at the DOJ. I'm sure they tried to keep that information on a need-to-know basis, but it's not like the nuclear launch codes. With the power and reach and accessibility that many of the people she's informing on have, it's possible, maybe even probable, that the DOJ targets were aware of her CI status."

Hurd nodded. "That's true, which then begs the question: what changed that put a bullseye on her back now? Regardless of how unpopular she was, she was still a sitting member of the US House of Representatives, and most people would think twice about such a high-profile hit knowing that the full force of the federal government might come down on them."

"We're what changed," JJ responded. "We know that she'd sat through a dozen or more interviews previously with DOJ prosecutors, but as far as we know—*and we should confirm*—there hasn't been a single indictment. Similarly, no prosecutor has convened any grand juries, filed for any arrest warrants, nothing, resulting from her testimony. If we can get access to the transcripts from those earlier interviews, I think we can quickly confirm what I'm thinking…"

Kristyn finished her thought. "We brought up names or events or connections that no one had touched on previously, and that set off alarm bells somewhere in the DOJ."

"Exactly," said JJ with growing excitement. "And I think I know exactly what set those alarms off: when we asked her about Brother Jacob and the people that support him and his ministry."

Everyone was quiet for several minutes, digesting all they'd heard and trying to find any flaws or weaknesses in her theory. None came. Finally, Isaksen asked for everyone's attention.

"Sadly, I can't help but agree with JJ. Assuming we're correct, that brings two things to the top of my mind. First, I find it more than a little suspicious that no one before us has thought to go down this road. Newton had sat for a dozen interviews, at least, yet no one explored this fairly obvious path, or at least it's obvious if you're the one managing and running this CI. I can only imagine that the DOJ teams handling her avoided this path at someone's direction, most likely Attorney General Honig or one of her lackeys."

"Much like she tried to do to you and me," Roberts added.

"Exactly. The second consideration is even more troubling. As much as it pains me to say it, I think there's little doubt that we have a leak, and it's not in this room. I don't know how it's happening, but the least we can do is minimize the chances of being compromised going forward. From this point on, no more voice or video calls related to this investigation using FBI and DOJ equipment or network connections. That means use your personal PCs or tablets if you have them, and no personal mobile phones if you're discussing anything to do with this case. I'd suggest everyone purchase one or more burner phones, and you should share those new phone numbers, new public domain email accounts, Zoom accounts, etc. with no one except the handful of people here. I'm not naïve enough to think we can keep our communications private forever, but hopefully long enough to get this in front of a grand jury."

Anxiety, even fear, was evident on every team member's face. When the anxiety and fear reach the point that you can't trust your employer, even fear them, it's cause for concern. When your employer is the top law enforcement agency in the entire United States, one of the most powerful agencies in the world, that lack of trust and fear can be totally debilitating.

38

Friday, November 7th

"He's a sneaky motherfucker, I'll give him that, but he ain't getting away from me. Oh, hell no, not on my watch!" After working nearly around the clock to dig into dozens of accounts and even more LLCs, Salter was buzzing on caffeine and ready for action.

JJ, Kristyn, Sue Vencill, and Keith Hughes were on the call with Salter, and as always, they could hardly contain their smiles and laughter at her exuberance. She had a way of lightening the mood, something they all desperately needed.

"Don't keep us in suspense, Diane. Bring us up to speed so we can start hating on him, too," JJ said with a broad smile on her face and, for the first time in several days, some lightness and humor in her voice.

"I started with the most recent bombing at Napa Custom Crush because it's really bugging me how it seems to differ from the others. This one seemed more personal and less political, at least that was my take."

"I think we're all in agreement on that point," Kristyn added.

Salter continued. "I dug into the financials for every single winery that uses that facility, as well as the owners, and in every case the ownership and all local and state permits, insurance, financing, etc. were in order. Nothing jumped out as suspicious. Except one."

"Gotta love it when the suspect list gets narrowed down to one," added Vencill.

"You got that right," Salter responded. "And what I found was that one winery, Beckett Estates Winery, had its ownership buried under enough different LLC shell companies with different names, different countries of registration, and different registered agents to make it all but impossible to trace."

"But not for you, obviously," JJ added.

"Modesty would normally prevent me from accepting such praise, but in this case, I'll fucking take it. The proprietor and 'face' of the brand is a lady named Ashley Beckett, but she's not the actual owner. I traced the ownership through a spiderweb of shell companies and also uncovered bank accounts in more than a dozen countries. They obviously spread the money out in a very disciplined fashion, parking it one account for a short time—sometimes minutes, sometimes days or weeks—and then moving it to a different bank in another country with less-than-open banking laws."

"You mean like the numbered Swiss bank accounts we've all heard of or seen in movies for years?" asked Hughes.

"The Swiss are somewhat out of favor, though a lot of old-school criminals still use them. More often we see money parked in accounts in Luxembourg, Belize, the Cayman Islands, Singapore, and the British Virgin Islands. Criminals, not to mention terrorist organizations, stay very up to date on changes to bank privacy laws and data sharing practices around the world."

"Tell me that after all the time and effort you invested digging into this that you're able to identify the person, or at least the company or LLC, that's at the top of this operation? Someone we can turn the spotlight on and focus on unraveling their organization from top to bottom and put these people behind bars?" JJ was ready to move on this information, and as usual, was just as open to putting every single one of the co-conspirators in the ground as in prison.

"I have, JJ. And before anyone asks, I've gone back and checked and rechecked my findings to be 100% certain. I know that everyone from Director Ferguson to SACs Isaksen and Roberts and all the way up and down the line are going to be fucking shocked and demanding ironclad proof. And then some."

"And we'll have your back every step of the way, you can count on that," Kristyn added to reassure Salter, who for the first time was looking nervous and anxious.

Salter finally just had to blurt it out. "Reverend Jacob Bernard of Sacred Waters Church in Texas leads, or at least finances, this entire enterprise. He's the head of the snake." She had to stop to catch her breath.

"So, once again his name comes up in this investigation..." said Kristyn, knowing deep down that this couldn't be a coincidence.

"Oh, one more small but interesting detail. After digging through all the bullshit, take a guess where Beckett Estate Winery just happens to be based?"

"They're not Napa-based?" said Hughes.

"They have a Napa-registered address, but that's mostly just a tasting room that's open to the public. They also own a few acres of vines with a small home on the property, but that's about it. Once you dig deep through all their BS, they're registered in Texas."

JJ just shook her head. "Why am I not surprised?"

39

Friday, November 7th

Everyone on the call took a moment to digest the information that Salter had just shared with them, though it was obvious from the look on their faces that JJ and Kristyn weren't quite as shocked as the others.

"Why do I have the feeling that this isn't as much of a surprise to the two of you?" Salter asked while addressing JJ and Kristyn.

JJ wanted to choose her words carefully because she didn't want to minimize the incredible work Salter had done or make it seem like they were using her simply to corroborate what they already knew. "We're surprised to hear that he's the one driving this, or as you said, he's the 'head of the snake'. His name came up yesterday on a call we had about the murder of Congresswoman Lavinia Newton. No one knows how deeply involved he is in this freaking nightmare, or for that matter, if he has any involvement beyond speaking at conferences where these rich, ultra-conservative businessmen and oligarch-wannabes gather."

Kristyn jumped in. "That's right. The congresswoman said that he pulled in boatloads of money from a lot of different sources, including the people attending the conferences. She attended a conference the week before in Sonoma, where Brother Jacob, as he's affectionately known to his followers, pulled in millions of dollars in contributions.

They supposedly earmarked this money for various conservative political causes, but based on your findings, it's obvious that at least some of that money is being diverted for criminal purposes."

Mollified, at least for the moment, Salter shifted the conversation a bit. "I dug into this Brother Jacob a bit this morning, and while I knew he was one of these TV and media evangelist assholes that has about as much to do with the teachings of Jesus Christ as a goddamn Satan worshipper, I didn't know how rich and how well-connected he is. I mean well-connected politically, and not just in Texas. In DC, too."

"Yeah, I just pulled him up on Google and there're all kinds of pictures of him with congressmen and senators, judges, and even the damn president. Gotta love this one picture of him leading a prayer breakfast for a bunch of far-right politicos that have made it their mission to ensure their rich supporters get richer while the rest of the people suffer." Hughes could barely contain his growing anger.

JJ asked a question that she was sure was on everyone's mind. "Diane, as you dug through Reverend Bernard's finances, what were you able to uncover? We all take it as a given that he's worth millions, actually tens of millions, based on the size of his church membership, the size of his home, the private jets, and all the usual trappings. Were you able to confirm that or put a reasonable estimate together that we can share with Director Ferguson that might help convince a judge to issue warrants to seize those accounts?"

"I was, but to be honest, I'm not finished yet and still have some digging to do. What I have may be enough to get those warrants, but you'll need more solid evidence before you hand this off to the US Attorney to present to a grand jury."

"Understood," said JJ, "and we absolutely expect that to be the case and respect that. The last thing we want is to jump the gun and bungle the case before it gets started. We're probably only going to get one bite at the apple before he either disappears or, at the very least, hides behind a team of lawyers the size of the Cowboys roster."

"To answer your question, I have been able to get an estimate of his present holdings based on what I've found in all the accounts that trace back to him as well as the 'legitimate' accounts he holds personally or as the 'owner', so to speak, of the Sacred Waters accounts. I'll only caveat this to say that there may be additional accounts in different shell companies spread around the world still to be discovered."

"So, these shell companies may have broken some laws, but those crimes are separate and apart from the criminal acts and groups that we're currently investigating?" It was a very astute question from Vencill, and one probably on everyone's mind.

"Correct," responded Salter.

"We understand and appreciate the caveat, so I think we're all aligned that the figure you share with us is preliminary and may go even higher." Kristyn knew intuitively that this could be the case.

"Based on what I've found so far, I can tell you that your estimate of 'tens of millions' is low. Just from his legitimate earnings from the church, his books, his media holdings, etc. his fortune would be north of $50 million."

"Damn," said JJ. "I guess being a fake man of God is pretty lucrative."

"True," Salter said with a smile, "but as they say, behind every great fortune is a crime. In Brother Jacob's case, his fortune from illegitimate activities far surpasses his legitimate millions."

"By how much?" JJ had to ask.

"Conservatively speaking, about $2.5 billion. Give or take."

40

Friday, November 7th

Everyone on the call sat in stunned silence. The look on their faces was one of pure shock and disbelief.

Finally, Isaksen spoke. "Did I hear you correctly? You said that Brother Jacob has control of more than $2.5 *billion*? With a '*b*'? How is that even possible?"

"Yes, sir," JJ answered. "You heard me correctly, and as I mentioned, that's an early, preliminary estimate based only on the vast spiderweb of companies and accounts associated with the crimes we're currently investigating. It's entirely possible that he has other accounts and shell companies connected to other ventures that Salter hasn't uncovered yet."

"But $2.5 *billion*? My God, do you know what kind of hell he could unleash with that kind of money? He could fund every far-right group of crackpots in the country, not to mention his own army of mercenaries, and barely put a dent in a fortune of that magnitude." Roberts was dumbfounded.

Hurd nodded her head in agreement with her boss. "You're right, sir, but it's not just that. Think of the political influence he can buy with that kind of money. Even though churches are supposed to stay outside the fray of politics, he could easily make multimillion-dollar contributions through his vast network of shell companies. And since the Supreme Court ruling in *Citizens United*, basically every politician and political office in the country is for sale."

"I agree," added Kristyn, "but what I've discovered is that Brother Jacob totally ignores the rules for his church's involvement in the political arena. I've reviewed at least a dozen videos on YouTube that were filmed over the past year, and he doesn't pussyfoot around when preaching to his flock about politics. He doesn't just ask his people to get out and vote; he flat out tells them *who* to vote for and how a vote for the other side is going to lead to this country's downfall and send them straight to hell."

For the next 45 minutes, the team batted around ideas about the best way to proceed and how to keep their investigation under wraps from both the people they were investigating and the government officials that were looking over their shoulders. Other than FBI Director Ferguson, they agreed they couldn't trust anyone further up the food chain. That realization spurred an idea for JJ.

"Hear me out on this before you sit back and take a crack at shooting the whole thing down, agreed?" JJ saw everyone on the call nodding in agreement, so she continued.

"We know that all the old, rich white men at the Sonoma conference donated tons of money to Brother Jacob, and according to Salter, most of them made their contributions directly from their respective corporations rather than their personal accounts. Nothing illegal about that, though their boards and shareholders might feel different, but we can put that aside for now. With me so far?"

Again, seeing nods all around again, she moved on. "I think it's time we expanded the search for his big-money contributors beyond the obvious corporate players and focused on the DC players, including members of Congress, judges, and members of the current administration. *Especially* members of the current administration."

"You do realize, I assume, that making contributions to religious organizations, of any faith, is not a crime? In fact, it would be very easy for anyone accused to say that it was simply a donation to help with the church's ministry and outreach. Any first-year law student could get the charges dismissed." Roberts was not wrong.

"No argument there. But I'm guessing that if DC power players made such payments, it still may raise red flags for a skilled forensic accountant."

"And Salter has more than proven that she's an incredibly skilled forensic accountant," added Kristyn.

"Right. Without a doubt. What I'm suggesting is, if we find that a certain congressman donates, let's say, $100,000 to Brother Jacob but his financial disclosures show a net worth that won't come close to supporting that amount on his measly $174,000 salary, it might drive a deeper investigation. Maybe they've been hiding assets that have been unreported, or at least under-reported, on their taxes. Maybe they've redirected funds from their campaign war chest to Brother Jacob to help him finance his culture wars."

"I see where you're going. We basically 'Al Capone' their ass and let the heavy hand of the IRS come down on them for tax evasion. I like it," said Hurd with a wide smile.

"And maybe after uncovering one or two big contributors and having the IRS crawl up their ass, we can convince them to flip on others. That could work." Roberts also couldn't help but smile.

"Let's keep one thing in mind, folks: just because people contributed to Brother Jacob to help fund his culture wars, it doesn't amount to incontrovertible proof they had any knowledge of his role in funding domestic terrorist groups or the recent spate of bombings. For that matter, we don't even have proof that Brother Jacob has any actual role in those actions, so we have to tread lightly." Isaksen always tried to be the voice of reason and caution.

"We don't have any proof *yet*." JJ couldn't hide her smirk.

41

Monday, November 10th

"**I**'m fully onboard with the plan you've proposed, but I know I don't have to tell you to proceed with caution," Ferguson said, the look of concern showing clearly on his face.

"We get it, sir," Isaksen offered. "We're talking about some potentially high-profile people with ties to powerful people in this administration."

"We're going to have to be extra cautious since we don't know who we can trust at this stage, and that goes for every department, every person, in the government. And since we're starting at ground zero here—basically on a fishing expedition for information—there's a chance that we may set off alarms at every turn." Roberts was confident that their plan was solid but was deeply concerned about secrecy. The internal leaks that contributed to the death of Congresswoman Newton were always on his mind.

***

After their call with Ferguson, Isaksen and Roberts looped-in Kristyn and JJ to let them know the Director was onboard. It was Kristyn who came up with the finer points of the plan for advancing the investigation since there would be enormous volumes of data to search through. Step one was narrowing the scope of the investigation. She and JJ created a target list of the 20 people they thought most likely to support someone like Brother Jacob, people that espoused the same rhetoric and goals. Trying to look at every power player in DC was like trying to boil the ocean, so narrowing the focus was critical. Kristyn would take the lead and work directly with Vencill, Hughes, and Salter to access as much publicly available information as possible on their targets, which included members of congress, people at all levels of the DOJ, DHS, and high-ranking members of the executive branch. Filing Freedom of Information Act (FOIA) requests would be a last-ditch resort and handled by Kristyn after reestablishing her 'cover' as an investigative reporter with the Dallas Morning News since the simple filing of such a request could set off alarms all over DC.

Since trying to sort through the expected huge volume of data on just the 20 initial targets could be daunting, at best, Kristyn asked Vencill and Hughes to develop a few prompts and search parameters that could expedite the process via ChatGPT or one of the other AI applications.

At first, Salter had taken offense at being 'sidelined', in her words, by technology. "You don't need any goddamn AI; you've got *me*, real HI. *Human Intelligence.*" It took 10 minutes to smooth her ruffled feathers and convince her she wasn't being replaced. Rather, they were merely augmenting their search capabilities so they could identify relevant data more quickly so that she could perform her forensic accounting magic. Finally calmed, Salter agreed with their logic and even offered to help define the search parameters and AI prompts.

"With JJ pitching in, that makes five of us focusing on these 20 targets, so let's divvy them up and we'll each focus on four," said Kristyn. "Let's spend the next hour defining the AI search parameters and then we'll plan to meet tomorrow at, say, 8am Pacific/11am Eastern to see what we've uncovered. Agreed?"

42

Monday, November 10th

His mind was racing a mile a minute, and his pulse was racing so hard he thought for sure he was on the verge of a heart attack. He didn't just feel like the walls were closing in; he felt like the entire world was collapsing around him. On him. Brother Jacob was not one prone to panic, but now he was teetering right on the edge of one. He tried taking deep breaths, even prayer, but nothing seemed to calm him.

If God wouldn't answer his prayers, then alcohol might have to fill His place. Instead of opening a bottle of red wine, his usual go-to, he reached for a bottle of scotch, in this case a bottle of 30-year-old Balvenie Single Malt. He poured himself three fingers worth over ice and practically gulped it down. That would have been considered sinful to any serious Scotch drinker, especially for a bottle as rare, not to mention expensive, as this one. But he didn't care. He coughed as it burned all the way down, but at least it brought his focus back to the problem at hand. He poured himself another and moved to one of the high wingback chairs near the fireplace in his study.

Dispatching Congresswoman Newton had been necessary, or so he had convinced himself, but it had unleashed more heat and chatter than expected. Admittedly, he'd probably let his ego and anger get the better of him, potentially resulting in an ever-increasing threat to his mission, if not his life. Now his only hope was getting the forces aligned against him to redirect their focus on someone else.

The more he thought about the mission and his divine right to lead the religious uprising that would free this country from the clutches of the secular humanists that he loathed—while siphoning billions to feed his own ravenous greed—the more he knew that this was the time for a grand gesture. Something so huge that it would be life-altering for most of his fellow countrymen, maybe even the world. Maybe it was more than one *something*, maybe a series of mass-casualty events that shook the country to its core. Most importantly, he had to ensure that no one could trace these events back to him while still being a tool for elevating his profile as America's savior.

One thing was certain: he needed to strike quickly to stop the growing momentum of the government's investigation. While he would have preferred to create large, disastrous events that rivaled 9/11, the time required for planning, logistics, and operative recruitment would take way too long. Similarly, while he had teams of highly trained mercenaries on his payroll spread around the globe in countries like South Africa, Serbia, and Chechnya, getting them in place for strikes against American targets was no small task.

As much as he desired an alternative solution, logistical considerations kept him coming back to the same groups of white supremacists and Nazis that he'd been working with. He considered them useful idiots at best, though admittedly they'd followed orders and performed well to date. Still, he didn't fully trust them; if one of them got arrested for even a minor infraction, they'd probably sing like a songbird to save their own ass. They all talked tough, especially when bragging about the hard time they served in prison, but every one of them would do or say pretty much anything, even throw their own mothers under the bus, to avoid going back.

By the time he'd finished his glass of Scotch, Brother Jacob had a plan of action mapped out. It wouldn't be just one strike; it would be three simultaneous strikes in different cities and using vastly different methods. Big. Audacious. Impossible to ignore and guaranteed to bring America to its knees. Best of all, it's not even critical that the attacks be successful. Someone's attempt at these brazen attacks alone might be enough. Then, non-stop news coverage would follow, along with political finger-pointing, hand-wringing, and the public's growing panic and perception that Washington was unable, or unwilling, to keep them safe.

Time was of the essence, so Brother Jacob wasted no time in reaching out to his minions. He gave each team an assignment, and no team was aware of the actions being planned for the others. It wasn't paranoia; it was simply good tradecraft to compartmentalize the operations. No one person or group could bring down the entire operation. He was even giving serious consideration to hiring another team to eliminate the foot soldiers involved in these attacks, thus eliminating any path back to him. He'd think that over, but right now he had more important tasks to take care of. Namely, making plans to be out of the country for the next few days. Nothing like a little extra insurance policy of plausible deniability, just in case.

43

Tuesday, November 11th

JJ and Kristyn were up early, though they were so wiped out, both mentally and physically, that they felt like they'd never gone to bed. They barely got any sleep, maybe a couple of hours at most, instead working late into the night diving into the personal and financial lives of their targets. They had little doubt that the rest of the team had probably done the same. Every member of the team had shown on multiple occasions that they were fully committed to solving this case and bringing those responsible to justice. Or the coroner.

After taking a few quick minutes to drag a brush through their hair, splash some water on their face, and brush their teeth, they fired up the video call precisely at 8am. When they saw how Vencill, Hughes, and Salter looked, they didn't feel as bad or self-conscious.

"I can see that everyone here is as tired as I am, so let's see if we can make this quick. When Kristyn and I dug into our eight targets—four for each of us—we discovered a lot of shady dealings like suspicious stock trades, some instances where congressmen and senators voted, shall we say, the opposite of their usual stances and proclamations soon after meeting with some of DC's slimiest lobbyists, and other suspect behavior. I think Diane will go deeper and uncover even more."

"But no direct contributions to Brother Jacob or any white supremacist or Christian Nationalist groups?" Salter thought she knew the answer; these people were smart and not likely to make things easy.

"No," answered Kristyn, "but since our research only scratches the surface compared to what you can do, we can't say with any certainty that they haven't contributed to the cause. Maybe it was through some third-party organization that didn't show up on our radar."

"I found the same thing when working on my targets, but I may have gotten lucky. I won't say that it's a 'smoking gun', but it may be the closest thing to one that we've uncovered so far." Vencill felt pretty sure she had a real nugget, but her brain was so fried from too little sleep and way too much caffeine that she didn't want to oversell and underdeliver to her peers.

"Let's hear it," JJ said while sitting up a little straighter and coming a bit more alert.

"OK, let me see if can lay this out succinctly. One of my targets was Senator Perry Reese, a Republican from Texas. I found dozens of contributions to Brother Jacob going back over 10 years; no real surprise, since they're both from the Dallas area and run in a lot of the same social circles, plus Reese never misses a chance to try to convince everyone of his Christian bona fides. Reese is also filthy rich, with family money coming from oil and ranching, so the fact that he's donated hundreds of thousands of dollars doesn't necessarily raise any red flags."

"So, what raises a red flag?" asked Hughes.

"I found that he's made dozens of payments to a guy named Colton Harper, ostensibly for construction work that Harper's company had done on his properties. When I cross-referenced Harper's name, I found that he's got a rap sheet as long as your arm and has ties to the American Nazi Party and the Aryan Brotherhood. In fact, the most recent information I found indicates that he's actually the leader of the Nazi party on the West Coast."

"That sounds pretty damning," admitted JJ.

"Yeah, but that's not even the best part. I can't find where there's ever been any legitimate purchase orders, work permits, county inspections, etc. for any work that Harper performed on Reese's behalf. For that matter, I can't find any evidence that Harper's company is anything but a front for his criminal dealings. There's a website that's pretty rudimentary, in my opinion, but that's about it. Bottom line, I think Reese is funding Harper and his group to the tune of hundreds of thousands of dollars per year. And if he's providing funding for Harper, who else is he funding?"

Salter had been listening to Vencill while banging away on her keyboard at the same time. "Hello, gorgeous! Motherfucker thinks he's slick, but you can't hide!"

"What did you find?" asked Kristyn. "We *need* that one piece of evidence that can blow this case wide open!"

"I found a whole shitload of communications between Harper and Brother Jacob going back several years. We'll need to spend some time digging deeper into them, but at first glance it's obvious that Harper was doing some nasty shit for him. If we dig deeper, we might get lucky and find references to some of the recent crimes, maybe even the murder of Keith and Loren Bryant."

JJ felt a surge of adrenaline, finally feeling like they had a solid lead after days, even weeks, of nothing but conjecture. "I'm going to reach out to Isaksen and Roberts immediately and ask them, via Director Ferguson, to request warrants for both Reese and Harper. We want to put a full-court press on both, see which one cracks first or begs for a deal. I'm sure Harper will expect Reese to throw him under the bus, so maybe that's our best approach. He's done multiple prison stretches before, so maybe he's not ready to do another."

44

Tuesday, November 11th

Supreme Court Chief Justice Michael Porter was already growing weary of the cases and overwhelming workload for this term, and they were barely into the second month of what promised to be a long, stressful time. He was used to the almost daily protests in front of the building; such protests were a fact of life in DC. What concerned him the most was the growing volume and vitriol from all sides, not to mention the almost weekly occurrences of outright violence. Almost every case being argued in front of the Court brought out dozens, if not hundreds, of protesters representing multiple interest groups and increasingly strident points of view.

The aggressive tactics of the far-right protesters exacerbated the increasingly dangerous situation. Where groups like the American Nazi Party and the KKK had stayed mostly in the shadows for the past few decades, they now felt emboldened and free, if not encouraged, to be out front and visible with their protests. The tone that the current administration had set had made hate speech 'acceptable', as were outright aggression and violence against their political adversaries. Certain powerful and influential voices in DC even encouraged them to take things further and use whatever means necessary to intimidate and silence the opposition.

President H.W. Bush had appointed Porter to the Court, and it was his son, President George W. Bush, that elevated him to Chief Justice. He'd always been a staunch conservative, as evidenced by his votes and rulings. The Court's current conservative majority ruled with a solid and virtually unshakeable 6-3 margin, the most lopsided court majority for either side in recent memory. It hadn't always been so, and though he would go to his grave denying it, he desperately hoped that things would swing back the other way before too long, even if he wasn't alive to see it. The nation's political leanings were like a pendulum: once it swung too far in one direction, it had to find its way back towards the middle and some semblance of equilibrium. He despaired to think of the long-term harm and implications of some of the Court's recent decisions, many of which he now regretted supporting.

The Stage IV prostate cancer that was ravaging his aged body made him realize his days on the bench were numbered. While he fully accepted his mortality, he was more worried about who the current president would pick to fill the empty seat if he died or retired. He knew it would be someone in total lockstep with the president's far-right ideology, dividing the country even more. He only wished that he could live long enough, and serve long enough, to step away when there was a Democrat in the White House, but he knew that was an unlikely scenario with the rampant voter suppression, gerrymandering, and other dirty tricks endemic to today's elections.

It wasn't prostate cancer that took Porter's life that day as he exited the Court building; it was a long-range and silenced shot from a sniper positioned nearly 500 yards away. Nobody saw the shooter. Nobody heard the shot. Dozens, though, heard the blood-curdling screams of the nearby pedestrians now covered in Porter's blood and brain matter.

***

Protest marches and demonstrations against the current administration have become an almost daily occurrence in cities across the country, particularly in 'blue' cities. The protests have been generally peaceful, at least until counter-protesters show up with the sole intent of instigating trouble. Most times, the white supremacists don't even bother to hide their telltale clothing and tattoos, though they go to great lengths to hide their faces from the omnipresent security cameras and press.

Chicago has a long history of protest marches, both peaceful and not-so-peaceful, going back decades. Today's demonstration was low-key by the usual standards, and rather than marching down city streets and obstructing traffic—a surefire way to turn even your staunchest supporters against you—the crowd of nearly 250 protesters lined the sidewalks along Dearborn Street outside of the Chicago Federal Center. The signs they carried touched on every grievance and complaint imaginable, from the administration's handling of the economy to the heavy-handed actions of DHS and immigration towards immigrants, regardless of their legal status.

Right at 5pm, as workers poured out of the building and packed the sidewalks, two large, lifted pickup trucks approached, one coming from each direction. Both had darkly tinted windows, bull bars on the front, and Confederate flags flying from each side of the truck bed. At precisely the same moment, both trucks sped up to almost 50mph and jumped the curb, taking aim and mowing down as many pedestrians as possible. People screamed and tried to run in all directions, but for many, their attempts were futile. Broken and battered bodies flew in all directions, many crushed under the massive weight of the trucks. The attack lasted barely 30 seconds, but the carnage was devastating.

It took hours for the first responders to transport all the injured and for the police and FBI to interview the witnesses. The attack killed 32 people, including almost a dozen federal workers heading home from their 9-to-5 jobs who were simply in the wrong place at the wrong time. Nearly 50 people sustained serious injuries that required transport to area hospitals.

* * *

It was a perfect day for a whale-watching cruise out of Mission Bay in San Diego. Clear skies, light breezes, and calm seas— exactly what the owners and crew of the 80-foot excursion boat *Sea Monster* desired for their guests. Built to withstand the rigors of twice-daily charters, her 30-year-old steel hull and reliable CAT diesel engines handled everything the Pacific threw at her. Her experienced crew knew that if the day dawned too rough for *Sea Monster* to venture out, it was a virtual certainty that no other tour boats anywhere in the San Diego area would risk it, either. Even if the boats could take it, the comfort and safety of their customers was always top of mind.

The morning charter had proven to be one of the better trips of the past month, with the nearly 100 excited guests seeing several humpback whales, including several picture-perfect breaches, as well as several pods of dolphins. As often happens, the afternoon trip that departed the docks at 1pm wasn't as fruitful, but the guests still spotted a few whales and dolphins, so the crew didn't hear any complaints. It was amazing how often the guests, especially the entitled tourists that descended on San Diego in the fall, bitched and moaned if they didn't experience a virtual Cirque de Soleil from Mother Nature. Some were just dumb or uneducated enough to believe that the animals stayed in one place 24/7 for their entertainment.

It was around 3pm when the captain slowly turned the boat around and pointed south back towards Mission Bay. They were moving slowly, only a few knots, as they knew there were whales relatively close by, and they wanted to give their spotters every opportunity to find more life for their guests to *ooh* and *ahh* over.

The explosion actually rattled windows several miles away on land, and the fireball that reached nearly 50 feet in the air was visible for miles in every direction. The fire continued to burn even as widely scattered debris floated on the surface. Boats rushed to the scene from all directions, but the fire was so hot that no one could get within 100 yards. Local San Diego police and the Coast Guard were on the scene in less than 15 minutes and searched frantically until dark, as well as the next day. There were no survivors.

45

Tuesday, November 11th

"**F**uck me, this feels like déjà vu all over again," JJ said, fighting hard to keep calm and not start crying in front of everyone on the video call.

It was not yet 5pm on the West Coast, but already Isaksen and Roberts had rallied the team together. Besides JJ and Kristyn, they'd invited Assistant SAC Hurd and Vencill, Hughes, and Salter from Quantico onto the call.

Kristyn looked just as shook-up as JJ, and for the exact same reason: having three major events, all happening at almost the exact same time in three different cities across the country, was eerily reminiscent of the modus operandi of The Murder Game. That was the case that had brought her and JJ together, and for that she was eternally grateful, but she had zero desire to live through anything like that again.

After Roberts questioned her about why this felt familiar, JJ explained the link back to the earlier case where she and Kristyn had nearly died at the hands of the Slayers.

"I'm not suggesting that these events are someone copying the Murder Game, I'm just saying that having three major events happen at almost the exact same time in three different cities is not a goddamn coincidence. It's a message. The message may not be directed at Kristyn and me—we don't even know if we're on their radar—but it's a message to the whole investigative team. Maybe to the entire country."

"While I see your point about the timing of the events, JJ, doesn't the fact that there were three drastically different targets and methods possibly indicate just the opposite?" Not an unreasonable question from Vencill.

"Not to be the devil's advocate," added Hughes, "but we don't even know for certain that the explosion on the *Sea Monster* was anything other than an accident. A terrible accident, to be sure, but still possibly an accident."

"Based on the preliminary information we have from eyewitnesses, as well as the early word from the marine police and Coast Guard, there's no way this was a typical explosion or boat fire. They're reporting that there's hardly anything bigger than a Yeti cooler lid floating around out there. The explosion completely obliterated the boat."

"I'd have to agree, Hurd." Roberts sat up straighter in his seat to face the camera. "While I'm not claiming to have a ton of expertise in explosives—and we'll make a final determination after everyone, including the ATF, provides their findings—I have a lot of experience with large boats, both yachts and deep-sea fishing boats. I spent a lot of time as crew on boats up and down the West Coast and the Caribbean when I was younger. Like all the excursion boats around here, the Sea Monster was heavily constructed from steel, not fiberglass. Fiberglass burns; steel doesn't. Explosives can blow up fiberglass, but the debris field would be radically different."

Seeing that everyone was following his logic, he continued. "The other reason that a simple accident isn't likely is because this boat had twin diesel engines, not gas. I'm not saying that diesel can't catch fire, but usually when it does, it's caused by something like a broken fuel line that sprays diesel fuel all over a hot engine. The key thing is that it may burn, but it doesn't have the explosive properties of gasoline. If this had been a boat fire that got out of control, it would have been visible for miles and there would have been time for survivors to take to the lifeboats. That wasn't the case; this was one catastrophic explosion, and as big and devastating as it was, there's no way this can be anything but a targeted attack."

Isaksen looked glum. "So, someone snuck aboard that boat, likely last night, and set one or more explosive charges large enough to destroy the boat and kill all the people onboard. They had no way of knowing how many people were going to die in furtherance of their cause, nor, I'm sure, did they care one damn bit."

"And the chance of recovering any usable evidence is probably slim to none. If anything survived the explosion, it's at the bottom of the ocean now, and based on the charts I just reviewed, the water is nearly 1,000 feet deep where the boat went down. There's no way to tie it to the other bombings, from a forensics standpoint," Hughes offered.

JJ had been half-listening for the past few minutes, her own ideas running through her head and blocking everything else out. Finally, she spoke up. "Not trying to shift the subject, but I think we need to focus on what these three incidents had in common and what someone had to gain by taking such enormous risks, not to mention the logistical nightmare of pulling them off simultaneously."

"Say more," encouraged Isaksen, trusting JJ's ability to collate a ton of data and variables and make sense of it.

"A Supreme Court justice in DC. A conservative justice at that. Protesters demonstrating peacefully against the current administration on a sidewalk near a federal building in Chicago, and witnesses say that the trucks that ran them down were displaying right-wing flags and bumper stickers. And a boatload of tourists on a whale watching trip in San Diego. Other than the fact that they occurred at almost the exact same time, they seem to have little to tie them together, right? One targets a high-profile conservative; another targets a group that's likely more to the left side of the political spectrum; and the other targets a random group of tourists."

Seeing nods all around, she continued. "I think that may be the point. Whoever is behind these attacks wants to create panic, to have people living in fear. Sow a lot of discord and distrust across the population. Convince them that the current government can't protect them. Create anarchy, maybe even start a civil war, to make the American people look for a savior. If I'm right, this may only be the beginning."

"I think you're on the right track, JJ." Kristyn looked at her and touched her hand. "But I think whoever is behind this is betting on this being more than just a way for them to create havoc and position themselves as America's salvation. I think that's secondary, at least for the moment, to diverting attention away from the ongoing investigations into their criminal activities. And who is this task force laser-focused on that has billions of dollars at stake and would likely do anything to shut us down, including killing hundreds, if not thousands, of innocent people?"

Nobody needed to even speak Brother Jacob's name. They were all on the same page.

46

Wednesday, November 12th

The view from the deck of his villa was breathtaking. Brother Jacob had traveled to the Los Sueños resort in Costa Rica many times over the years, ostensibly on church outreach missions but, true to his nature, primarily to indulge his hedonistic tendencies.

Though this was a last-minute trip to put some distance between him and the investigations into his activities back in the US, not to mention the three simultaneous attacks he had ordered his followers to carry out yesterday, he wasn't exactly roughing it. A beautiful three-bedroom villa overlooks the 200-slip marina filled with beautiful sportfishing boats. A fully stocked kitchen and bar, and several great restaurants and bars just a short walk away within the resort property. And best of all, two beautiful young ladies, Marcella and Isabella, that he had procured for the duration of his trip, or until he was tired of them—whichever came first. He loved that prostitution was legal in Costa Rica, and a bargain when compared to most other places he traveled. Since he was paying well above their normal rate, essentially promising them more for 3-5 days than they would normally make in a month, he had demanded and received assurances of their discretion. Not to mention their willingness to comply with all his twisted sexual penchants and inclinations.

He slept well last night after seeing the internet reports about the attacks his people had carried out. Each team completed its mission exactly as he'd commanded, even though they had thrown the plans together on a wing and a prayer. Usually, each operation takes days, if not weeks, of planning. And three operations *simultaneously?* That should have taken weeks or months, and even then, there was a high risk of failure or exposure for any of them. The joy he'd felt at seeing his vision realized led to some overindulgence last night, to say the least. He'd probably celebrated a bit too much, but the champagne was going down way too easily. As were his companions.

Shortly after 10am, his satphone rang unexpectedly. That phone was his constant companion and lifeline when traveling in case he was out of cell range or desired a more secure connection. Still, the fact that someone was reaching out to him did not bode well.

"I take it this is not a social call, am I correct?"

Attorney General Honig hesitated before replying, the barely suppressed venom in his voice making her blood run cold. "No, Brother Jacob, it's not. There have been developments here in DC that you need to be made aware of, especially considering your current trip to Costa Rica. Circumstances might be such that you'll want to extend your trip a few days or possibly change locations."

He wasn't surprised that she knew he was in Costa Rica, though he hadn't shared the destination with her or anyone. Since he'd flown one of his own jets and even booked the villa under his own name, it would be easy for her to track him down. He could have gone somewhere totally off the grid, but that would only raise suspicions if someone started tracking him. And he felt certain that someone soon would, if they hadn't already. At least now he was out and about in public and showing the world he had nothing to hide.

"Tell me."

"This morning the FBI obtained arrest warrants for Senator Reese and someone named Colton Harper. I don't know this Harper person, but I'm assuming that since they applied for and approved both warrants, he has a connection to you."

"You told me you'd shut this down and squash the FBI's investigation, did you not? So, tell me: who the fuck has disrespected and ignored you this time, *actually openly defied you*, and jeopardized our mission, not to mention your life?"

Honig could barely breathe as she fought her rising panic. "It's FBI Director Ferguson, that bastard. I told him in no uncertain terms to stand down and to redirect his focus elsewhere, but it's come to my attention that he's been running a shadow investigation completely off the government grid. The only reason I found out about these warrants was because I have a loyal informant planted in the federal court clerk's office."

Brother Jacob's head was about to explode. He paced around the villa and screamed in anger and frustration as he threw the pitcher of mimosas against the wall, shattering glass everywhere.

Marcella came rushing out of the bedroom, naked other than the black lace thong she'd slept in, to see what had happened. "Mister Jacob, what is wrong?"

"Shut up! Get out. Now! Grab your stuff and get out of here. Both of you!" The fire in his eyes and the tone of his voice left no doubt that he was serious, so she ran back into the bedroom and grabbed Isabella and their things and rushed out the door. They didn't even bother to get dressed until they were well away from the villa, fearing for their lives from this crazed American.

Once again turning his attention to the satphone, he fought to control himself enough to continue the conversation. "You understand Reese can blow this whole thing up, right? He may not know where all the bodies are buried, but he knows enough to destroy our mission and put both of us in prison for life. You understand that, right? So, what are you planning to do about it?"

Now Honig had gone beyond scared all the way to terrified. She was already scrambling to figure out a way to disappear before the bottom fell out, and that's if she was lucky. If she wasn't, she knew Jacob wouldn't hesitate to have her taken out. What she was about to say might very well be the final nail in her coffin.

"My plan was to quash the warrant as soon as I heard about it or at least get word to Reese in time for him to flee. Maybe lawyer up, worst case. But Ferguson and some people apparently loyal to him arrested Reese early this morning and have already spirited him out of the DC area. We don't know where. Yet."

Brother Jacob flew into a rage, breaking and smashing furniture, dishes, and pretty much everything in sight. He didn't know which was going to explode first, his pounding heart or his pounding skull.

"You find him, and you put him down. And that goes for that motherfucker Ferguson and anyone else that he's working with, too. Do I make myself clear?"

"Yes, crystal clear. I will find them and end them. You have my word."

"For your sake, you'd better not fail. You've already failed me enough times recently that your assurances carry little weight."

"And what about this Colton Harper? Is he going to be a problem?"

As he was hanging up, Jacob simply responded, "I'll deal with Mr. Harper. You just take care of things on your end."

47

Wednesday, November 12th

FBI Director Ferguson was no dummy. While he would have preferred to put Senator Reese on a rendition flight to a CIA black site outside the US, he knew such action would give Honig and others loyal to the administration a reason to come after him and disavow Reese's detention. That would mean game over before it even got started.

Instead, Ferguson had Reese arrested in broad daylight and, by providing a few well-placed tips to the media, had every broadcast and cable news network in attendance. He also prepared a written statement detailing the senator's crimes and conspiracies that the government suspected him of funding and supporting. It was a multi-dimensional chess game, for sure, but one that he was determined to win. By publicly arresting Reese and putting his alleged crimes out there for the world to see, he knew it would be difficult, politically speaking, for Honig or anyone else in the administration to intervene. He was counting on it. Politics is all about survival, sometimes literally.

Agents handcuffed Reese and put him in the back of a large black Suburban with agents on each side of him. As soon as they were out of range of the cameras, one agent placed a black cloth hood over Reese's head to disorient his sense of direction. It worked almost too well; he was hyperventilating almost to the point of hypoxia. They drove for nearly two hours, though that was really just a ruse: Ferguson had 'borrowed' a safe house from another DC three-letter agency that was barely 40 minutes away from downtown, near the outskirts of McLean.

Once at the safe house, one of Ferguson's men removed the hood and handcuffed Reese to a table. For the first couple hours he was belligerent, expressing outrage at his arrest and screaming all the expected clichés of the famous and powerful: *Do you know who I am? I'll have your badges for this. When my lawyers get through with you, your career will be over.* Ferguson and his team didn't respond, only smiled, which only pissed him off even more. Exactly as they intended.

Reese demanded loudly and repeatedly that they contact his attorneys and reiterated for probably the hundredth time he would not say a single word without his lawyers present. That just made the FBI team smile once again; so far, they had not asked him a single question, nor did they intend to. They were just letting him stew, letting him become increasingly panicked. They had no intention of contacting his lawyers either, but they weren't ready to share that fact with him, at least not yet. *Fuck him.*

Finally, after almost two hours, Ferguson stepped into the room where Reese was being held. It had not gone unnoticed by Reese that this was far from a typical interrogation room, at least by Hollywood standards. No large two-way mirrors. No visible cameras or recording devices. No witnesses. His fear only grew, as did the sweat pouring from his body and already soaking through his bespoke shirt and jacket.

"I thought I made myself clear: I have nothing to say to you, or anyone, without my lawyers present. But please, go ahead and violate my constitutional rights, even more than you already have. That will just make it that much easier for me to walk away a free man and to see you and your team behind bars."

Ferguson smirked, intentionally trying to irritate Reese that much more. Like all narcissists that have enjoyed money, power, and sycophants kissing their ass for years, anyone showing them no fear or deference, or outright disrespect, sent them over the edge.

"Well, Senator, we'll see how that goes for you. In the meantime, though, I think you'll have to agree that we've been nothing but cordial and hospitable to you. We arrested you based on a warrant signed by a federal judge, so it's all nice and legal. Then we gave you a nice car ride out to the country and provided you with these lovely accommodations, which I think you'll have to agree are much nicer than the supermax prison where you'll spend the rest of your life. We've fed you, given you plenty to drink, and even let you use the bathroom. And through all that, we haven't asked you a single question. You've been yakking and bitching and complaining, but we haven't even started having a conversation yet."

"So, what's your point, Director Ferguson? Or should I say, *former* Director Ferguson, since you'll be out of a job and thrown in prison for the illegal abduction of a United States senator."

Ferguson laughed out loud at this one. "As much as you brag and try to flaunt the fact that you're a lawyer, it's so obvious that you graduated from a second-tier law school, at best, and have never practiced law a day in your life. As I already stated, we had a duly signed and authorized warrant for your arrest. We have proof of enough campaign finance violations, federal and state tax fraud, and millions of dollars in offshore bank accounts to send you to prison for decades."

Reese smirked, giving Ferguson a condescending look that said, '*You can't touch me*'. "You'll never even get those cases to court, and even if you did, the president would grant me an immediate pardon. I'm one of his key allies and most loyal supporters in the Senate. You don't have a fucking prayer."

"I guess you could be right, Senator. I know you and the president are close, practically butt-buddies, if the rumors we hear are true. But that's OK. We've actually filed additional charges that will take things to the next level, and I don't think the president will want to touch you with a 10-foot pole once it goes public. Much less his little five-inch pole."

"And what would those so-called charges be?" Reese practically spat, humiliated and pissed that Ferguson would dare bring up the DC gossip about him and the president. *Nobody can prove that. Nobody.*

"Oh, just little things like domestic terrorism. Murder. Conspiracy...."

"Now wait a goddamn minute..."

"And let's not forget the biggest one of all: treason."

"Wait, wait, I don't know what you're talking about. I'm not involved with anything having to do with treason."

"It's okay to deny it, Senator. We have the receipts, as the kids like to say nowadays. That includes your contributions to Brother Jacob, both directly to him and through his proxies. We also have witnesses prepared to testify that you've conspired to destabilize our government, the whole damn country, in order to install Brother Jacob and his merry band of Christian Nationalists as leaders. I wonder if the President will still be your special friend when he finds out that you're conspiring with someone who wants to take his job?" Those last bits were speculation, at best, but he wanted to put it out there to get a reaction. It worked.

"Now wait, while I may have supported Brother Jacob's ministry..."

"Save it, Senator. Remember, we're not having a conversation because your lawyers aren't here. But since we're charging you with treason and domestic terrorism, including an active and ongoing threat, you can forget about seeing your attorneys anytime soon. And believe me when I tell you, the courts will back me on this because of the exigent circumstances. You see, I learned that in law school. A real law school. But I digress; for now, you only have one decision to make."

Ferguson's threats had shaken Reese to the core. He could barely speak, and his voice was barely above a whisper. "And what might that be?"

"After we put the word out that you're cooperating with our investigation and completely spilling your guts to save your own ass, which I'm sure will reach Brother Jacob quickly, which of our non-US black sites would you like to be transferred to so we might continue this conversation? And believe me when I tell you, it will be a long, drawn-out conversation. Names. Dates. Places. I want to know everything that you know and everything that you *think* you know. If the people leading the discussion think you're holding out on us, well…Let's just say you don't want them to think you're holding out on us."

Reese fought to hold back the tears, not wanting to look weak but fighting a losing battle. He was practically sobbing, knowing that his life of privilege and luxury and power was over.

"So, it's your choice, Senator. What's it going to be? We can do Guantanamo, but that's almost cliché at this point. How about Thailand? It's not exactly the beaches in Phuket, but it's still pretty exotic. Or maybe Romania, Poland, or Lithuania if you like that old Eastern European vibe?"

Not getting any response from Reese, who continued sobbing like a scolded child, Ferguson took it up a notch.

Snapping his fingers, he practically jumped up in excitement. "I've got it—the perfect place. Traveling there is a bitch, admittedly, but once there you'll have plenty of privacy. No prying eyes or nosy neighbors. The weather may be a bit warm for your taste, and the food may not agree with you, at least not right away, but you'll get used to it. But the people? Lovely people, actually, but very serious about their work. If they're getting paid—and they're being paid handsomely, believe me—they guarantee results."

Ferguson grabbed his laptop and pulled-up Google Earth and entered the site name. He brought his chair around to sit next to Reese and excitedly shared the screen with him as the application continued to drill down to the chosen site. It took less than 30 seconds to drill down to what appeared to be a scruffy encampment in the middle of a forest about 10 miles from the coast. "What do you think, Senator?

Say hello to the Temara interrogation center just outside of Rabat, Morocco. Glamorous city, from what I remember. The interrogation center, not so much. It's only a few klicks from the Atlantic coast, but I don't think they're planning any trips to the beach for you. I mean, you might get to experience a bit of watersports if you don't cooperate, if you get my drift." Ferguson laughed at his own little joke, especially at the growing terror in Reese's eyes.

"Rabat, or at least Temara, will be your new home-away-from-home for a while. How long depends on you and your level of cooperation."

Ferguson slapped his hands on his thighs and stood up from his chair with a smile. "We'd better get you packed! Wheels up at 0600 tomorrow."

48

Thursday, November 13ᵗʰ

"So, I take it that Reese has seen the error of his ways and chosen to cooperate?" Roberts asked of Ferguson. Today it was just the two of them and Isaksen on the call since the situation called for even more security.

The call was being conducted old school: no Zoom or Webex or Microsoft Teams, just an old-fashioned conference call. The only thing that brought it into the 21ˢᵗ century was their use of satphones registered to people or companies that weren't on anyone's radar instead of their office phones or cell phones. Even with this precaution, they took great pains to keep the call short and cryptic.

"He has," responded Ferguson with a smirk. "He was crying like a little bitch when I told him we were sending him to a CIA black site for enhanced interrogation. If it were anybody else, I might have almost felt sorry for them, but in this case, to hell with him."

Isaksen chuckled at his boss's disdain for Reese. "We don't need to know where he's being held—that's safer for everyone—but are you comfortable telling us who's babysitting him?"

"I called in a few favors and managed to recruit a few off-the-books operatives who have the experience and taste for this kind of thing. As far as his location, even I wasn't told where he's being taken, and I don't want to know. I fully expect that Honig is doing everything in her power to find him and have me thrown under the jail. I'd be willing to bet that at this very minute she's working to create some kind of trumped-up charges against me so she can get a judge to issue a warrant."

"The media mouthpieces are already going crazy and blowing this story up more by the hour. Thank goodness your people put out that statement that Reese is being charged with treason and terrorism; that at least gives you some cover about his little disappearing act." Isaksen admired how Ferguson was playing this entire operation like a game of three-dimensional chess. While he wished they could publicly name Brother Jacob as the primary target of their investigation, there was no way that could happen with Honig, and surely others within the administration, aligned with him.

"Hopefully you're somewhere safe?" Roberts was more than a little concerned that Honig would do more than have Ferguson arrested; she'd have him killed without a moment's hesitation, especially if Brother Jacob ordered it.

"Yes, or as safe as anyplace I can think of. I thought it prudent to get out of DC for a few days, and, considering the circumstances, my wife felt the same and was agreeable to taking a bit of time off to go on an adventure. I'll stay in touch as things develop, and you can reach me on this number 24/7 if needed. And I know I shouldn't have to say it, but I'll say it anyway: *watch your six.*"

* * *

Colton Harper was on the run. While normally a man that would use any excuse to engage in a fight, even when the enemy had superior numbers and superior firepower, Brother Jacob had sent word for him to get the hell out of town. *Now.* He wanted to argue the point, but Jacob's go-between made it clear, in no uncertain terms, that the subject wasn't up for debate or negotiations. While Harper wanted to stay close to his Oakland base, where he had friends and several safe houses, that was not an option.

The proxy continued. "The full force of the FBI and federal law enforcement, not to mention state and local cops, is coming for you. You're much too valuable to our organization to risk having you captured and in their hands. Trust me: if they find you, they'll do whatever it takes to make you talk and compromise our mission."

"There's no way they can make me talk. I've gone toe-to-toe with these motherfuckers before and never given them a goddamn thing. If it comes down to it, I can do the stretch. I won't turn on you or the mission."

"It's more than that. The Prophet says you're too valuable to the mission to be sidelined, especially this late in the game. You're a leader, and you're needed now more than ever. If they track you down and arrest you, even if they can't make charges stick, you're still taken off the chessboard for the duration of our mission. We can't afford that. The Prophet was very clear that *he* can't afford that."

Harper finally agreed to follow The Prophet's commands. He was to head south from Oakland and go directly to a safe house in Salinas, the gritty, crime-infested capital of Monterey County. The trip would only take a couple of hours, depending on traffic, since it was only about 100 miles away.

It was just before midnight when Colton Harper stepped into the Salinas safe house. It was less than 30 seconds later when more than a dozen shots rang out. This being Salinas, where daily gunfire was as common as fireworks on the 4th of July, no one took notice or even bothered to call 911.

49

Friday, November 14ᵗʰ

Spurred on by multiple influential conservative politicians in DC and the conservative mouthpieces of Fox and other media outlets, large protests erupted in several cities. Ostensibly, the protests were against the 'unlawful arrest, detention, and rendition' of Senator Reese, but there was more to it than that. The protestors could use their outrage, some of it real, some of it manufactured, to continue to press their case that the 'radical left' was trying to suppress any person or group that was not sufficiently 'woke'. Their real purpose was shifting the national conversation away from the actions of the alt-right and putting the forces aligned against the current administration under the microscope.

Brother Jacob, having now relocated to Belize after being not-so-politely asked to vacate the premises at his damaged Los Sueños villa, watched the protests unfold via his computer's Starlink connection. He was happy with the size and scope of the protests, especially since it had taken only minimal effort comprising a few phone calls to certain parties back in the US. While some protests arose organically as grassroots events after Fox News reported Reese's arrest as a 'deep state kidnapping', he wasn't leaving anything to chance.

With Colton Harper eliminated, he could now focus his efforts on having Reese tracked down and killed before he could further compromise their mission. There was no way of knowing what, if anything, Reese had already shared, and that kept him on edge. He still seethed at the incompetence of Attorney General Honig and the people under her command for letting the FBI director's investigation continue unimpeded, resulting in Reese's arrest. The realization that Honig was clueless about who was holding Reese, or where, only fueled his anger. For hours he'd been having an internal debate about having her eliminated versus hanging the whole conspiracy around her scrawny neck should the authorities get too close to him.

Jacob sent an encrypted message to his key leaders in California instructing them to join him on a video call at 1pm Pacific; Belize, like Costa Rica, was two hours ahead, the same as Texas. He always loved doing international travel that was north/south oriented instead of east/west because it minimized the impact on his body's internal clock. His wife was always confused by time zones and could never understand how it was possible to fly thousands of miles to Central and South America with little or no time change, but the same wasn't true for travel to Europe or Asia. She may have been an effective shill for the church, but to put it nicely, she was undeniably geographically challenged. *Bless her heart.*

Once the call kicked off, Brother Jacob assumed his role as The Prophet and sat with his face obscured and his voice digitally altered. He skipped the pleasantries and got right to the point.

"I've made certain that the protests we saw today in major cities will continue tomorrow. There may even be some demonstrations in additional cities that pop up organically; if so, so much the better. Regardless, your assignment is simple: I want you to send in groups of counter-protesters to disrupt the demonstrations and create panic, sending people scrambling. I want them to bust some heads, make sure it's bloody, ugly, and violent enough to require a large police response, maybe even the National Guard, to restore calm. If you want to destroy some property—cars, stores, whatever—I'm fine with that, just don't allow any evidence to be recovered that points back to us."

"Do you want our people to be the ones out there creating the disruption?" asked one leader of the Aryan Nation.

"Absolutely not. I want you to hire others to do the dirty work. And let me be very clear: you need to make it appear that the people disrupting these otherwise peaceful protests are our enemies, not groups we're aligned with. Antifa. Illegal immigrants. BLM. Most of those groups will jump at the opportunity to create havoc since they hate anyone supporting the current administration, and the people protesting at these events clearly fit the bill. Do whatever you have to do, say whatever you have to say, to ignite the flame. If it requires funneling money to them to cover expenses, use your third-party cutouts to keep us at arm's length from this. You can choose which cities you want to target based on your available resources, but get it done. I want this to make the protests for Rodney King and George Floyd look like a fucking kids' birthday party by comparison."

<h1 style="text-align:center">50</h1>

<h1 style="text-align:center">Friday, November 14th</h1>

The Prophet had made it clear to members of the Coalition, his core team of most trusted leaders, that they were to use members of the radical left to disrupt the protests planned for more than a dozen major cities. He also instructed them to stay far away from the protests and ensuing violence and, if The Prophet got his wish, full-blown riots.

To his followers, The Prophet's word was law. Anyone who opposed his wishes or questioned his plans and methods too loudly was never seen or heard from again. While Coalition member Gary Maltby, head of the Blood Tribe group of white supremacists, didn't want to go against The Prophet's orders, he had serious reservations about the probability of success.

He had driven three hours from his compound outside of Yuma, Arizona, to Phoenix planning only to observe the protests and violence, not take part. Being from Yuma, barely a stone's throw from the Mexican border, he had no problem recruiting one of the more violent Latino gangs that dealt primarily in illegal drugs and human trafficking to lead the attacks. He didn't question the gang's ability to unleash untold violence and destruction, turning the streets into a virtual war zone; it was his fear that the liberal media would spin this as a needed response to the administration's policies.

He had tried to raise his concerns on the call with The Prophet and his Coalition brothers, but they quickly shut down the discussion. Even though he believed that some of the other Coalition members had the same reservations, none of them seemed to have the balls to speak up and question The Prophet's logic and reasoning. He tried to be respectful and deferential, hoping that the collective group would express their ideas, both pros and cons, without raising the leader's ire. He expressed his concerns that the attacks by far-left groups like BLM and Antifa against peaceful demonstrators marching to show support for the administration might embolden them to engage in even more violence against groups aligned with the alt-right. In Maltby's mind, this was a recipe for disaster, not success.

Maltby traveled alone and kept to himself, even while having a leisurely lunch and a couple of beers. He sat at the bar of a popular area restaurant called 'Cold Beers & Cheeseburgers' where it was busy enough that he doubted anyone would remember him. He enjoyed his lunch, but more than that, he liked the fact that it was miles from the protests that were scheduled to start later in the afternoon.

He quickly downed his third beer and then signaled to the bartender that he was ready to pay his tab. As he exited the restaurant, he saw that the dreariness and light drizzle from that morning had cleared, and he regretted not having his sunglasses in his pocket. Not that he had to walk that far to reach his truck, but he'd always been highly sensitive to bright sunlight and even a few minutes of exposure gave him a crippling headache.

Today was no different; having to walk about 100 yards in the blinding light, plus the anxiety and stress he was feeling about today's protests, was more than enough to send him digging through his backpack for a few of the Oxy he kept stashed there. He shook out three of the pills and swallowed them dry, then sat in the truck for at least 20 minutes waiting for the pain behind his eyes to subside. Starting the big F250 truck and making his way slowly to the exit on W. Germann Road, he waited for the considerable traffic to clear. It didn't help matters any that he had to turn his head and face almost directly into the sun to see the oncoming traffic. Finally, after nearly two minutes of waiting, he pulled out into the lane closest to him.

What he failed to see was that traffic from the cross street was now turning towards him with a leading green arrow, and before he pulled all the way into the road, a dark gray Hyundai Palisade SUV plowed into the side of his truck. Despite his pickup's size and weight, the SUV knocked him partially up onto the curb and caused major damage to the driver's side front wheel and steering. Maltby was dazed, and blood was pouring heavily from a deep gash over his left eye. Reaching for the handle, he didn't realize that his door was so damaged that he'd never be able to get it open despite multiple attempts. He tried taking stock of his injuries, already feeling like he'd just gone a few rounds with an MMA fighter. His brain was telling him he needed to get the hell out of there *now*, but he wasn't sure why. It was just a traffic accident. Even if there were injuries...

He was barely conscious when he realized sirens were approaching. Even in his current fog, he sensed that there was danger in being confronted by the police. He redoubled his efforts to move, to get out, but his body wouldn't cooperate. It took the arriving EMTs nearly 20 minutes to extricate him because the collapsed steering column had his left leg trapped. Until then he had felt no pain, just some pressure, but once they cut the column away and the weight lifted from his leg, the pain came on with a vengeance.

One paramedic was about to administer morphine for the pain when a police officer stepped up. "I need you to hold a few more minutes before you give him that shot of morphine. According to the information I just received, there's a BOLO out for Mr. Maltby's arrest. I need just a couple of moments with him before he heads off to the hospital. We'll also want to be sure that he's restrained during transport, and we'll be following right behind."

Like most professionals in the medical field, the paramedic was much more concerned about the well-being of his patient than about whatever nonsense the police were investigating. *Probably some bullshit charges for making an illegal U-turn or something stupid like that.* "I need to give him something for the pain. He's got a compound fracture of the left tibia and damage to the fibula and knee. What the hell is so important that it can't wait until we get him to the hospital and take care of his injuries?"

"He's wanted in connection with domestic terrorism, multiple bombings resulting in more than a dozen deaths, and too many weapons charges to count."

The paramedic was shocked. "In that case, officer, he's all yours. I'll just wait over here by the ambulance until you're done."

51

Saturday, November 15th

"He's awake, but I can't promise you how alert he is. We've had him loaded up with narcotics since admitting him, but even with enough morphine to drop a charging rhino, he still isn't resting comfortably. His leg injury is the most serious; the doctors aren't sure if he'll regain full use of it." The charge nurse was cooperating with Isaksen and Roberts, at least to a degree, though it was clear from her demeanor that she wasn't in favor of granting them access to her patient. Unfortunately for her, the hospital administration had overruled her concerns.

"Thank you for that, Nurse Markham. We'll try to keep things civil and calm when questioning him. The last thing we want is to have his hospital stay prolonged unnecessarily," responded Isaksen. He didn't add that they wanted the SOB released into their custody as quickly as possible, so any medical setback was not in the government's best interest.

"Is it necessary for all four of you to be in the room at the same time? I recognize that you're not visitors in the normal sense of the word, but our policy is only two visitors at a time." She was wondering why JJ and Kristyn were even here when it was clear that Isaksen and Roberts were in charge.

JJ spoke up politely. "It is necessary, unfortunately. Admittedly, it will be a little tight in there, but each of us has special knowledge and areas of interest in this case that require our involvement." *If you can't dazzle 'em with brilliance, baffle 'em with bullshit.*

"May I ask that you at least keep the patient's door open so I can monitor him during your questioning? In case of any medical concerns or emergencies."

It was Roberts who answered. He chose his words carefully since his first impulse was to rip her a new one. "I understand your concerns, Ms. Markham, but we're going to be questioning Mr. Maltby about some very serious national security concerns that must remain private. Think of it as *beyond* top secret. If he weren't in the hospital, his questioning would take place in a secure government facility, possibly even outside the US, if you catch my drift." He was laying it on thick, but he'd do or say anything to get her the hell out of there at this point. They were wasting time—time that they didn't have.

"As we told your CEO and Hospital Administrator, we will limit our time with Mr. Maltby to only 30 minutes and do our best to keep him from getting overly agitated." Isaksen was being truthful about the 30-minute time limit, but he couldn't have cared less about the man's comfort. Normally he was a by-the-book guy, but right now he was more than willing to make the suspect squirm. Or worse.

They entered the room and saw that Maltby's leg was in a cast and elevated, and there was a large bandage over his left eye that covered the twelve stitches that had been required to close the wound caused by his head hitting the steering wheel. Dozens of wires and IV tubes connected to different parts of his body, and the tangled mess probably meant he would strangle himself if he tried to get out of bed. Nurse Markham had briefed them on the importance of not jostling or disconnecting anything lest it set off alarms at the nurse's station; a single alarm going off would surely have them thrown out. Fortunately, that didn't include the Patient-Controlled Analgesia (PCA) pump or 'magic button' that patients press to self-administer morphine. Isaksen immediately took control of that button and placed it out of reach.

Maltby stirred as they set up video equipment and microphones to record their interview, then watched as they spread out their chairs around the room, making it impossible for him to see all of them at once. That was part of their strategy to keep the suspect off balance. He was obviously in a lot of pain but tried hard to play the role of the hardened, stoic criminal and ex-con that he was. He tried nonchalantly to reach for the morphine button and couldn't hide a hint of panic when he found it wasn't there.

Roberts started things off. "Gary—I hope you don't mind if I call you Gary—let me get right to the point. No dancing around, no bullshit. When you're released from here, you're going to be taken to a really bad, really dark place, and you can rest assured that the care you've received here in the hospital will be a thing of the past. No morphine, no Oxy, not even a goddamn Tylenol. And that leg of yours? I can almost guarantee it will get infected with some third-world nastiness that would turn most people's stomach. Probably some kind of flesh-eating bacteria shit. And when we finally have to cut that nasty fucking limb off, you can forget about anything for the pain. You think you're a tough motherfucker, a badass terrorist who kills and maims innocent people? Well, you'll have your chance to show just how tough and badass you are."

Maltby reached once again for the morphine, fear and panic evident in his eyes. "I don't know what you think I've done, but you've got the wrong guy. I'm just a simple auto mechanic."

"Right," said Isaksen. "A simple auto mechanic from Oakland that comes all the way to Phoenix for lunch, right? Nice try. We know who you are, Gary. We know about your affiliation with the Blood Tribe, and we know you came here to incite violence during yesterday's demonstrations. And we know one other thing, Gary. Something that you wish we didn't know that's going to bury you. Maybe literally."

Maltby could see the look of satisfaction on Isaksen's face, knowing that he held all the cards. There was probably no way out of the predicament he found himself trapped in. Death would be a welcome relief versus months of interrogation and spending the rest of his life in prison. And even that might be better than what The Prophet would do to him for his failure and capture.

Saturday, November 15*th*

JJ jumped in, forcing Maltby to turn his head to focus in her direction. JJ and the others noticed that even this slight movement made him wince and moan. "So, Gary, let's cut through the preliminary bullshit right up front. We'll tell you what we already know, even what we can *prove*, assuming you live long enough to make it to court, so you don't waste your time denying it. That will give us more time to talk about more important and substantive stuff. You know, the stuff that might make it possible for you to avoid the death penalty, maybe even walk out of prison before you're 75, if you cooperate."

"Fuck you, lady."

"As eloquent as I'd assumed, coming from a classy individual such as yourself. Getting back to what we know, let's start with the fact that you're the leader of the West Coast faction of Blood Tribe, a known domestic terrorist organization as identified by the FBI and other law enforcement."

"It's not a crime to belong to a club that's exclusively for white, Euro-descended members. We choose not to affiliate with mongrels and those of lesser races. That's our right, last time I checked."

"True," responded JJ with a smirk. "There's absolutely no law against being a racist and hating anyone who doesn't look like you or rise to your standards. It's when you blow things up—buildings and people—that you cross the line. And the evidence we have proves you've crossed the line multiple times."

Kristyn weighed in: "And here's the craziest part, Gary: you and your friends think that you've been doing these bombings as part of some cultural war, or as an attempt to 'own the libs'. In reality, you've been nothing more than a useful tool to the man you look to as your leader. And like any tool that has outlived its usefulness, he will quickly discard you."

Maltby looked confused, even fearful. He was fidgeting non-stop, as much from the anxiety as from the actual pain. *Where is that goddamn morphine button?*

"Let's get down to the most important point, Gary. Tell us about The Prophet." Kristyn gave him a withering stare that was so intense it stunned the others, especially JJ.

The startled look on Maltby's face was priceless. He obviously had expected no one outside of their close-knit band to have ever heard of The Prophet, much less know about his role as the leader of the coalition of anarchists and domestic terrorists.

"We want to know who he is, where he is, how he built his organization, how he contacts you, how he compensates you, *everything*. You provide that information, and you just might live through this." Isaksen's voice was as cold, direct, and menacing as JJ had ever heard from the man. It almost gave *her* chills.

53

Saturday, November 15th

The mere mention of The Prophet sent Maltby over the edge. He tried to scream, but Roberts immediately shoved a pillow over his head to make sure the hospital staff couldn't hear him. That would bring this session to an immediate halt. The pillow was a good short-term solution; the piece of duct tape Isaksen put over his mouth would have to suffice until they were done. There were barely 10 minutes left before Nurse Markham, and maybe even the hospital executives, would come knocking on the door. Maltby continued fighting against his restraints, whether to attack his tormentors or to tear out his IVs and wires to make a run for it. Maybe both.

Thirty minutes was not nearly enough. Hell, 30 hours probably wouldn't be enough time to get everything they wanted from this racist scum. Isaksen tried another tack. "It looks like the pain is getting to be a bit much for you, Gary. Is that right? Maybe you'd like a little relief? You answer our questions, and maybe I'll consider pressing this button." He held up the PCA button in front of Maltby's face, and the begging, almost pleading look in his eyes was clear.

Isaksen looked at Kristyn and nodded at her to continue.

"First question, Gary: who is The Prophet?"

Roberts reached over and removed the tape, surprising everyone with how gently he did it. "I don't know, I swear. I've never seen his face or even heard his authentic voice. None of us has. He always has some kind of electronic voice distortion." He looked at Isaksen pleadingly.

"Oh, not yet, Gary. We can't give you a morphine hit after every question; you'll either become incoherent and useless to us, or maybe you'll die. Not that we'd mind." Isaksen was bluffing. He knew they needed to keep this guy alive.

Kristyn continued. "Tell us about your position within The Prophet's organization. We know that you're one of his key people, but tell us about the others. We want to know names, locations, groups they're affiliated with, and the crimes they've been involved with."

"And then you'll give me a push of morphine?" he practically begged.

Wanting to keep him cooperative, Isaksen gave the button a brief press, and the effect was immediately evident. "Just a taste to let you know that I'm a man of my word."

Roberts looked at Isaksen and gestured to him to step out into the hallway. As Isaksen stood, he motioned for JJ to take his place as the master of the morphine.

Once in the hall, Roberts shared his concern that their 30-minute limit was almost up, and they still had a lot of ground to cover. "I just texted Director Ferguson and asked him to reach out to the hospital CEO ASAP to request more time. I let him know that we're at a critical stage and that if we get pulled out now, we may never get another chance."

"You're right, of course. Did Ferguson respond?"

"He agreed to do it immediately. I just hope he can reach the right people before they throw us out. Ferguson agreed to even embellish the criticality of our investigation by implying that there's an imminent terrorist threat that we're trying to stop."

Isaksen smiled. "Can't help but love that guy. He's always got our backs, and he's got a damn steel-trap mind to go with it."

A moment later, Nurse Markham came around the corner, with a look on her face that was a mix of anger, confusion, and fear. "I don't know who you guys know, but you must have friends in high places to get our administration to extend your time with our patient. I tried asking the CEO what was so freaking important that we'd accommodate your outlandish request, but he just spouted something about national security and cut me off. Now I'm not just pissed, I'm frightened."

"You don't need to be frightened, ma'am, if we're allowed to do our job," Roberts said. "And if you want to check in on the patient every once in a while, to make sure he's OK, we can live with that. Trust me, it's in our best interest that he stays alive and gets better ASAP. In the meantime, please keep our conversation and your conversation with your administration to yourself. We don't want to create any kind of panic among the staff or patients and visitors."

Over the course of the next couple of hours, Maltby reluctantly provided as much, if not more, information that they could have hoped for. Mostly it was his need for frequent presses of the magic morphine button, as they'd all come to call it, but it was also the information that JJ had shared with him that rocked him to the core. The look of betrayal, anger, and hurt on his face confirmed what they'd suspected: he, as well as the rest of the group's leaders, had been clueless.

Finding out that the cause that you believed in, fought for—*even killed for*—was nothing but a sham and that The Prophet had lied about the reasons behind every operation they undertook was enough to push anyone over the edge. To find out that it was nothing more than the man's greed and his own selfish desire for power made it that much worse. When Maltby could no longer fight back the tears, they knew it was a sign that he would do anything to take the man down.

54

Sunday, November 16th

I t was nearly 10pm Saturday night when they walked out of Maltby's room and headed out for a late dinner, finally making it to their hotel for some much-needed rest around midnight. They had planned to leave the hospital by 9:00 but had to sit around for another half hour waiting for the Arizona state trooper assigned to guard the patient/prisoner to arrive.

They spent nearly six hours with Maltby over the course of two days, and even Nurse Markham had given up on trying to run them off. She could at least take solace in knowing that her patient was doing well and, despite the hours spent with the investigators, was resting comfortably. That was mostly because Isaksen relinquished control of the magic morphine button as a reward for his cooperation.

They had all arranged flights for Sunday evening out of Phoenix Sky Harbor (PHX) airport, all thankful to have relatively short flights after a couple of mentally draining days. JJ and Kristyn were heading back to Carmel via Monterey Regional Airport, Roberts was traveling to SFO, and Isaksen was heading to DFW to see his wife and family for the first time in weeks. Since they had several hours before heading to the airport, they spent the afternoon over a long, relatively relaxing lunch while debriefing on all that they'd learned over the past two days. There was also a lot of time spent reviewing all the pieces of the puzzle the team had collected over the past weeks, even before JJ and Kristyn joined the investigation. The team made sure the puzzle pieces aligned with, or at least didn't contradict, what Maltby had shared.

"Am I the only one who is still shocked that, at least according to Maltby, none of The Prophet's leadership team, this so-called 'Coalition', has any idea whatsoever who he is? Don't you find it almost inconceivable that these asshats, who have dozens or hundreds of followers of their own, are taking orders from someone that they've never seen, never even spoken to directly? I gotta tell you, that just blows my mind." JJ had probed that point several times with Maltby, as had the others, but his answer was always the same.

"For many reasons, yes, it does," responded Roberts. "But you also have to consider that these guys all talk a tough game about racial purity and standing up for the white man in America, but the bottom line is that at their very core, they're just your basic criminals. They're all just coin-operated. *Show me the money*."

"Good point." Isaksen had been thinking along the same lines as Robers. "The Prophet threw vast sums of money at them to carry out his warped vision—or more accurately, his selfish crimes *disguised* as his vision for America—to ensure their loyalty."

"Can you imagine what the Coalition would have done if they'd known that The Prophet was a mega-rich TV evangelist who was only in this for his own financial and political gain? I'm not sure I can envision these neo-Nazis and assorted white supremacist riffraff following some so-called 'man of God'. It's hard to envision these guys as a bunch of born-again Christians, to put it mildly." Kristyn had little respect for the *Christian charlatans*—her words—that preached the prosperity gospel before this case even started, but now she was all in favor of bringing back the Roman Coliseum gladiator games to see how they fared.

"I know we struggled with this while we were with Maltby, but I think we ultimately made the right decision not to tell him that Brother Jacob is The Prophet. I don't think it would have served any grand purpose at this stage, plus it's probably best to keep it as quiet as possible. The last thing we need is for his millions of followers to interfere in the investigation and provide him cover." JJ knew that Brother Jacob was aware of the investigation and was already taking steps to cover his tracks, up to and including killing a Supreme Court justice and members of his own Coalition.

Isaksen looked pensive before speaking again. "I know it was not the focus of our interviews, but I am so thankful that JJ and Kristyn got Maltby to open up about the killings of Keith and Loren Bryant. You did a fantastic job of making that just another topic of conversation, just like the multiple bombings that we talked about. It never even occurred to me to question him about those murders, but I'm so grateful that you did."

JJ blushed a bit at the praise. "It was Kristyn's idea. She suggested we handle it just like we were going down a list of questions about various incidents, and it seemed to work. We didn't want him to realize that we had a special vested interest in their murder versus the others. We didn't want to risk him trying to use that information as leverage for a better deal, or even another hit of the magic morphine button."

Kristyn nodded in agreement. "Right. And now that he fingered the Coalition member that planned the attack on Keith and Loren, as well as the man that actually pulled the trigger, we can hopefully bring those people down ASAP. And giving Julia and the kids the closure they deserve is the icing on the cake."

***

"Glad to see you. Sitting here for an entire shift is not exactly the police work I signed up for," Trooper Wilson said as he stood to shake his replacement's hand. "I wasn't sure if they were assigning someone from my barracks or someone from Phoenix PD."

"Yeah, I guess I drew the short straw. Must have pissed someone off, that's for sure. I'm Officer Harris, nice to meet you," he said as he shook Wilson's hand. "Doing the 11pm to 7am shift is going to be tough. I'm sure it will be quiet, but I'll probably be fighting to stay awake by midnight." He smiled at his plight.

Wilson headed out, and Harris took his seat just outside of Maltby's room. He peeked into the room to confirm that the patient was sleeping and resting comfortably, and seeing that all appeared normal, sat down and retrieved his Kindle from the backpack he'd brought with him. Reading the latest Brad Thor thriller would keep him occupied and alleviate the boredom during the few hours he had to wait until it was time to make his move. Probably between 2-3am, when there were only two nurses on the floor and they were performing their patient rounds at the other end of the long hallway. That's when he'd strike. Gary Maltby had been way too chatty with the FBI, and now The Prophet was taking steps, via his surrogates, to ensure that he didn't live to see the inside of a courtroom.

55

Monday, November 17th

Julia had scrambled to get the kids off to school on time, with Patrick insisting on playing his video games for 'just a few more minutes' before getting dressed, and Karen going through her daily routine of sorting through at least five outfits before settling on today's fashion choice. It was touch and go to see if they were going to make it to school before the opening bell, but Julia dropped them off right at the school's front entrance just in the nick of time.

It was 8:30 when she finally found a parking space less than a block from Katy's Place, the local restaurant where she was meeting JJ and Kristyn for breakfast and an update on their investigation. She was anxious and jittery, but it was purely nerves and not caffeine. That would come later. For now, she was just concerned about what new information they had. She said a silent prayer that all the time they'd invested, and all the danger they'd faced, hadn't been for nothing.

She found JJ and Kristyn sitting at a corner table near the window. They both stood and greeted her with a hug. It wasn't the most private spot, but it would have to do since this was such a cozy place and had such a large clientele.

"We're glad you could meet with us on such short notice. I hope we didn't mess up your morning schedule with the kids." JJ gave her a warm smile. With Julia, she never had to fake the warmth.

"No, not at all. This morning was the usual routine, basically herding cats to get them dressed and fed and out the door on time to get to school. I swear, if I don't get a ticket one of these days racing to get them there before the morning bell, it's going to be a miracle."

Kristyn reached out and placed her hand on Julia's. "How are the kids doing? Hopefully, they're adjusting well. And you? How are you doing? This has to be a big change for you, too."

"It's a major change for all of us, but truthfully, even after this short time, I can't imagine life any other way. I love having them with me and doing everything I can to help them get to a 'new normal'. They're spending time with their friends, taking part in after-school activities, and seem to be adjusting as well as one could hope."

They talked for a few more minutes until the waitress came by to get their order. As soon as she headed off to the kitchen, JJ figured it was the right time to get down to business.

"We've made some progress in the case, and we wanted to share what we can with you. Let me cut to the chase: we now know who killed Keith and Loren, and we know who ordered the hit on them." She saw the look of confusion and grief and a million questions on Julia's face, so spoke quickly to get it all out before Julia lost it altogether.

"Let me explain. We know who's responsible, but the police haven't arrested them yet; we're trying to get the case in front of a special grand jury ASAP, and as soon as they hand down the indictments, we'll be able to say more. We hope to have the arrest warrant for the shooter in our hands within the next 24-48 hours. That also goes for the leader of the neo-Nazi group that planned the murder and a few of his followers who took part. We expect prosecutors to charge six people with conspiracy, murder, and murder for hire."

"Was this neo-Nazi the leader of this whole thing, or was he just another hired player?"

It was Kristyn who responded. "While he's near the top of the organization, he takes his orders from someone else, the person who leads this oddball assortment of domestic terrorist groups. We can't share his name yet, but I can tell you that the FBI and other law enforcement agencies are laser-focused on taking this guy down. Getting an indictment of this guy, who's the very definition of rich, powerful, and politically connected, will not be easy, so that's why everyone involved with the investigation is working hard to make sure they can make the charges stick."

"Not to mention making sure that some very influential people in our government, reaching to the highest echelons of this administration, don't block us. They've already taken steps to derail this whole thing."

Julia's eyes grew wide. "My God, are you talking about the assassination of Justice Porter at the Supreme Court?"

JJ knew it was information that she probably shouldn't share, but she moved forward anyway. "What we're saying can't leave this table, but yes. And while I can't share names and details, just know that Chief Justice Porter isn't the only person involved in this conspiracy that these people have assassinated."

Julia grew even paler and struggled to hold back the tears. "So, the bottom line is they killed Keith and Loren because they'd dug up enough incriminating information on these people to take them all down. As we'd suspected all along."

"Exactly," said Kristyn. "The information they uncovered went well beyond what the local police, the FBI, ATF, and other federal agencies had found. They still may not have had enough to guarantee successful prosecutions, but they certainly had enough to take to a grand jury and secure indictments."

56

Monday, November 17th

"Thanks for coming together on such short notice," Isaksen said as he kicked off the video call. "I know we need to get updates on several items from the Quantico team, but first things first: the suspect we arrested and interviewed in Phoenix, Gary Maltby, was found dead this morning in his hospital room during the nursing shift change. And to answer your first question, no, he did not die from injuries he sustained in the accident. He was murdered."

There were shouts and confusion all around, everyone struggling to be heard. Roberts raised his hands to plead for quiet. "Let's allow SAC Isaksen to finish before we pummel him with questions. Please."

"Thank you. As I was saying, the Phoenix PD were able to confirm murder as Maltby's cause of death, not that there was any doubt. Someone slipped into his room and put two bullets in his chest and one in his head. And before you ask, nobody heard a thing. Obviously, the shooter used a suppressor, and they also found his pillow with bullet holes and burn marks indicating that it was used to muffle the sound even more."

"But we had guards stationed outside his room 24/7," JJ practically shouted in frustration. "How the hell did this happen?"

"That's where it gets even worse. A hospital orderly discovered a dead body this morning inside one of the hospital's storage closets.

Phoenix PD has confirmed the victim is Officer Paul Davis, the officer assigned to work the overnight shift guarding Maltby. He died of multiple gunshots as well. As best they can tell, after reviewing CCTV, the killer entered the hospital disguised as a cop, right down to the uniform, the shoes, even the ID. He killed Officer Davis and then took his place stationed outside Maltby's room. Phoenix PD has spoken to the Arizona State Trooper that was to be relieved by Davis, and he's provided an excellent description of the killer. He's upset and feeling guilty as hell, as we all would, even though he had no reason to suspect that this guy was anyone other than Phoenix PD."

"Am I the only one that's freaked out that The Prophet got to Maltby so quickly? As far as we know, Brother Jacob is still in Belize, right? I mean, my God, we had the man shackled to a hospital bed thousands of miles away; we never released his name to the media; and he was under 24-hour police protection! It's not like The Prophet has a bunch of goons at his beck and call in Phoenix the way he does in northern California, where the Coalition is based." Kristyn found this disconcerting.

"That's a good point," offered Isaksen, rubbing his temples to keep the growing tension headache at bay. He knew he was fighting a losing battle on that front; all the temple rubs and Advil in the world had been little help over the past few weeks as he dug deeper into this case.

"If I may," offered Vencill as she spoke up a bit more shyly than usual. "I think the data we uncovered while looking at Maltby's and Colton Harper's mobile and social media trails may provide a clue."

"Please tell us you've got something that connects these people to The Prophet and his leaders," responded Roberts. "We need some solid evidence that can convince the prosecutors and the grand jury, especially in the face of the political pressure that's going to come raining down on us from the DC power players."

"Hughes and I sorted through the raw call records we got from Verizon for both Maltby and Harper, and we found several instances where they were talking to each other. From there, we branched out and looked for phone numbers they had in common; that is, numbers that they'd both called or received calls from. The good news is that we found more than a dozen people that they have in common over the past few months."

"Have you been able to associate names and contact information for those numbers yet?" JJ was feeling the anticipation.

"We have," responded Hughes, "plus we've been able to pull financials on each of these new players, and Salter is doing her deep dive on each of them now."

"Before you jump in, Diane, let me add one more important point for the team because this might be critical information as you put together your case for the grand jury."

Vencill looked to Salter to apologize for jumping in, but Salter just smiled and responded, "Please, finish. I can wait."

Vencill picked the ball back up. "We determined the users' locations for many of these calls, and we can show with near 100% certainty that many times these people were together at the same location when these bombings occurred. For example, we have one instance where Colton Harper's phone pinged near the Lofton Renewable Energy building in San Jose at the same time three others on the list pinged. That can't be a coincidence."

"That's great work, guys. This could very well become the linchpin in the conspiracy case that gets presented to the grand jury. Brilliant!" Isaksen was uncharacteristically effusive in his praise, a sure sign that he felt at least a bit of relief from the enormous stress he was under.

"I don't want to be a Debbie-downer here, because you guys have done a *fantastic* job. But I have to ask, was anything found that can tie one of these numbers directly to Brother Jacob?" Kristyn wasn't getting her hopes up.

"No, that would have been too easy," said Hughes. "It's quite possible that one or more of the burner numbers appearing on the Verizon records belong to him, but we haven't been able to tie any of them definitively to him, or anyone else for that matter. I can't say for certain that we ever will."

After a few more minutes of discussion about the phone records, they shifted gears to hear what information Diane Salter had to share.

Salter could barely suppress her smile. "It's cool. I don't mind going last. You're going to see, though, that you saved the best for last!"

Just her smile and her joy and ever-present humor lit up the call and put everyone more at ease.

"That's a helluva introduction to live up to, Diane. What ya got?" JJ loved Salter's briefs.

"What I got is these motherfuckers dead to rights! Ya'll talked before about pulling an 'Al Capone' on their ass? Well, I got the goods that'll bury every goddamn one of them!"

She wasn't wrong.

57

Tuesday, November 18ᵗʰ

The day had dawned bright and sunny in Carmel, a welcome change from the usual marine layer that blanketed the area most mornings this time of year. There was still a bit of a chill in the air, but JJ and Kristyn had taken advantage of the nice weather and gone for a long walk on the beach. They needed the time to breathe, to decompress, and nothing provided relaxation like a walk by the ocean. It's not like they took a walk on the beach every single day when they're home in Santa Monica, but they didn't skip many. This investigation had kept them so busy that they'd hardly taken any time to relax, feel the sand between their toes, or just sit and watch the waves crash on the shore.

As they sat on the sand, snuggled together in a blanket and staring out at the seemingly infinite ocean in front of them, they felt relaxed for the first time in days. Last night they'd agreed to set work aside and focus on each other, actually take time to be present, to reconnect. Since arriving in Carmel and getting involved with this case, it felt like they hadn't had a moment to just *be* with each other, to talk and connect and remember why they fell in love in the first place.

Last evening they'd relaxed over a quiet, almost three-hour dinner at Grasing's, a popular restaurant in the village, and felt the tension slowly melting away. As the tension melted, they both sensed something more: a spark, a warmth. By the time they paid the bill and made it back to their house, the spark had grown into a *four-alarm fire* of passion. The rest of the night was a blur, one long marathon that left the bed practically in shambles. It was the hottest, most desperate sex they'd had in months. While hot sex wasn't the only reason they'd fallen in love, it was right up there near the top of the list.

JJ sat staring at the ocean, transfixed, as always, when gazing out at the endless blue expanse and large whitecap-tipped waves all the way to the horizon. Kristyn lay beside her, cocooned inside the warm blanket and snoring lightly. JJ couldn't help but snap a few pictures and record her dainty snoring and occasional snorts; it was a running joke between them about which of them snored the loudest.

While in the middle of taking another picture, JJ's phone rang. Her first impulse was to ignore it; she didn't want to be interrupted from this blissful relaxation. Sadly, that was not her nature. Never has been. During her time at the FBI, her instructors had emphasized over and over that an ignored call could mean the end of someone's life. Or your career.

Seeing that the call was from Sue Vencill, she never gave serious thought to ignoring it anyway. "Hi Sue, what's up?"

"We've uncovered something from the phone and text records we need to share, but none of us here in Quantico feel like we have the standing to just call members of the leadership team to insist they get everyone on a video call ASAP."

"So, you think that Kristyn and I, as civilian consultants on the case, have that kind of juice?" JJ said lightly, not wanting to come down hard on the Quantico team.

"Very funny. You know you do. These guys trust you; they brought you in on multiple cases to help with their investigations. That says a lot about how much they value you. So yeah, I think you guys have the juice, and if you reach out to them, Isaksen especially, I think he'll drop everything for you. And don't bother denying it; you know it's true."

"OK, you got me. So, who do you want on this call? I'll ask them to set something up for 11am PT; that will give us time to get back to the house and hopefully everybody else enough time to clear their calendars."

"Not to sound too dramatic, but I think you should get the entire leadership team, everyone that's had a key role in the investigation. That includes FBI Director Ferguson."

By invoking Ferguson's name, JJ realized that Vencill and the Quantico team must really have something critical to share. She didn't waste any time discussing things further, just immediately woke Kristyn and started heading back to the house. They were both on their phones the entire way back to the house as they reached out to everyone that needed to be part of the call.

At precisely 11 the call started, and while it was usually Isaksen and Roberts that took the lead, this time it was Ferguson. Whether that was because he realized the urgency of the situation or because he was pissed that someone had dragged him away from his already-packed schedule to join, no one was sure.

"Ms. Vencill, since you requested this little soiree, please get us started. What have you and the Quantico team found?"

Vencill was nervous and practically sweating through her jacket. Having the director of the FBI put her on the spot was new, not to mention terrifying. "Yes sir. While digging into the phone records and comparing them to the times of the attacks, we could identify multiple instances of our suspects connecting with each other and placing them in the vicinity. We covered that point yesterday with the rest of the team. But as we continued digging, we uncovered multiple instances where one phone pinged in or very near the FBI office in downtown San Francisco."

58

Tuesday, November 18th

"Say what?" Roberts almost screamed as he jumped out of his seat, nearly sending his chair flying backwards. "Are you suggesting that Brother Jacob and his crew have an asset inside my house?"

Vencill looked at Hughes and Salter, hoping one of them would step up. Hughes saw her discomfort and spoke up. "Yes, sir, that appears to be the case. If it happened once, or maybe even twice, we might put it off to coincidence, but we've got correlation to every single attack. Including the attack on Gary Maltby in Phoenix."

Assistant SAC Hurd asked, "Were you able to trace the owner of this phone? I'm assuming it was a mobile phone and not a landline inside our HQ building, correct?"

"Correct," Hughes responded. "As you would probably expect, it's another burner phone, so we haven't been able to determine the owner, only that someone used it in the building and nearby."

"This is deeply troubling, and that's putting it mildly," interjected Ferguson. "Can we track the phone's purchase history, such as the purchase date, place, and buyer?"

"It's possible, sir, given enough time, but there are no guarantees. Someone could have purchased the phone in thousands of places, and that's just in the US. If the person is smart, they may have bought it months, or even years, before activating it. For what it's worth, if we're able to identify the user, I can probably work backwards through the cell records and the suspect's credit card history to provide enough evidence for a grand jury to indict them." Salter knew it was a long shot.

Isaksen spoke. "Assuming of course that this inside person paid by credit card and purchased the phone themselves; not a very safe assumption. It's entirely possible that one of the other conspirators purchased the phone and provided it to them."

"Without question, sir," Vencill responded. "But there's one other angle we've been pursuing that may provide a clue. I don't want to get everyone's hopes up, but..."

"Spill, please," Roberts said, fighting hard not to take out his growing frustration and anger on her. *Don't shoot the messenger.*

This time Hughes didn't come to her rescue. He knew that what she was about to share could be a stretch. Not that he wouldn't normally be ready to take a bullet for her, but this felt like laying your head on the chopping block and dropping the guillotine on yourself.

"We've been trying to review the text messages shared between the conspirators. Mostly we've come up empty; as I'm sure you would expect, they likely used Signal or a similar program where the messages disappear whenever they needed to communicate via text."

"You said mostly..." Kristyn said hopefully.

"Right, we've found several instances where they used regular text/ SMS to communicate about something innocuous. The texts may not directly relate to the attacks, but they help us narrow down the identities of the senders and receivers. I don't think what we've found so far would hold up in court, but we may have a lead on the person we're assuming is inside SAC Roberts' office."

Vencill hesitated, half expecting an interruption from one of the team. None came. She took a deep breath before continuing. "We've seen several references where different conspirators have referred to someone named 'Dawn', and through a lot of digging and the process of elimination, we've concluded that the phone connected to the FBI office belongs to this 'Dawn' character."

Roberts looked stricken, his face ashen. He struggled to find the words, any words, just to formulate a response. He knew all eyes were on him, and they were expecting something, anything.

"I take it from the look on your face that this name rings a bell for you?" Ferguson asked calmly, not wanting to sound accusatory to one of his trusted SACs.

Roberts struggled to get the words out, his voice barely above a whisper. "Yes, sir. One of my lead administrative assistants is Dawn Lewis, and as much as I'd hate for this to be true, I frankly don't believe in coincidence."

"I take it she's a trusted employee and someone with access to information that would compromise our investigation?" asked Isaksen.

Hurd saw Roberts was struggling, so she responded in his stead. "A very trusted employee, sir. She's been with the Bureau for nearly 20 years, including the last six under SAC Roberts. Before that, she served in the same capacity for his predecessor for nearly 10 years. Suffice it to say that she has access to virtually every case file, every calendar entry, every meeting transcript, everything. In a million years I wouldn't have suspected her, but if Brother Jacob was looking for the perfect inside asset, he couldn't have found a better one."

Ferguson said what they were all thinking. "Now the question becomes: how do we take this traitorous bitch down? *Now.*"

59

Wednesday, November 19th

The morning air was unusually cold for this time of year, and the fog covering the Bay and much of the city only added to the chill. Fortunately, the walk from the Civic Center station to the FBI HQ office was only about five minutes. Dawn Lewis had taken the BART commuter rail from her home in Concord, a commute of just under an hour. Most days she used the time to listen to her favorite podcasts or scroll through Instagram and Facebook, but today her focus was on the encrypted message she'd received from The Prophet. She read it once again, from start to finish, even though she'd already read it so many times she could have recited it word for word.

The Prophet's words could not have been clearer: find out where Senator Reese is being held and by whom. *Now.* His underlying, not-so-veiled threat didn't go unnoticed: *I pay you for results, and if you can't deliver those results, perhaps you've outlived your usefulness.*

She didn't want to disappoint The Prophet, not only because she feared for her life, but because she believed in *him*. She believed in the *mission*. Mostly she believed that America, and California in particular, was in a freefall brought on by years of liberal democrats and 'woke' politicians and their propensity to solve every problem by spending taxpayer money instead of letting people pick themselves up by the bootstraps, as her ancestors had done.

When she was first recruited, the money had been the big enticement. While her role at the FBI paid well, it would never make her rich; for that matter, it was barely enough to allow her to cling to one of the bottom rungs of the middle-class ladder here in northern California. As a woman in her late-40s who looked like she was in her mid- to late-50s, widowed for nearly 20 years, and zero likelihood of finding a future romantic partner to help carry the load, she knew that life was going to be a struggle from here on out. A traditional retirement somewhere down the line? Probably out of the question; she'd more likely end up on public assistance. She was too proud for that, and too bitter.

The Prophet had dangled an offer to pay her a very generous retainer, and she bit. After proving her value and willingness to be his inside asset, he sweetened the deal with a promise to pay her generously for information relating to FBI investigations into him and his organization. He was as good as his word: in the five, almost six years that she'd been his asset, he had paid her more than $150,000, all of it tax free and secreted away in an offshore account he had helped her establish.

She was the first to arrive on the 13th floor, and she went straight to her desk and, once again ensuring that no one was around, inserted the special flash drive into her PC as she booted up. The flash drive, a 'gift' from one of The Prophet's tech geniuses, created a 'virtual machine' that connected to an encrypted VPN running off a Starlink connection rather than the Bureau's internal network. As she entered the commands to access the untraceable backdoor path—also created by The Prophet's tech wizards—she navigated quickly to Roberts's calendar and recent communications.

It only took a few minutes to drill down several layers and locate the information related to Reese. She downloaded the information to a secure server location and committed the file destination to memory (*never leave a written or electronic trail*, The Prophet had emphasized repeatedly), then quickly backed out of the network connection and returned her computer to its normal operating mode.

Lewis wasted little time, walking straight to the ladies' bathroom on her floor and ducking into the stall furthest from the door. Her hands shook as she removed the burner phone from the concealed compartment in her backpack and turned it on, anxiously counting the seconds until it was ready for her password. She pulled up the encrypted messaging app on the phone and sent a quick and succinct text to The Prophet, including the link that would provide access to everything she'd found about Senator Reese. It was out of her hands now; she felt no guilt or shame about providing access to information that might lead to his execution, including the location where he's being held, the security arrangements, the communications protocols, everything. *Anything to help Brother Jacob in the furtherance of his divine mission.*

60

Wednesday, November 19ᵗʰ

"Did you get all of that?" Roberts asked the Quantico team.

"Yes, sir. All of it. The software we loaded remotely to capture her keystrokes worked perfectly, and that's really just for a 'belt & suspenders' kind of arrangement. Even without that, we captured the path to her network connection, the VPN connection, and her path through the system to reach the documents we'd planted for her to find. I'd say it was 100% successful." Hughes couldn't contain his smile.

"What about the text between Lewis and The Prophet? I'm assuming that she was smart enough to use Signal or another end-to-end encrypted service?" asked Isaksen.

"She did, but with the trojan horse we sent via an attachment within a text message, which she so graciously opened, we linked our devices with hers and captured the messages in real-time on the device." Vencill was justifiably proud of that move.

"And we can get a warrant to request the metadata from Verizon as well. That will be another nail in her coffin if this goes before a grand jury and to trial. It will provide evidence of who sent the message, who received it, and when. Hopefully, that will help us definitively tie the receiving phone to The Prophet." Salter could barely contain her excitement as things seemed to turn their way.

Roberts smiled, probably for the first time in days. "Great work, everyone. We've got the bait in the water, now let's see what kind of big fish we can catch."

"My money is on one or more members of the Coalition and their minions. I know it won't be The Prophet himself, but hopefully it brings us one step closer to taking him down." JJ had that giddy feeling she always gets when the end is finally in sight—even when she may need binoculars to see all the way to the end.

Kristyn had been uncharacteristically quiet for most of the call. Her thoughts finally coalesced into something she thought could be clearly articulated, she spoke up. "This is significant progress, and we're definitely going to take some key players—and very dangerous people—off the board when this operation goes down."

"And that's a good thing, right?" asked JJ.

"Of course, but the question is, does it get us any closer to putting the cuffs on Brother Jacob and ending this reign of terror? If he sees his people being picked off one after the other, what's stopping him from either finding new soldiers, or maybe just disappearing altogether? With his resources and unlimited funds, he could fly off to any of dozens of countries without extradition treaties with the US."

"What are you proposing?" Isaksen trusted her instincts.

"We need a scenario that is so utterly compelling and irresistible to him he can't resist returning to the US. Maybe it's dangling his end-goal in front of him, almost within reach. Or, conversely, putting his end-goal in so much imminent danger of collapse that he feels he has no choice but to return and take direct hands-on action. I'm not sure which at this point. Maybe neither. But I want to spend some time thinking it through."

"Not to rush you," Roberts said, "but if you can come up with a plan before tonight's operation, that would be great. Assuming The Prophet will have his people raiding the decoy house tonight—I can't imagine them waiting even a single day—it would be great to know our next steps."

JJ answered, even though Roberts had directed his comment at Kristyn. "She and I will spend the day trying to come up with some workable scenarios, and then we'll see you this evening at the rendezvous point near the decoy house. I assume you'll have your guys ready to rock and roll and in place around dusk?"

"Count on it. And we're coming in heavy." Roberts smiled at the thought.

"I love the sound of that," JJ responded with a wide smile. "One other quick point that we haven't touched on: I think we should take Dawn Lewis into custody tonight as soon as the operation starts. Maybe even a few minutes before. We don't want her in touch with any of the men raiding the decoy house, much less The Prophet."

"Excellent point," added Isaksen. "And we might want to consider offering her a deal, some sort of limited immunity, for cooperating with the investigation moving forward. She might be a wealth of information and eager to make a deal, especially after she hears the long list of charges against her."

61

Wednesday, November 19ᵗʰ

JJ and Kristyn took advantage of the beautiful, sunny afternoon and worked on the patio despite the temperature being only in the high-50s. The firepit came in handy and provided just enough warmth to keep it comfortable. They'd been at it for nearly two hours and were getting frustrated with their lack of progress. Flaws were immediately apparent in every plan they came up with, but not because they were being overly critical; it's just that the probability of success seemed too low and the risk factor too high. There was no way they'd ever put forth a plan that The Prophet could easily see through or, even worse, turn to his advantage. They also weren't about to champion a plan that put their team, and law enforcement and innocent civilians at undue risk.

"This is frustrating as hell," griped JJ.

"I can't argue with you there. Too bad we can't slip out to the Cypress Inn for a bite and early happy hour. I could use it."

"I'm sure we both could, but obviously it would be our ass in a sling if we showed up tonight three sheets to the wind. Or even one sheet."

"Let's at least take a break and fix something here. Neither of us is at our best when we're hangry."

They dug through the refrigerator, immediately regretting they hadn't made time for a grocery run but scrounging enough ingredients

"

together for a couple of salads. Kristyn was tearing the lettuce while JJ sliced cucumber, tomato, and deli ham to go on top, both quiet and deep in thought. JJ was so engrossed in her thoughts that she wasn't paying close enough attention and cut the index finger on her left hand.

"Ouch, dammit, that hurt like a mother." She backed away from the counter lest she get blood on their food.

"Let me get you a bandage. Here, take this paper towel while I look for one."

Kristyn was gone for several minutes searching through the medicine cabinets in both bathrooms. As JJ looked down at her bleeding finger, she had a fleeting idea that seemed to fade as quickly as it had appeared. She squeezed her eyes shut and tried to focus, to block out all other sights and sounds and the pain from her cut. Her brain was working at seemingly warp speed, but the images and thoughts weren't coming together in any kind of coherent fashion. It felt to her like those times when you're trying hard to think of a word and it's right there on the tip of your tongue but just won't come.

"Are you OK?" Kristyn asked with a noticeably concerned tone of voice. "Are you getting ready to pass out?"

JJ jumped. She hadn't even heard Kristyn come back into the kitchen. "No, I'm just struggling to remember a fleeting idea that I had, trying to bring it back to the front of my stupid mind. It felt—it *feels*—like I was onto something good, but now I can't remember it."

"Here, let me clean your finger and put this bandage on the cut. We'll sit down outside and eat, and maybe you'll relax enough that it will come back to you."

Eating helped with the hangry feelings, but it didn't help JJ recover the epiphany she'd had earlier. She tried putting it totally out of her mind for a while, though that was hard to do when time was quickly ticking away. They had only a few more hours before they had to be at the rendezvous spot up in the hills above Salinas and the 101, and that would take an hour or more.

"You know, other than in the shower, I think we both do our best thinking on the beach, just gazing out at the ocean. Let's grab a blanket and walk down there. Good idea?"

"Probably a great idea."

The rhythmic crashing of the waves, the seagulls squawking and squeaking, and the barking of the dogs as they chased balls and sticks and played tag with each other soon had JJ in an almost hypnotic state. Kristyn sat quietly, just letting JJ's mind do its thing. Hopefully. It didn't happen as quickly as Kristyn had hoped, but eventually JJ's eyes fluttered open, and she was back to reality and some semblance of presence.

"I think I've got a plan, or at least the start of a plan. Let's run through it; you ask questions, play devil's advocate, whatever you need to do. Shoot holes in it if you see weaknesses, but let's try to flesh it out now so we can share it with Isaksen and Roberts tonight."

"Thank God for the restorative powers of the ocean. It never fails."

62

Wednesday, November 19ᵗʰ

JJ and Kristyn sat in the backseat of the big SUV along with Assistant SAC Hurd, while Roberts was in the driver's seat and Isaksen riding shotgun. Both SACs were eager to hear what they'd come up with. They agreed to keep this discussion to just the five of them for the time being and share it with Director Ferguson and the Quantico team after tonight's operation—assuming that tonight was the night.

"The plan is not that complicated, but there are a lot of moving parts. A lot will depend on timing and our ability to sell this whole thing." JJ looked at each of them to see if they were ready for her to jump into it. They were.

"After we take these guys down tonight, hopefully without a lot of shots being fired, we hold back on the announcement for 12-24 hours. That does two things. First, it probably has Brother Jacob stewing because he won't have heard from either Dawn Lewis or the leader of tonight's little party. And second, assuming that we can make good on the promise we made to Lewis granting her limited immunity in exchange for her cooperation, we'll be able to secure arrest warrants for other members of the Coalition. Or at least some of them. With me so far?"

Seeing that they were she continued. "Once we've arrested these other key people, hopefully we can pump them for some real and easily verifiable information that we can use against Brother Jacob, but if not, we can probably leverage some of what we've already gotten from Reese, Maltby, and others."

"To what end?" asked Isaksen. "I'm not sure I understand your endgame."

"Sorry, sir, you're right. I've probably given you more backstory and detail than you need. Here's the hoped-for end game: we let word get to Brother Jacob that all his followers are now aware of his identity and have turned against him, partly to save their own skin and partly because of their anger and resentment of his hypocrisy."

"Interesting..." said Roberts, obviously thinking things through.

"Not to make light of the situation or sound too much like an old TV commercial, *'but wait, there's more!'*" Kristyn smiled at her own brief attempt at humor. She was the only one.

"Here's the trickier part of the plan, and where we need to put our heads together. I think what will absolutely push Brother Jacob over the edge and send him rushing back here is if we convince him that there is a new player in the wings that is laser-focused on taking his place and completing the mission. A player who is rich enough, powerful enough, and high-profile enough to slide right into the organization he built and see it through to its logical conclusion."

"Which is?" asked Hurd.

"Brother Jacob apparently has the ultimate delusion of grandeur. Even though he professes to be this politically conservative 'man of God' and supporter of the current administration, his ultimate goal is to replace the President and his entire administration and install himself as the leader. He wants to turn our already fucked-up government into a theocracy with him sitting on the throne."

"I'm not clear on how he plans to pull something like that off," Isaksen added.

Kristyn jumped in. "That's why he was doing everything in his power to create anarchy, like the attacks on the demonstrations last week around the country. Notice that in every case the people instigating the violence were left-wing operatives, like Antifa and BLM, while the protesters they attacked were ostensibly supporters of the current administration. According to Maltby, it was Brother Jacob who planned those attacks and paid those people. His plan is to create chaos and confusion; to make everyone question their politics, their personal safety, and the country's leadership."

"And who would you suggest as this new power player that wants to push Brother Jacob aside?" Roberts was mostly onboard but unsure how realistic this part of the plan was.

JJ sighed. "I'm not sure, sir. My first thought was another preacher or priest; surely there's a lot of them out there that have some major skeletons in their closet. I mean, you can't swing a dead cat without hitting one that's been accused, if not convicted, of being a pedophile. The problem is very few of them have the large following, deep pockets, and media empire of Brother Jacob."

"Maybe we need to look in another direction. Maybe to a politician? Or someone in Hollywood?" Isaksen looked around at the others to gauge their reaction.

"Brilliant, sir. Absolutely freaking brilliant." JJ was smiling ear to ear and already thinking about how to leverage their industry connections to find the right candidate. God only knows there are enough people in Hollywood with secret lives who would do anything to keep them hidden from the world.

63

Wednesday, November 19th

Isaksen was growing concerned about tonight's operation. Did Brother Jacob's people see through the ruse and not take the bait? Are they planning their attack for a different time, like 1-2 days out, after scouting the location and refining the plan? Or even worse, is there another mole in the FBI or local law enforcement that has tipped them off? The stress had him reaching for the roll of Tums antacids he kept in his jacket pocket. He'd gone through almost an entire roll since the morning.

The assembled team had years of experience in similar operations, and they never expected the assault to start until well after midnight. That's pretty much how raids work, whether it's the good guys raiding the bad guys or the other way around. Wait until everyone at the target location is asleep and then make your approach. Knowing it and liking it are two very different things. Sitting around for hours waiting for something to happen isn't anyone's idea of fun. Luckily, they're all skilled professionals; they rested and ate in shifts to stay alert and ready for action.

Isaksen and Roberts relied on the skill and leadership of the San Francisco-based SWAT team led by Special Agent Thomas Nelson. Nelson, with Roberts's guidance and assistance, also pulled in SWAT team members from Sacramento and Fresno; they weren't taking any chances with weapons or manpower because they didn't know their enemy's size, resources or capabilities. They brought in drones with infrared cameras, multiple armored personnel carriers stationed in the surrounding hills, and enough weapons and ammunition to start and sustain a small war for days.

Shortly after 1:30am, a message came across the tactical radio frequency from the drone team. "We've just picked up movement coming from both directions of Nacimiento-Fergusson Road. Two vehicles approaching from both east and west, currently about a half mile from the target and approaching at normal speed. All vehicles appear to be large SUVs, so assume multiple occupants."

"I'm surprised they're on that road. It's a dark, winding road and kinda tough to navigate even in the daytime. Kristyn and I have driven it on one of our previous trips to Carmel, and while it's admittedly rustic and beautiful, it's not an experience I'd like to repeat, especially at night."

"Where does that road end up? The ocean?" Like almost everyone from outside the immediate area, he had never heard of this road.

Kristyn responded. "It runs through the Santa Lucia Mountains and connects the San Antonio Valley in the interior with the coastal areas of Big Sur. So, as you said, sir, it basically runs into the ocean."

"One quarter mile and closing," came the voice over the radio.

"Hold your fire until my command," Nelson ordered. "Once they've entered the property, block the exits. All team members guarding the perimeter, priority is containment of all suspects. Nobody makes it to the tree line, period. And hold all civilian traffic for a half mile in each direction."

Isaksen deferred full operational leadership to Nelson but felt compelled to reiterate one important point. "Our goal tonight is to apprehend as many attackers as possible and hold them for questioning in the recent spate of bombings. That's especially true of the leaders; they'll probably hang back in one or more of the SUVs until it's over. Lethal action should only be taken if that's your only option; let's hope it doesn't come down to that. Be safe and watch your six."

The attackers came in heavy and obviously intent on killing every single person in the house. Twelve men stormed the house spraying automatic weapon fire; unfortunately for them, it took a few moments to realize that they were firing at mannequins wearing FBI and US Marshals jackets.

"It's a trap!" yelled one of the shooters. "Everybody out, now!"

As the shooters turned and ran towards the front and rear doors, they heard the booming voices of the police and FBI teams descending on them. Searchlights from two helicopters and multiple sets of klieg lights positioned near the edge of the woods made the battlefield as bright as the midday sun. Most of the attackers heeded the amplified voices of the FBI team ordering them to throw down their weapons and give up, but several of them tried to fight their way out and escape. It did not end well for them; the human body doesn't stand much of a chance against a skilled FBI shooter and his or her M4 carbine. Shooting 5.56 NATO rounds traveling at nearly 2,900 feet per second and with the ability to switch from semi-automatic to 'burst' automatic fire, it's the weapon of choice for thousands of law enforcement teams.

At least the Coalition leaders in charge of tonight's operation could take solace in knowing that their men fought bravely, however stupid and ill-conceived their plan was. That solace was overridden, though, by the anger of being tricked and overwhelmed by superior numbers and firepower, not to mention their anger at being taken into custody and facing intense interrogation and long prison sentences. All tried to remain defiant and stoic as they were placed into the police transport vehicles, but they knew their mettle was going to be tested like never before.

After it was over and the dead were heading to the coroner's office, the injured to the hospital, and those placed under arrest heading to jail, JJ and the others stood by their SUV and tried to decompress.

Even though they hadn't been in the middle of the action, thankfully, they were still experiencing varying levels of adrenaline crash.

JJ summed up tonight's action. "I feel we were doubly blessed tonight. First, because our plan worked. I was hopeful, maybe even cautiously optimistic, but we've all seen the best-laid plans go to shit. Second, we didn't lose anyone from our side. With the exception of the one agent who twisted his ankle running through the woods, we didn't even incur any injuries. I'll take that as a win."

"And I don't think any of us are going to lose any sleep over those five idiots that thought they could shoot their way out of this. Morons." Roberts wouldn't lose sleep, but he still would have preferred them all alive and under arrest. The more people they interrogate, the more they'll learn—and the more pressure they can put on Brother Jacob.

64

Thursday, November 20th

"You know there's not a snowball's chance in hell that Attorney General Honig is going to grant any kind of immunity deal to Dawn Lewis or any of the other conspirators, regardless of their role or rank. If anything, I can practically guarantee that she's going to swoop in there and take control of the witnesses and the overall case." Director Ferguson was pleased with the successful operation from the night before, but he didn't see how it was possible to continue pushing this case with Honig dead set on shutting it down.

"Exactly, sir, which is why we're keeping this out of the federal system. For now, maybe forever, we're only charging them with state crimes, so she's got no standing to interfere. Doesn't mean she won't try to throw her weight around, but we've already spoken with the governor and his attorney general, and they are 100 percent committed to pursuing this case. After all, most of the attacks perpetrated by Brother Jacob have been here." Isaksen had been working this angle since first thing this morning.

"Smart move. I love it. But I don't expect her to take this lying down. It wouldn't surprise me one bit if she hopped on her broom and flew out here to force her way into the case."

Roberts laughed. "When we talked to the governor and attorney general, they made one thing very clear: in their words, *'If that bitch sets one foot in California, we're throwing her ass in jail.'* Let's just say there's not a lot of love, and zero respect, for Honig. The governor even promised to have the National Guard standing by at the airport if they needed to have a show of force."

"I always liked those guys," Ferguson said with a chuckle. "And my God, what I wouldn't pay to see that bitch in handcuffs!"

*****

The representative from the California attorney general's office addressed Dawn Lewis directly. JJ and Kristyn were in the room as observers along with three armed officers; there were another three just outside the door in the hallway.

"Ms. Lewis, the governor and attorney general have granted the State's request to provide you with limited immunity from prosecution in exchange for your full and complete cooperation in the investigation into the recent acts of domestic terrorism. You should understand that we retain the right to rescind this offer at any time if the investigating team finds that you have lied, withheld critical information, or tried to deceive them in any way. Is that clear?"

"Yes, sir."

"And let me also be clear that this is *not a 'get out of jail free card'* for your crimes. You are still going to be held accountable and prosecuted for your involvement in this conspiracy, but if you live up to your end of the agreement, then our commitment to you is that we will request no more than 10 years in prison upon your conviction. Is that also clear?"

Lewis could no longer hold back the tears. *Ten years may very well be a death sentence.* "Yes, sir."

With her attorney's agreement and encouragement, she signed the papers presented by the state. Looking at JJ and Kristyn, the attorney asked, "Thank you for arranging a safe location and protection for my client. Are we still in agreement that she can check-in with me every day to consult on her case?"

JJ nodded. She'd been down this road with clients and their attorneys before. "Yes, we're in total agreement on that point. Unless something unforeseen comes up that would necessitate meeting in person—and I can't even imagine what that might be—your communications will be via phone or Zoom. Your choice. However, if we agree that a face-to-face meeting with Ms. Lewis is warranted, we will choose the location to ensure full operational security.

"Agreed."

"Come on, Dawn, let's get you settled. We have a lot to talk about. We may even become BFFs." JJ smirked, enjoying the opportunity to get a little jab in at this person who, in her mind, was getting off way too lightly for what she'd done.

"Will the two of you be leading the interviews with Ms. Lewis?"

Kristyn answered. "No, we're only going to be there today for some preliminary discussions. Hopefully, they'll be fruitful. Starting tomorrow the FBI will take over, and I can only assume that they're not nearly as fun and easygoing as us."

"But they do usually draw the line at torture," added JJ, getting in just one more dig. "Usually."

The attorney saw no humor in their comments; in fact, he wanted to protest but held his tongue. Better to get this over with.

Dawn Lewis just cried harder, almost to the point of gasping for air. She had to be helped to her feet and supported all the way to the SUV that would transport her and her guardian angels to the safe house.

JJ didn't feel the least bit guilty.

65

Thursday, November 20th

Brother Jacob was livid, and for the first time ever, was starting to doubt himself, his organization, and his entire vision. Word had reached him, despite the FBI's attempts to keep most information under wraps, about both Dawn Lewis' arrest and the failed mission last night to locate and terminate Senator Reese. The fact that several of his followers died in the failed raid didn't concern him in the least; there were plenty of men just like them ready to do his bidding. What concerned him the most was the fact that the FBI had lured his men into a trap, and along with the dozen or so men that were arrested, two of them were part of the Coalition leadership team. Those men knew almost everything there was to know about the inner workings of his organization, including the details behind the bombings and targeted killings that had been carried out under his direction. He needed to eliminate them, and quickly.

Even with all his many resources and informants in law enforcement and the court system, there was still no solid information on where Reese or any of the others were being held. The only thing his informants knew for certain is that the FBI and US Marshal Service had charged them and then immediately secreted them away. Whether they were all being held together or separately was unknown. Hell, almost *everything* was unknown at this point, and that fact ate at him more than anything. He was a man who prided himself on being in control of every detail, every decision, and every emotion. A recent sermon he'd delivered popped into his head, a most disconcerting thought: *Pride goeth before destruction, and a haughty spirit before a fall.* Proverbs 16:18. He tried to put that out of his mind. What the hell did a bunch of illiterate goat herders from 2,000 years ago know about the world? *Fuck them.*

He needed to regain control of the situation. Grabbing the satphone off the kitchen island, he called Honig. As much as he had grown to despise her incompetence and recent failures, his back was against the wall. When she answered, his message was straight to the point. "We need to talk. Now. Call me back when you can talk securely. I'll expect your call within five minutes." He didn't even wait for her to respond, simply hung up.

It was every bit of five minutes before she called back. "I had to excuse myself from a meeting and leave the building to find some privacy. I don't trust that all our supposedly secure and private locations at the DOJ are 100% secure and private. And I certainly can't trust the people."

"What does that say about our fine government, or about you, for that matter, since you sit atop that department? Very disappointing."

"I don't really give a shit what you find disappointing or concerning. If you hadn't let your greed and your ego get so fucking out of control, we wouldn't be in this mess."

No one had ever spoken to him like that before, and even if he had to push down his anger for the moment, he would make sure that she lived to regret her insolence. He took a deep breath before speaking, and in a voice much calmer than expected in this tense situation, he said, "What I find disappointing is that, despite our multiple conversations and my explicit instructions, you have failed to shut down the FBI investigation. That has now led to multiple arrests of people who could ruin our mission if the government convinces them to talk. And you and I both know that even though these cretinous idiots talk a tough game, they'd likely roll over on their own mothers if it short-ened their sentences."

"And I've told you more than once that I've instructed Director Ferguson to shut down this operation on multiple occasions, but he and others under his control are running a rogue, back-channel investigation. We've been working hard to track them, but they're well trained in spy craft. They've disabled their personal cell phones and are now using burners to communicate, and they're using personal subscriptions for publicly available video conferencing services. From what we've ascertained, they never use the same conference link or access codes twice, and they're changing personal email addresses every couple of days."

"So, you're no closer to shutting them down than you were when I first directed this action. Is that the bottom line?"

"Yes, that is the bottom line. Whether or not you like it, and I've reached the point where I couldn't fucking care less either way, that is the situation that we're in."

Strike two. "Then I suggest you get yourself to California *immediately* and exert your authority—the full authority of the US government—to take control of these prisoners away from the state. Once under your control, you can shut down this investigation and do whatever you want with the prisoners. Free them, kill them, I don't care. Just get it done."

"You just don't understand, you clueless bastard. There have been no federal charges placed against any of those arrested, only state charges. And I've already received back-channel notification that if we try to take over, they'll fight us every step of the way. Even if we prevail, and we probably would, it will take weeks or months before it's settled. By that time, your people would have told them everything."

Strike three. "And am I to assume that even the US Attorney for that part of California, who reports directly to you, as I understand it, isn't taking steps to get this away from the state and into your hands?"

"Are you kidding? That son of a bitch, who's such a fucking RINO he may as well be a fucking Democrat, hates me and wants to see me fail. Ever since the President picked me over him for this job he's been pissed off and looking for a way to settle the score, maybe even take my place.

"Well, then. It seems that we've hit a major bump in the road, and it's going to fall to me to figure out a way around it. I'd hoped that you might provide a solution, but apparently you have nothing further to contribute."

Honig said nothing, sensing an underlying threat in his words and the cold, almost detached delivery. She felt a bead of sweat forming on her face and a rising sense of panic.

"Be sure to take a few moments to say goodbye to your friends and family and wish them well. And make sure they understand you brought this upon yourself through your incompetence, your unchecked ambition, and your insolence. Goodbye, Ms. Attorney General."

***

Reports of her untimely death, and the baffling circumstances surrounding it, was the lead story on every news broadcast that evening. Other than her immediate family, no one shed a tear. The feigned sincerity evident in every statement on TV and social media, including from the President, members of Congress, and the DOJ, became fodder for some of the most shared and 'liked' memes in recent years.

66

Friday, November 21ˢᵗ

"Oh, it's a glorious day!" Ferguson said with a wide smile as he started the video call. "For some unknown reason, the tune *'Ding dong, the witch is dead'* keeps running through my head. Does that make me a bad person?" He could barely suppress his laughter.

Everyone on the call got a chuckle out of that. Nobody seemed to have any tears or tug-at-the-heartstrings eulogies to share about the dearly departed Honig.

"Not only does it not make you a bad person, but you should get the award for finding the most appropriate song of all time to sum up how we all felt about her. I'd say that's probably true of most Americans, too." Isaksen was never a fan. Good riddance and may she rot in hell.

"Who will replace Honig? And is he/she any better than Honig? I know that none of us wants an 'out of the frying pan, into the fire' situation." JJ's biggest fear was that the President could appoint Honig's replacement. That would be a disaster.

Ferguson answered. "There's actually a federal statute that defines the line of succession for the Attorney General in the event of their death. First in line is the Deputy Attorney General. That's a guy named Joe Hruska, and he's one of just a handful of holdovers from the last administration. Let's just say that he and Honig didn't see eye to eye on most things."

"Can't the President just fire him or demand his resignation so he can replace him with someone who will push the administration's agenda?" Kristyn knew the Attorney General was part of the Executive branch, of which the President is the leader.

"That's correct," Isaksen offered. "But we may have a couple of things working in our favor. First, the lines of succession after Joe Hruska are also long-term Associate and Assistant AGs that have served under both Democrat and Republican administrations, so there's no guarantee that any of them would toe the administration's line the way Honig did. And second, if the President tries to put his own AG in place, which he undoubtedly will, that person must be confirmed by the Senate. While it's a slam-dunk that the Senate will eventually confirm his pick, it takes time. Hopefully, by the time they'd get that process started, we'd have this case signed, sealed, and delivered."

***

The FBI interviews with the men captured during the attempted raid on Senator Reese's safe house started slowly. They housed the suspects in separate sections of the same large facility and allowed no communication between them. Agents interviewed each man separately, and they all started off brash, cocky, and tight-lipped about the organization. One key fact was immediately clear: not even one of them had any idea about The Prophet's true identity, even though they had pledged their lives and their freedom to do his bidding. When presented with evidence—incontrovertible evidence—that The Prophet was none other than Brother Jacob Bernard, every one of them flew into a rage. Though many of them claimed to be 'Christians', they were the very definition of Christian Nationalists and couldn't be living a life more diametrically opposed to the teachings of Jesus Christ if they were full-blown Satanists.

When the FBI interviewers presented further evidence proving that the bombings and attacks that they'd done at The Prophet's behest were purely for his personal financial gain rather than some high and mighty fight against the liberal/progressive establishment, they were all ready to hang him out to dry. Even those that waffled for a bit eventually came around to that way of thinking when presented with evidence that the bombing at Napa Custom Crush was nothing more than retribution after the facility caught him committing fraud on a multi-million-dollar scale and evicted him.

Now it was a matter of having enough FBI investigators to conduct so many simultaneous interviews, because the suspects were all talking. They were all more than willing to give up everything they knew about the organization, about the inner workings of the Coalition leadership team, how they communicated with The Prophet, how they moved money from Point A to Point B, and what they thought his end game was. It was on this last point that nobody had a simple answer; everyone assumed that taking it to the liberal establishment *was* the endgame.

Authorities also interviewed Reese and Lewis separately, and both shared everything they knew about the man, the mission, and his long-range plans. Any feelings of loyalty or fealty they'd had towards The Prophet were long gone. Having someone you worship try to kill you tends to cause a change of heart.

Initially, Reese tried to claim that he was being wrongly accused, and when that didn't work, he tried asserting his authority as a member of the US Senate. The FBI team quickly disabused him of that notion by showing him video of Wednesday night's attack on the decoy safe house that Brother Jacob ordered. When Reese saw how many people literally invaded the farmhouse with only one thing in mind—killing him—he realized his only chance at saving his ass was to cooperate. From that point on, he was the very personification of the cooperating witness. Still cocky, but at least cooperative.

67

❧

Friday, November 21ˢᵗ

It was Dawn Lewis who finally provided one of the most important pieces of information, if not *the* most important: the name of The Prophet's bomb maker. She confessed it was she who had done the initial search of the FBI's extensive criminal database to find someone with the skills, experience, and willingness to set aside their own personal beliefs and allegiances for the almighty dollar. After developing a list of five potential candidates, she forwarded it to Brother Jacob to make the final decision. He, in turn, reached out to a few of his many assets at the Pentagon, and they were unanimous, and effusive, in their recommendation.

Brother Jacob had found the perfect man for the job. His name was Dave Woodstra, special forces-trained demolition expert, dishonorable discharge for suspicion (never proven) of blowing up an Afghan market that killed 15 people and injured dozens more, two arrests and convictions in the US for possession of explosive materials, and another arrest for domestic violence. Aside from his less than stellar military and criminal record, every report and evaluation praised his expertise in building the perfect bomb for any situation or environment. That is, if they needed a shaped charge to take out a certain individual with minimal collateral damage, he could deliver. If they needed something with a bit more *oomph* to take out a large, hardened target—collateral damage be damned—he was the man. The fact that he still had all 10 fingers and toes was considered proof positive of his expertise with explosives.

Lewis admitted she didn't know Woodstra's current whereabouts but said that he lived just outside of Coeur d'Alene, Idaho. She had several phone numbers for him though, including one satphone number, and she provided all of that to the interview team. So far she'd been holding up her end of the immunity agreement, which pleased the FBI team. Of course, what didn't please them was the constant minimization of her direct involvement in any of the crimes, but that was a tale as old as time in the criminal world. *'I was only following orders.'*

***

"You gotta be kidding me? Coeur d'Alene, Idaho? Why's it always fucking Idaho? Is there anyone who lives there who's *not* a goddamn white supremacist?" Deputy Attorney General—now *Acting* Attorney General, a role and title that could be, probably *would* be, rescinded at any moment by the President—had prosecuted too many cases of domestic terrorism, weapons charges, destruction of government property, and murder to count, and many of them emanated from that immediate area.

Ferguson couldn't help but laugh. "Sadly, you're right. It's one of the most beautiful places in the US, right up there with Lake Tahoe if you're focusing on inland sites. I don't know how it became the *très chic* hangout for every Nazi and Nazi wannabe in the country."

"We can get a warrant for his arrest, but assuming he's even up there in the hills, you're going to need a damn army to take him down. You know the kinds of weapons they claim to have up there. Supposedly everything from heavy automatic weapons to rocket-propelled grenades, even enough explosives to take down the entire mountain. One group has even bragged online that they've acquired some shoulder-launched surface-to-air missiles that were stolen from a Belgian armory last year. If that's true, that would rule out helicopter insertion." Ferguson hoped to avoid another FBI raid; so far they'd been fortunate, but he knew their luck could run out at any moment, especially in the face of a well-equipped and determined enemy.

He continued. "If we're going to do this without it looking like the start of World War III and major casualties on both sides, we're going to have to approach this another way. Not to mention that we don't have the time to put an operation like that together; even if we did, it's a sure bet that SecDef would shut us down since he's beholden to the administration."

"So, what's your plan then? And what can the DOJ do to help?" Hruska knew he was a short timer, but he intended to do everything possible to stop this descent into fascism before being fired. Or jailed. Probably both.

Ferguson smiled. "What's that old saying? Something like, *'If the mountain won't go to Mohammed, then Mohammed must go to the mountain'*. We're going to have to get Woodstra to come to us."

68

Saturday, November 22nd

At its core, the plan was simplicity itself: lure Woodstra into a meeting, supposedly with The Prophet but in actuality a trap set by the FBI and then pump him for information. Maybe even offer him some sort of deal for information and testimony. Simple.

Yet, like most 'simple' plans, there were a million moving parts and a million ways to totally screw the pooch. As JJ and Kristyn thought through the plan with Isaksen and Roberts, they realized they had one thing in their favor: Woodstra, like all the other co-conspirators, had never heard The Prophet's actual voice. He had always used a voice filter to disguise it, so logic would dictate that they could call him and arrange a meeting without tipping their hand. Woodstra should have no reason to suspect that anyone other than The Prophet and members of the Coalition had his phone number, especially for the sat-phone he carried.

"We should re-interview the Coalition leaders and Dawn Lewis to find out if there's any kind of security protocol when talking to Brother Jacob, like any kind of password or challenge/response phrase. She should also be able to tell us what kind of voice modification app he uses so we can use the same one. I know that there are several you can just download to your mobile phone, but it's possible that he's using something a lot more sophisticated and professional sounding." JJ knew that was often the case, especially in the spy novels and movies she relished.

"Good point," added Kristyn, "and we should also get their input on where we should set up the meet and with whom. We know that Brother Jacob never meets with these people in person; he does everything through one or more cutouts. That means it's critical that we not only come up with *why* he's asking Woodstra to come to a meeting but also *where* and with *whom*."

Roberts spoke. "I think the 'why' is the easiest part: he's bringing him in to meet about a job that requires his specialized skills. The 'who' might be a little trickier; my first instinct is to use the two Coalition leaders that we already have in custody, but my biggest concern is that word of their arrests has already reached Woodstra. I know we've tried to hold that information close, but we've seen multiple times that Brother Jacob seems to have eyes and ears everywhere."

"While our Coalition guests are still being cooperative, let's see if they'll offer an opinion about whose name we should dangle as bait. There's something like a dozen members of the Coalition, so hopefully they can suggest someone that Woodstra knows and trusts that won't set off any alarms." Isaksen not only feared Woodstra seeing through the ruse and disappearing, but he also worried about what kind of booby traps he might leave behind as payback to the authorities that pursue him. It wouldn't be the first time a crazed bomber left trip wires and other assorted explosive 'surprises' for the cops that come sneaking around.

Roberts was ready for action. "Let's jump on these details ASAP. I'd like us to have everything in place to make the call to Woodstra this evening at the latest, and unless anyone has a different idea, I think we should set up the supposed meeting for tomorrow. We don't want to give him time to grow suspicious, for whatever reason. We'll keep the call and the message from The Prophet simple and to the point: be at this place, at this time, to meet with whoever to put together a major operation for this coming week. The end."

69

Sunday, November 23rd

Woodstra arrived at the airport in San Jose around 11am after a nonstop flight on Southwest Airlines from Spokane. After he picked up his Hertz rental car, he entered the address for his meeting with Andre Hitzig, a Coalition leader and, based on conversations with Dawn Lewis, one of The Prophet's most loyal and trusted lieutenants. According to the GPS, the destination was just about 26 miles and should take less than 45 minutes this time of day on a Sunday.

The FBI team had picked what appeared to be the perfect spot for the meeting, at least on paper. Anderson Lake was a popular spot, but the area they'd chosen was near the dam, currently closed for repairs, so they knew it would be empty even on a weekend. What really sold the FBI on this spot was the ease of sealing the area off once Woodstra reached the site. Coyote Road was the only road in or out, so as soon as he exited his car at the abandoned park ranger building, they would spring the trap. Their only concern was Woodstra abandoning his car and trying to get away on the many trails of the large county park surrounding the lake, but they'd taken steps to mitigate that risk, including stationing additional men on foot and ATVs around the area.

The arrest itself was almost anticlimactic. Armed agents immediately swarmed Woodstra as he stepped from his car. He offered no resistance. When the agents searched his car and its contents, they found nothing; when asked, Woodstra simply said that he never traveled with explosives or the tools of his trade, for obvious reasons.

SAC Roberts read the bomber his rights, and when asked if he'd be willing to speak with the FBI and answer some questions before consulting with an attorney, he readily agreed. That was an unexpected response, and the surprise registered on every agent's face. They all knew of Woodstra's criminal record, his prison stints, his trials, etc., so they fully expected him to lawyer-up immediately.

JJ whispered to Kristyn. "Watch. He's going to answer a few questions to whet our appetite and then demand some kind of plea deal for his continuing cooperation."

Kristyn had to smile when, barely 10 minutes later, Woodstra did exactly as JJ had predicted. He'd answered a few questions, readily admitting that he'd flown to San Jose from Idaho at what he believed was The Prophet's direction to take part in a conspiracy to destroy a federal building. He also conceded that he had built the bombs that destroyed Napa Custom Crush, Lofton Renewable Energy (*'that was one of my greatest masterpieces ever'*), and others.

It was when the questions shifted to The Prophet that Woodstra got tight-lipped. He tried the usual tact, saying that he'd be as good as dead if he talked, that he had no idea who the man was because he was just a lowly cog in a big machine, and so on. When Roberts tried pressing him, his response was direct, to the point, and obviously well-rehearsed. He asked for full immunity, drawing laughter and derisive comments from the FBI team.

JJ smiled at Woodstra. "Let's set aside the fact that we know, and you've even confirmed, that you've taken part in multiple acts of domestic terrorism that have resulted in hundreds of millions of dollars in damage and killed or injured dozens. What could you possibly offer that would be so valuable that we'd consider even partial immunity?"

Now it was Woodstra's turn to smile. "I can give you The Prophet's identity, for starters. These other lunkheads that you've been chasing and arresting have no freakin' clue who they've been working for. And trust me, it will be the biggest news story in years, probably decades. I guarantee you it will break the internet."

"Sorry to have to be the one to break it to you, Dave, but we already know who The Prophet is. We've known for a while and we're already prepared to take him down. I agree with your point, though: the story will be huge when it breaks. Probably even knock the Taylor Swift and Travis Kelce engagement off the front page."

Woodstra was dumbstruck. Nobody was supposed to know The Prophet's identity. No one. It was only because of a small technical glitch and a bit of dumb luck that he'd learned it. He hadn't been searching for it and didn't really care about it. For him, it was all about the money, and he couldn't have cared less about The Prophet's so-called 'mission'. Admittedly, he was totally shocked when he realized the leader's identity, or at least when he had enough evidence to raise his suspicions to a 90% level of confidence.

"Since we already know his identity and your big bombshell revelation—excuse the pun—is no longer so earth-shattering, why do we even want to consider any type of break for you? Personally, I wish we could add capital murder with special circumstances and death penalty eligibility, but this being California, the courts are too touchy-feely." Roberts was more of an Old Testament, eye-for-an-eye kind of agent, so the fact that California had instituted a moratorium on carrying out the death penalty since 2019 really rubbed him the wrong way.

It was obvious from the look on Woodstra's face that he was scrambling to come up with something to prove that he was still useful and relevant. "You say that you know his identity, but can you *prove* it? Enough to get an indictment? Enough to convince a jury beyond a reasonable doubt? Those are vastly different thresholds."

"Thank you for the refresher from Criminal Law 101, but we are familiar with the burden of proof. Convince us you have something worth sharing that reaches the threshold for indictment and conviction, and we might consider your request. Otherwise, I see a very bleak future for you, if you catch my drift." Roberts was not about to over-commit until he knew what he was dealing with.

"How about recordings of every call I've ever had with The Prophet, including one call where his voice modulation application failed for several minutes without him being aware? I recognized his voice almost immediately, but I'm sure you guys can take it to the next logical step and have your hotshot tech people analyze it for a match. I've also got every email he's ever sent and snapshots of every text he's ever sent."

JJ asked, "So even though he used an encrypted messaging system like Signal, you captured it before it disappeared?"

"Exactly. My momma didn't raise no fool. I'm a big believer in CYA, cover your ass. You never know when the shit's going to hit the fan and you need a bit of leverage. I'm guessing this is one of those times."

Woodstra may not be a lawyer, but he'd done a damn fine job of stating his case. Not well enough to walk away from all charges; that would never happen in this lifetime. But it was one of those rare times when it was truly a win-win.

70

Monday, November 24th

"Your bomb maker was telling the truth. We've analyzed the voice recording that you sent over and compared it to multiple recordings of Brother Jacob taken from his website and YouTube. We can show with 100% confidence that it's him, and before you even ask, it will absolutely stand up in court when the time comes." Hughes never looked forward to testifying in court and getting grilled by defense attorneys whose only goal is to call into question his character, his methods, his conclusions, and any past mistakes that are a matter of record. Fortunately, there were very, very few of those.

"What about his bank accounts and wire transfers from Brother Jacob? Any luck there? I know you've only had a few hours to dive into it." Kristyn directed this to Diane Salter but was aware she might need more time to get any answers.

"Since Mr. Woodstra opened the kimono for us regarding his bank accounts, including his offshore accounts, we've been able to track every payment he's received for each of the attacks. It looks like Brother Jacob tried to cover his tracks by using different banks to make payments at different times, but since we'd already uncovered those accounts, it was a simple matter of matching up the date and amount of payment to the attack. That goddamn Brother Jacob thinks he's slick, but with his people taking pains to cover their own asses, it's going to be his undoing."

"How about you, Ms. Vencill? Have you had any luck digging into the emails and text messages?" Isaksen was hopeful but not optimistic. While far from a tech guru, he understood enough about the challenges presented by cryptography, VPN networks, and other ways that criminals hid their communications that he hoped that texts and emails would just be icing on the cake if needed.

"Sorry, but no real breakthroughs yet. It may be helpful, if this goes to court, to show that an email was sent on a certain date and time with instructions to do 'X' and then 'X' happened shortly thereafter. If we can show that enough times, it will probably sway a jury even though the defense will argue that it's all circumstantial since we can't definitively tie the messages to Brother Jacob. Keith and I will keep working this angle though. Maybe we'll find enough instances where instructions sent via text or email correlated with some of the phone call recordings we have. Again, the defense might say circumstantial, but in my relatively limited experience, a few dozen 'circumstantials' adds up to a conviction.'"

"Can't argue with you there," responded JJ.

Isaksen shifted the conversation. "While we have all this incredible brainpower together at once, I'd like us to take some time to explore possible next steps. We know for certain The Prophet's identity, and we have enough evidence, not to mention enough people willing to testify, that I feel pretty good about getting a conviction if we go to trial. However, what we don't have is him locked up and awaiting trial. I'd love to hear your ideas about how we proceed from here."

It was Salter who kicked things off. "I think we freeze his assets, including every bank account, and squeeze the hell out of him financially. We also shut down his credit cards so he can't buy fuel for his jet or even pay the airport fees. He's nothing without access to his money."

"That's good," JJ said as she warmed to the topic, "but I think there's a step we need to take before that. We need to get him indicted to give us a legal leg to stand on to do what Diane suggested. The question becomes, do we pursue this in state or federal court? I know we shied away from federal court before because Honig was still in charge, but might we go a different route now while Hruska is calling the shots?"

"Great question, and a lot depends on how certain we feel Hruska will survive to fight another day. Part of me wants to file both state *and* federal charges. Not the same charges in both, of course, but file certain crimes in California and others under federal. We should make sure that we have at least one or two slam-dunk wins in each court system so there's no chance of anyone walking away totally free. Especially Brother Jacob." Roberts missed his calling; he would have been a rockstar federal prosecutor.

"Once we have him indicted, we should be able to reach out to the government of Belize through diplomatic channels and have him extradited. Of course, that presupposes two things," Isaksen said, still formulating his thoughts before continuing.

"One, that he'll still be in Belize when we finally get the federal indictment in hand. As far as we know, he's still there, but if he feels the walls closing in, he may head to a country without extradition. And two, that our own State Department doesn't screw us and refuse to pursue extradition. For that matter, they'll likely try to get the DOJ to quash the indictment, and if that doesn't work, they'll go crying to the President."

Kristyn spoke up. "While I agree with the plans as you guys have laid them out, I think we need to consider some 'what if' possibilities. What if we can't get a federal indictment? What if he flees to a non-extraditable country, or simply disappears?"

"I'm not clear on what you're getting at, Kristyn." Isaksen wanted to see where this was going.

"Simply, I think we need to develop a contingency plan for luring him back to the US. We need to find something that is so important, so critical to his...his mission, or his ego, his whatever, that he *has* to come back. From what we've learned, that's certainly not his wife and kids, or even one of his mistresses. It may not even be anything material, like his collection of exotic cars or his thoroughbred horses. But there's got to be something that drives him, something that he can't bear to leave behind."

"I like where you're going with that, and I think it may be a simpler plan to put into motion versus our earlier discussions about trying to recruit someone from politics or Hollywood to take his place as the purported 'savior' of America," said JJ.

"In fact," she continued, "I think we need to try your angle *before* going through official channels. If we try to go the extradition route and are unsuccessful, whether because the other country refuses to honor the extradition request or because we get cockblocked by the Secretary of State, there's no way Brother Jacob will fall for any kind of subterfuge after that."

Isaksen summed it all up with one sentence. "We need to find his Achilles' heel, and we need to do it ASAP."

71

Monday, November 24th

"Two video calls in one day? Don't you guys ever take some time off?" JJ was only half joking since it was almost 6 o'clock on the West Coast, meaning that it was 9pm for the Quantico team. She knew that they'd started their day almost 14 hours earlier.

"Trust me, JJ, I'd love to be curled up on the couch with a glass of wine, my dog, and a good Netflix movie, but I didn't think this should wait." Salter was eager to share what she'd stumbled upon, feeling like it could be just the break they needed.

Isaksen had at least had dinner since it was 8pm in Dallas. He and his wife, Valerie, had hoped for a quiet and relaxing evening at home, something that seemed to happen less and less these days. She was a rock, though, and understood the demands, and importance, of his job. If there was a break in the case, she was the first to say that it demanded his full attention.

"OK, so as you know, Vencill and Hughes have been focusing on the communications between Brother Jacob and his co-conspirators while I've been doing my usual follow-the-money forensic accounting work. The three of us got together this afternoon and reviewed the phone records again, and we noted that there was one number that Brother Jacob called weekly without fail. No specific day or time, but there was never an instance where more than 5-7 days passed between calls. No one had done a deep dive on the number earlier because, unlike every other number we ran which multiple suspects had called, Brother Jacob was the only person who ever called this one. And when we checked the location data—where the called number pinged—it was always in the same place. It never moved, at least not in the months that we checked."

"Leading you guys to conclude, I assume, that the person owning that number was never at any of the crime scenes and likely not part of the larger conspiracy." Kristyn thought that was a logical conclusion.

"Right," answered Vencill. "We, meaning Hughes and I, just assumed that it was a number to one of the key people or departments at the church, like maybe one of the assistant pastors. Like Diane said, beyond the fact that he called this mystery number weekly, it didn't raise any flags."

Hughes jumped in. "Diane came up with the idea of digging a bit deeper to see who the phone number is registered to, and rather than an individual, it's registered to an LLC. While the fact that it's registered to an LLC is not necessarily a red flag, we noticed the LLC name was very similar to one we'd seen before during this investigation."

"That's right. The phone is registered to BEW LLC, and that rung a bell," Diane explained. "The fire at Napa Custom Crush destroyed the production facilities and a lot of the wine stored there, including wine from Beckett Estate Winery. 'BEW'. You probably recall that the ownership of Beckett was buried under a shit ton of other LLCs and shell companies, but after digging through all those records, I found it was owned by Brother Jacob."

"I recall you sharing that Brother Jacob had everything he owned and controlled buried multiple layers deep to keep it hidden from the authorities," said Roberts.

"Right," Salter said, nodding her head in agreement. "But I think I've found another asset that may be an angle we can play to draw him back here. BEW LLC is based in Fredericksburg, Texas. After a bit of digging and calling around, it's clear to me that BEW LLC is just another piece of the Beckett Estate Winery empire. That actually makes total sense because there are over 400 wineries in Fredericksburg, and I'm convinced they were the source for many of the 'mislabeled' grapes that got them kicked out of Napa Custom Crush."

"Are you suggesting that we can lure him back by threatening to seize his vineyards and winery? No offense, but that sounds like a bit of a pipedream," said Isaksen.

"No, sir, not at all. What I'm suggesting is that we can lure him back by arresting his mother."

72

Monday, November 24th

They all sat in stunned silence for several moments.

"Wow," said JJ as she gathered her thoughts. "That sure as hell came out of left field! You're going to have to give us a bit more to go on, because I'm totally lost."

"OK, so it's well known that Brother Jacob's father, Reverend Ashford Bernard, was the founder of Sacred Waters Church and died in a plane crash in 2008. What's kind of been lost to history is that his mother and father divorced back in the late 90s. According to the filings I could access, Ashford accused her of abandonment. Whether or not she abandoned them, she more or less fell off the face of the earth; there were even a lot of rumors that she'd died as well. After a lot of poking around in a lot of databases, I'm certain that she's actually alive and living under a new name: Ashley Beckett."

"As in Beckett Estate Winery, I assume?" It was starting to become clear for JJ and the others.

"Exactly. She's in her mid-70s now but still alive and kicking. I've found some pictures of her from the 80s and 90s and compared them to current photos of 'Ashley Beckett' and you can tell that extensive work has been done. Bitch is damn near unrecognizable, but I'm convinced that it's the same woman."

"And Brother Jacob has apparently remained close to her all these years, even buying the land and establishing the winery in Fredericksburg as her new playground." The possibilities intrigued Roberts.

"Before we settle on arresting the mother, I think we need to dig a little deeper on one other possibility," added Kristyn.

"What? You don't think leveraging the mother will work?" asked Vencill.

"No, I think it's possible, just that there may be another layer that we need to consider. Maybe I'm just being cynical, but I wonder if there's more here than meets the eye. I just did a cursory Google search about the father, and according to the articles back in 2008, the NTSB investigation concluded that contaminated fuel caused the crash. I'm sure that's possible, but maybe there was more to it..."

"You're thinking sabotage, I assume." Isaksen didn't look convinced. "And presumably it was Brother Jacob that sabotaged his father's plane? To what end? Sacred Waters was little more than a local church back in 2008 when he took over. He may have had grand visions of what the church could become, but that would have been far from a certainty back when he stepped into the leadership role."

"Look, I could be way off base here but let me paint you a scenario and see if it at least bears digging into. We know that his mother is alive and well and acting as the matriarch of this winery. We know he calls her about once a week, and he funnels a boatload of money to Beckett Estate Winery; I'm not sure why it wouldn't be self-sustaining by now, but maybe we can look at that, too. Can I continue?"

"Yes, definitely. Go on." JJ was interested to see where Kristyn was going with this, too.

"From everything I've ever read about the father, he was a devout Southern Baptist. Totally a 'fire and brimstone' kind of guy, cut from the same cloth as Billy Graham. He was all about leading people to Jesus and being saved, and while I'm sure he wasn't the most liberal or progressive man in the world, he was reportedly a good and decent man who did his part to help those in need. Brother Jacob, on the other hand, is less Billy Graham and more Joel Osteen or Kenneth Copeland. For them, it's all about the money; religion is just the tool they exploit to get it."

Kristyn paused for a second to catch her breath before dropping the real bombshell. "A cursory internet search shows that the mother and the estate she calls home have been featured in everything from *Wine Spectator* to *Architectural Digest*, *Fortune*, and *Condé Nast*. If there's a common theme through those magazines, it's *money*. *Big money*."

"OK, but we know that Brother Jacob is funneling her money..." added Roberts.

"Right, but what if it's more than that? Maybe she's the power behind the man, or the man behind the curtain, or whatever metaphor you want to use. She's obviously as obsessed with money and possessions as her son. Maybe she helped elevate him to his current position by getting the father out of the way, and she influenced him to get on the prosperity gospel bandwagon to make millions."

"Interesting..." said Salter. "That would take one devious bitch, but it's not out of the question."

"Let me play devil's advocate for a moment," offered Isaksen. "Aside from the possibility that she's complicit in her ex-husband's death, nothing you've talked about is illegal, at least on its face. There may be some IRS implications, but beyond that, pushing her son to be a religious con man isn't something we can easily charge and prosecute."

"I don't disagree, sir, but I can imagine the possibility that it goes well beyond that. Maybe she's the one pulling the strings, the brains of the operation, if you will. Not him."

"But why? To what end?"

Kristyn was all-in at this point. "In a word, sir: *legacy*. She's getting up there in years and knows that she can't live forever, but she wants Brother Jacob to assume the 'throne', for lack of a better term, as America's savior. Maybe deep down she is religious and wants him to rid the US of the dreaded secular humanist leaders that have turned the country away from God. Or maybe she could give a shit about God and religion and just wants him at the helm of an autocratic government that bends to his will and further enriches him. I don't know the *why* with any certainty, but deep down I feel like this is a scenario we need to investigate."

JJ couldn't help but smile. *So freakin' brilliant. One of the many reasons why I love her.*

73

❦

Tuesday, November 25ᵗʰ

The FBI re-interviewed each member of the Coalition and the men arrested with them. JJ and Kristyn had another conversation with Dawn Lewis. Unless they were all lying, it quickly became apparent that since none of them had been aware of The Prophet's identity, they had even less clue about his family, if any, or his possessions and properties. None had even heard of Beckett Estate Winery in Fredericksburg, Texas.

JJ and Kristyn were getting the same answers from Dave Woodstra, or they were up until they broached the topic of the BEW property.

"You seem confused or hesitant about the BEW property. Why is that?" JJ asked him.

"You asked me if I knew about that property and if I ever traveled there, and as I think it through, the truth is a bit more complicated. I'm not certain."

"How can that be? Either you've been there, or you haven't," she pressed.

"Let me explain. There was a time shortly after I started working on behalf of The Prophet that he arranged for me to do a job for him. This time it was different. He had his men pick me up in Idaho, and we drove to the small airport in Coeur d'Alene. Once we boarded the plane, they put a black hood over my head so I couldn't see out the windows. We flew for about 3 hours, and when we landed, they drove me to the final destination. And yes, they kept the hood on me the entire time."

"And you didn't see any signage or anything to indicate that you were at Beckett Estate Winery? How long were you there?" Kristyn didn't see how it was possible to keep him from learning the location.

"I didn't see any signage at all. They didn't remove the hood until I was inside a building, which was basically a bunk building, where they kept me for 3 days except while I was working. And every time I left the bunk building, I had to wear the hood until we reached the location where I would start work that day. And when it was time to move to a new building or location on the estate, they made me put on the hood again."

"What kind of work were you doing that took three days? I'm guessing you weren't working in the vineyards or harvesting grapes. And they must have given you some kind of site plan or blueprints so you could plan your work, am I right?" JJ wasn't sure she believed him, at least not yet.

"You're right, they gave me site plans and blueprints, but they didn't have any company name or address on them. The plans just showed buildings with generic numbers or names. It was crazy, to tell you the truth. While I had no actual idea where I was, it was obviously a winery. I mean, I saw the tanks and the barrels and the production facilities; they can't hide that shit. And I've been to enough wineries in my time that I know that smell anywhere. I'm not sure why they were going to so much trouble to keep it a secret, but I played along. The Prophet was paying me enough that I didn't question his orders."

Kristyn followed up on JJ's question. "So, again, what did The Prophet have you do during the three days that you were there?"

"He had me rig explosives at several of the buildings that he could trigger remotely if needed. His orders explicitly called for the total destruction of those buildings, not just damage. I mean, I don't think he was looking for an insurance payout. I think he was setting up some sort of defensive position or escape plan in case the cops ever raided the place."

"Did any of the local workers see what you were doing and question things?" Kristyn wasn't sure how he could have pulled this off unseen.

"No, the only people I saw the entire time were my guards, or, if we're being polite, my 'escorts'. I was there on a Saturday, Sunday, and Monday, and the place was closed. Now that I think about it, it must have been a holiday...probably over Labor Day weekend, if I had to guess. I seem to recall it was late summer, but whenever it was, it felt like the depths of hell there."

JJ looked at Kristyn and said, "That would be consistent with Texas hill country, for sure."

The next step required getting the BEW site plans and blueprints from the Gillespie County, Texas, municipal government and having Woodstra mark them indicating the locations and types of explosives he'd deployed. They hoped that contacting the local government there wouldn't set off alarms for Brother Jacob. The number of assets under his control in the federal and state governments seems to be endless. Hopefully, that didn't extend all the way to the little city of Fredericksburg.

"One last thing," JJ said, an idea having just popped into her head. "Have you ever done any similar jobs on behalf of The Prophet? I mean, like wired explosives at homes or estates that you think have ties to him the way BEW does?"

Woodstra smiled. He'd hoped not to have to go down that road, but now that she'd asked him the question directly, he knew that any lies or attempts to muddy the water would jeopardize his shot at leniency. "Now that you mention it, there was a time a while back when his people transported me under similar circumstances and I ended up at a massive estate and ranch outside of Fort Worth."

"Oh, now that I mention it..." JJ was pissed.

74

Wednesday, November 26th

Woodstra cooperated and provided detailed information regarding the location of each bomb, the materials used, and the triggering mechanisms both at BEW and at Brother Jacob's estate. JJ and the team viewed it as a good news/bad news situation. The good news, such as it is, is that he'd used C4, which, under the right conditions, is stable for the long term. Woodstra had designed his explosive packages to be airtight and watertight, plus they were all placed in relatively cool indoor environments. Under those conditions, C4 should be stable almost indefinitely. The bad news, not unexpectedly, is that he used a *lot* of C4 for each bomb since The Prophet had given explicit orders to build each bomb to guarantee complete destruction, not merely damage.

As the team considered all the pros and cons of each approach to getting Brother Jacob back on US soil, they were concerned by Woodstra's admission that he had placed explosives in strategic locations around Ashley Beckett's home on the BEW property. They still had no information about her security detail, including the number of operatives, their schedule and rotation, how they were armed, and in which buildings or sectors of the estate they were deployed. There could also be any number of cameras, ground sensors, and other technology in place that could ruin their surprise entry and endanger the whole team. None of them liked the idea of a blind approach, but there didn't appear to be any other option if they wanted to take her into custody first to use as leverage against her son.

It took hours of back-and-forth discussion before they agreed on the best, or more accurately, the least bad, approach. Isaksen and Roberts committed to discussing the plan with Ferguson and Hruska by the close of business.

****

JJ and Kristyn were sitting on the patio of their Carmel rental house, enjoying the relatively mild afternoon temperatures. They'd been looking at the site plans and aerial photographs of both Brother Jacob's ranch and the BEW property, and something looked off to JJ, but she couldn't quite put her finger on it.

"Nothing about the size or building materials or architectural style seems to be the same, at least as far as I can discern. What else do you think it might be?"

JJ was quiet for a few minutes, looking back and forth between the two site plans. Then her eyes lit up. "That's it! I think I see it."

"Tell me!"

"Look at his estate. He's got the main house, then about a quarter mile in one direction is the barn and about the same distance in the other direction is a detached garage that houses his exotic car collection. His house sits at the top of a triangle, if you will. Now look at the BEW site plan. It's got almost the exact same layout between the house and two other buildings."

"OK, I see that, but why does that matter?"

"According to Dave Woodstra, he wired both houses with explosives. At Brother Jacob's estate, he also wired the barn but not the building housing his cars. Now look at BEW. Again, the house is wired to explode, as is the building housing their production facilities but not the storage building where the wine is racked," she said while pointing at the plan.

"And why do you think that is? I'm not sure I'm getting it yet."

"Look at the site plans. What do you see on both within just a few hundred yards of the buildings that aren't rigged to explode?"

Kristyn looked more closely, and then it finally hit her. She couldn't help but smile. "Damn, you're right. There's a helicopter landing pad close by in both cases. So you think their plan is to fight their way from the other buildings to these, blowing up the other buildings to slow our approach and provide cover?"

"Maybe, but I think it's even more well-planned than that. If I were Brother Jacob and had basically unlimited funds and resources, I would have taken it to a different level. In this case, *down* a level. I would have at least considered building tunnels to connect these buildings and possibly others."

"I like it. What better way to hide your escape than to blow up the building you were in while you're scurrying underground to another location. It would be hours, maybe days, before they realized you weren't in the building when it blew up. By that time, you could have made your escape."

"Exactly. Depending on the size and scope of the law enforcement raid, maybe you can escape by helicopter and make it to your private airstrip that's on the ranch property. Or maybe that's not an option, so you use a car or ATV or whatever to get up into the hills. Regardless, it's all about escaping and living to fight another day. Or living long enough to escape for good."

"How do we determine if there are tunnels on either or both properties?" Kristyn was ready to put a plan into action.

"We get Isaksen and Roberts to get authorization, including warrants if needed, to deploy drones with Ground Penetrating Radar (GPR). Assuming that the tunnels aren't too deep, the GPR should be able to see them."

75

❧

Thursday, November 27th

"No offense, gentlemen, but this isn't how I'd hoped to spend Thanksgiving Day. I was looking forward to good food, a lot of football, and a much-needed nap. I hope we can make this quick." Hruska maintained a sense of humor, at least.

Isaksen and Roberts were at first taken aback by the concerns and hesitations expressed by Director Ferguson and Acting Attorney General Hruska, so what they'd hoped would be a quick meeting to garner their leaders' approval and blessing wasn't that easy. Both SACs were grateful for the pushback, however, because it led to consideration of other ideas and approaches that everyone liked better, especially since it minimized the risk of an all-out war. The last thing the Bureau wanted or needed was another Waco or Ruby Ridge.

It was Hruska who'd come up with the idea that they eventually agreed upon, and no one could fault his logic or reasoning. First, because they believed it had a better chance of success than the original plan, and second, because they'd get the added benefit of exposing one or two additional conspirators in the DOJ.

The plan focused on getting Ashley Beckett away from BEW and seeking refuge at Brother Jacob's ranch. They knew that would be the trickiest part since there was no evidence that she'd ever traveled there since obtaining her current identity. Rather than storming BEW to arrest her in what could be a very bloody, violent, and public show, they planned to exert some external pressure on her and her son to force the move.

"Let's spend a bit of time crafting the documentation showing that we plan to arrest Ms. Beckett and charge her with whatever charges we can throw at her, whether or not real, and get it out there as soon as possible. Hopefully tomorrow. I hate to pull my people in during Thanksgiving break, but I don't think we can afford to let this slide until next week. My guess is that it will take only a few hours for it to work its way through the system enough to be leaked to Brother Jacob, even with the holiday." Hruska had confidence in the solution.

"I think we might want to take it one step further." Speaking directly to Hruska, Isaksen added, "You'd mentioned that there were likely multiple people acting as his assets throughout the DOJ. Why don't we create a few memos and charging documents but make them slightly different, like maybe an additional charge, or a different target date for the arrest, whatever. That way if we find the documents in Brother Jacob's possession or even hear reference to something that was in one document but not in the others, we can zero in on that mole and have more leverage with them when we prosecute."

"Won't he be suspicious of the differences if he acquires the documents from multiple sources?" asked Ferguson.

"We can probably mitigate that risk by showing one document as Version 1 and changing the version numbers in subsequent copies."

"I think it makes sense," agreed Hruska. "I'll have the most trusted members of my team draft them up."

* * *

Isaksen and Roberts got JJ, Kristyn, and the Quantico team together for a quick video call to update them on the current plan. They all agreed that it had a lot of positive points compared to the original, not the least of which was the probability of less bloodshed and loss of life. None of them could deny that the original plan, with its emphasis on overwhelming manpower and firepower while storming an unknown enemy stronghold, could lead to catastrophic results from both a body count and public relations perspective.

"So, let me make sure I understand how we expect this to work," Kristyn said with a slight bit of skepticism or concern in her voice. "We're counting on one or more of Brother Jacob's moles in the DOJ leaking the FBI plans to arrest his mother on multiple charges. We'll make sure those charges are serious enough to carry a sentence of life without parole, meaning she'll die in prison. And then Brother Jacob will come swooping-in like a superhero to save the day?"

"Sarcasm noted," Roberts said, "but yes, you're basically correct. We know that Brother Jacob has built his empire with her help and, putting on my Dr. Freud hat for a moment, probably to please her. We know that he's spent millions building BEW and keeping her in the lap of luxury. Since she's all the family he's got left—we don't think he gives two shits about his wife and kids beyond being props for his ministry—we think he'll do whatever he can to protect her."

JJ nodded. "True, and one other thing we shouldn't forget: we believe that the father's fatal plane crash may have been sabotage, and if that's the case, it's a near certainty that one of them was directly responsible. My money is on him, but I'd bet my last dollar that she was part of the planning and conspiracy. Knowing that she could have a charge of first-degree murder hanging over her head should set off his Oedipus alarm."

That last comment brought a chuckle from everyone on the call.

Vencill asked the obvious question. "How do you see this playing out? Is he going to rush back from Belize or wherever the hell he is now and rescue mama and rush her out of the country? And leave his empire behind?"

"No, I think he'll play it a bit cagier than that. I expect he'll move his mother to his estate ASAP, probably by air. I don't think he'll risk having someone drive almost 300 miles to get her there. Too many chances for her to get stopped along the way. He can charter a private plane or a helicopter at the Gillespie County Airport near Fredericksburg and fly directly to his ranch." JJ was familiar with the drill: air travel is faster and gives you much better odds of evading the authorities in almost every situation.

Kristyn spoke. "He has to suspect that we're going to be watching for him to fly back to the US, like monitoring the airports, his flight plans, even his passport."

"You're right, but he's prepared for at least some of those obstacles," offered Salter. "I found two other passports under different names that are tied to him and his church, and I've also found past checks and wire transfers to air charter companies like NetJets. If I had to guess, I'd say he's going to fly to some location, like maybe Mexico City, as if he's on a business trip or extending his 'vacation'. He knows we're likely tracking him, so he'll want to make sure we know he's there. Then he'll take a charter using one of his aliases from there back to the US, maybe even make it a two-hop trip on different charters, to cover his tracks."

"I don't know if you're a criminal genius or someone who's watched one too many spy movies," Roberts said with a wide smile.

"Maybe I'm both. I just know I'm way past ready for this motherfucker to be out of our lives."

76

❧

Friday, November 28ᵗʰ

Friday morning started with good news for a change. The FBI had sent a drone equipped with GPR over Brother Jacob's estate and found tunnels between several buildings, including the ones that JJ had suspected. The subterranean maze connected practically every building on the estate; fortunately, the tunnels weren't big enough to drive a car through, but they appeared to be large enough to accommodate a scooter or motorcycle. Something to keep in mind.

JJ hoped that the good start to the day was an omen that today would suck less than the others they'd lived through recently. Maybe it would even be the day they put the plan to take down Brother Jacob into action and start bringing this whole mess to an end. She and Kristyn had delivered on their promise to find out who killed Keith and Loren and helped provide Julia and their kids some measure of closure. They'd had no idea when this whole thing started that it would snowball into a conspiracy of this magnitude. They weren't naïve; they knew that having multiple neo-Nazi and white supremacist groups involved was going to make it a complex and dangerous investigation, but having it expand to include one of the wealthiest and most influential media personalities in America was not on anyone's Bingo cards.

As Kristyn walked into the room, JJ filled her in on the news about the tunnels at Brother Jacob's ranch. "Even if the tunnels aren't big enough for a car, there's got to be lights and ventilation, obviously. I wonder if there's any way to track down blueprints or construction drawings? It would be nice to find out if there's a central point where we can shut down the lights or the air to force people out."

"Good thought, but I've got one that feels even more pressing: I want to sit down with Dave Woodstra one more time, look him right in the eye, and make him convince me that those tunnels aren't also wired with explosives. He needs to have the fear of God put into him that if one single person gets hurt by hidden explosives down there after he assured us, on multiple occasions, that there aren't any, that he'll never see the light of day again."

77

Friday, November 28th

Brother Jacob's Gulfstream G700 was cruising at 43,000 feet and nearly 575mph on the way from Belize to Monterrey, Mexico. He was so nervous and keyed-up that he could barely sit still. He'd gotten up from his seat several times and paced the aisle, but nothing seemed to calm his nerves, at least not until he took an Ativan and washed it down with a glass of Blanton's. That relieved some of the anxiety and, unusual for him, a bit of claustrophobia. Luckily for him, the flight was only about two hours, and he was more than halfway there.

When he'd received backchannel notifications from two different assets, one at the DOJ and another stationed at FBI headquarters, he knew the information was legitimate and not to be ignored. Not that he would have ignored it anyway; he was not about to risk his mother being arrested. If the feds had discovered her true identity and involvement in his activities, then it was just a matter of time before they unleashed the full power of federal law enforcement. They would arrest her, parade her in front of the cameras and make her stand trial like a common criminal. He couldn't abide that. He wouldn't.

He finally settled down enough, now that the sedative and alcohol had done their magic, to check to see if his mother had made it from BEW to his ranch in Fort Worth. Since the indictment had yet to be issued and probably wouldn't be until early next week when America awakened from its turkey-day coma, he felt certain that her security team had done as ordered. They would have chartered a helicopter or small private plane from the small regional airport in Gillespie County using a credit card from one of the virtually untraceable LLCs under the BEW banner. They would also use fake names and IDs on the passenger manifest. Unless someone has eyes directly on her—and that's always a possibility when faced with the entire federal law enforcement contingent—there should be no way of tracing the steps of her disappearance.

He dialed the number for his top lieutenant, Scott Harris, whom he had put in charge of his mother's security upon her arrival in Fort Worth. Harris was Brother Jacob's closest confidant and personal security chief; he was also the one charged with overseeing and managing the security contractor for all his properties. He had instructed his mother to throw away her personal cell phone before leaving BEW; no sense in giving the feds an easy way to track her. "Scott, I assume my mother is nearby."

"Yes, sir. She's right here. Let me hand her the phone."

"Before you do..." he quickly interrupted.

"Sorry, sir, you wanted something else before you talk to Ms. Beckett?"

"Yes, something extremely critical and something that I trust you with, nobody else."

"Anything at all, sir. Just tell me what you need."

"Has my wife returned to the ranch?"

"Yes, sir. She arrived last night around 7pm."

"And are the two little fuck trophies with her, I assume?"

His harsh reference to his two children caught Harris off-guard for a moment, but maybe it shouldn't have. After all, he could never recall having seen Brother Jacob spend a single minute with either of them the way a father should. "Brett and Angela are both here as well."

"Good. Thanks for letting me know, and this stays strictly between us. Please put my mother on now, and I'll see you soon."

"Hi, son. I trust you're having a pleasant flight?" It's just like her to ignore the tension and danger and act as though everything is fine."

"Yes, Mother, and hopefully your trip was uneventful, as well?"

"It was. Though I hate to be driven out of my home and away from the winery and everything that I love by these bastards." A bit of anger broke through, which was understandable under the circumstances.

"I wish I could say it was only temporary, Mother, but I'm not sure that will be the case. The government is pursuing some fairly serious charges against you, and there's little doubt that they're using you as a steppingstone or leverage to get to me."

"Well, we'll just see how well that works out for them. They can't prosecute what they can't catch, and I trust you've put plans in place for us to travel to a country without an extradition treaty with the US?"

"Of course. I've already dropped a few breadcrumbs in a couple of countries, including Namibia, but our final destination will be the Maldives. Perfect weather, beautiful beaches, absolutely paradise."

"Sounds perfect. Just the place for an old lady to live out her last days."

He wished he could be there now to comfort her and to get their plans in motion. With his organization in shambles after the recent arrests and defections—*traitorous bastards!*—the mission would have to be put on hold. At least he still had access to his fortune and would survive to fight another day. Even with the deck stacked against him, he was still narcissistic enough to believe he could continue the fight to become the leader of the free world even while in 'exile'.

First things first. Get to his ranch and put everything in place to leave the country, possibly forever, within the next 48 hours. There were still 45 minutes left before he was scheduled to land in Monterrey, Mexico, and from there he would travel on a charter jet under another fake name, the destination Phoenix. The last leg of his long and very circuitous trip would be from Phoenix to Ardmore Municipal Airport, a small town just across the Oklahoma border from Texas and a three-hour drive to the Dallas/Fort Worth area. Even though he could fly straight into the private airstrip on his ranch, he couldn't risk there being any record or flight plan that connected him, or anyone for that matter, to his home. He was counting on the FBI thinking that he was in Monterrey or the surrounding areas in Mexico.

78

Saturday, November 29th

The conference room inside the Dallas FBI field office was jam-packed with law enforcement from federal, state, and local jurisdictions represented. It said a lot about the respect these people had for SAC Ken Isaksen as the leader of one of the largest FBI offices in America that they had shown up on a Saturday—on a holiday weekend, no less—when they had no information about the mission. Just the fact that he had called and requested their help was all that mattered. One thing they all appreciated about him was that he didn't waste time worrying about jurisdictional pissing contests, plus he was never one to 'cry wolf'. If he asked for their help, that meant something major was brewing. They couldn't have been more correct on that point.

JJ and Kristyn were in the room as well, Isaksen having requested them as part of the planning team since they could speak to the general layout of the property, the locations of the subterranean tunnels, and the specifics about the explosives deployed by Dave Woodstra. Isaksen had also requested their help in overseeing the raid from the safety of the Mobile Command Vehicle (MCV), a massive 18-wheeler equipped with its own generator, video conferencing equipment, multiple workstations, and virtually every communication and technology device and application one could imagine.

"While I wish we had a few more days to rehearse the raid, adjust plans as necessary, etc., we don't have that luxury of time. We go tonight at 2200 hours. I know that's not a lot of time to prepare, but is there anyone here who thinks they cannot have their teams and equipment ready and in place by then?" Isaksen knew it was asking a lot, but he had faith in the professionalism of the assembled teams. Plus, now that they knew who they were going after and why, they were more than eager to get a crack at taking Brother Jacob down.

"I'd hoped to have four choppers, but one is down for maintenance. I will have three MD500 choppers in the air, two from Texas DPS and the one that your office is providing, so that should suffice for oversight and exfil, if needed. We can also have a shooter onboard each," said Major Frank Tulley, the highest-ranking DPS official in the room.

SAC Roberts responded. "That should work, Major. And SAC Isaksen and I have talked and would like to request you to take full operational control of all ground and aerial assets for this operation, including the drones, if that's OK with you. We know your history in handling these kinds of large, multi-jurisdictional operations."

Tulley was shocked. Another law enforcement organization, Feds at that, asking someone else to take control? That was unheard of. One more example of why he trusted and enjoyed partnering with Isaksen and the team he'd assembled. "Thank you, sir. I'd be happy to take operational lead on the operation."

Isaksen addressed the room. "I know that everyone on this team is a professional and experienced in this kind of operation, so I probably don't need to remind you we want to maintain operational secrecy until the moment we hit the ranch. Let's coordinate our entrances and routes; the last thing we need is a traffic jam of assault vehicles going down the same country roads outside Fort Worth. We're going to give each assault team a designated point of entry and building to hit. I don't need to remind you: make your entry, clear the building, and get everyone out of there, including anyone you take into custody, as quickly as possible. Most of these buildings are wired for explosives, but we don't expect Brother Jacob or his people to take that step until they've tried to make their escape in the tunnels. Our goal is to flush them towards the building you see on your plans that sits right next to the helipad."

"'You don't *expect* Brother Jacob to take that step'? Not too reassuring, sir," one of the local Dallas PD officers said with a chuckle. While it had the effect of lightening the mood a bit, nobody could argue that he hadn't raised a valid point.

"No argument there, Officer. Unfortunately, we have no way of being 100% certain what he, or any suspect, for that matter, will do when their back is against the wall. Here, though, we're counting on the fact that he'll do everything possible to (a) protect his mother, and (b) escape to God-knows where."

Roberts jumped in. "Remember what SAC Isaksen just said; most of the buildings on the ranch, including the main house, are wired to blow. I think it would be foolish of us to expect him *not* to blow each one to kingdom come once he's clear to slow or stop our pursuit. Do not dawdle, gentlemen. Get in, clear the building, and get your asses out. Quickly."

"I wish the asshole who built these bombs was the one leading us through each of these buildings. I'd like his ass to be on the line to get us safely through." This from a member of Isaksen's local team. He was saying what they all were probably thinking.

"I can't give you that, but we may have the next best thing," said JJ. Everyone looked at her with a mixture of concern and uncertainty. She'd experienced those looks from others many times, so nothing to do but move forward.

79

⚜

Saturday, November 29th

The room immediately devolved into chaos. The uproar was not unexpected, but the volume and vitriol were more than JJ had hoped for.

"Let me make sure I heard you correctly," a tall, muscular Texas trooper said with his voice barely below a shout. "You're telling us that the man who built these bombs, the same man responsible for nearly a dozen recent bombings at the behest of Brother Jacob, not to mention the large number of people killed and injured, is actually taking part in this operation?"

JJ understood their concern, even their anger, but she wasn't about to back down. She stood up straight and looked the man directly in the eye. "Yes, that is exactly what I'm telling you. He will not be here on site, but he will be connected to us via video conference and will help guide and protect the teams on the ground as they move from building to building. Nobody knows more about the layout of this ranch and the location, blast radius, and safeguards of these explosives than Woodstra, and he knows that it's in his best interest to work with us."

"And you trust this murdering son of a bitch not to drop the hammer on us? Am I the only one who has some concerns about this guy looking for a little retribution against law enforcement since his ass is sitting in jail right now and facing a long prison sentence?" This from a local Dallas PD SWAT team member.

Isaksen jumped in, not that JJ needed defending, but to assuage everyone's concerns quickly and get them focused on the big picture. "So far, Mr. Woodstra has been extremely cooperative, and we've promised him substantial leniency for his continued cooperation. He knows that without a deal he would likely die in ADX Florence," referring to the supermax prison in Florence, Colorado.

"And," Kristyn interrupted, "don't forget that we requested *his* help for this operation, *not* the other way around. If he'd asked to take part, we may have gotten suspicious, but we made him this offer less than 18 hours ago. And before anyone asks, *yes*, we sweetened his deal in exchange for his help tonight, but with the proviso that if even one member of this team gets hurt because of his actions, the entire deal is off the table. Not just the new sweetened parts; the entire deal."

"You said that Woodstra won't be on site for the operation. Where will he be?" asked FBI Special Agent Douglas Stephens. "And who will be guarding him to make sure we can shut him down in real time if he double-crosses us?"

Isaksen answered the question from his agent. "He's being held at a secure location in California and has a revolving contingent of nearly a dozen guards providing protection from loyalists to Brother Jacob. Assistant SAC Hurd from SAC Robert's field office is in charge of security and overseeing the interrogation of all prisoners, including Woodstra. JJ will communicate with him from the MCV; all communications from Woodstra are filtered through her. I don't want him, or anyone outside of this command, to be in your ears and in your head. All orders are from me, SAC Roberts, Major Tulley, or Ms. Jansen. Is that clear?"

Everyone nodded. It was still a while before the complaints, concerns, and gripes settled down, but the team reluctantly accepted it. Isaksen and Roberts probably could have shut down the conversation sooner, but they wanted to give everyone a chance to be heard, to feel like a valued member of the team and not just a warm body holding a weapon.

80

Saturday, November 29th

As 10pm approached, JJ was feeling increasingly anxious. Her palms were sweaty, her breathing and heart rate much too rapid. She'd been involved in similar operations before, so she wasn't sure why she was feeling more anxiety than usual. Maybe it was because they were going in partially blind, having had no time to penetrate the ranch and discover what they might face in the way of electronic security. Woodstra had said there were some cameras, which is to be expected, but he didn't know how many or where they were all located. He didn't know if there were ground sensors to pick up their approach, thermal imaging that could 'see' their body heat, roving guards, or even worse: dogs.

The one aspect of the operation they felt confident about was their control of the airspace. Between their helicopters, drones, and the plan to secure the ranch's helipad and airstrip, there was no way that Brother Jacob was flying out of there. That didn't mean he didn't have other plans in place for eluding them; no question that he had the home-field advantage. They'd discussed the possibility of an escape attempt via motorcycles, ATVs, or even horses. Perhaps there's an SUV concealed somewhere on the property that's capable of navigating through the rough terrain. All he has to do is reach it. The question of how much of a hindrance Ashley Beckett will be to his escape—a 70-something year old woman is likely to be a liability in that regard—was a consideration.

Isaksen had his own concerns. "I don't like the fact that our primary target, the residence, is nearly a quarter mile from the entry point. When we breach the gate, it will take us a good 30 seconds to get to the house, probably another 15-30 seconds to be in position to breach the front and back doors. I don't enjoy giving them that much time to prepare for our assault or make it to the tunnels. Or open fire on us."

Major Tulley spoke up. "Maybe let's call an audible. Let our birds fly your assault teams in, one to the front door and one to the back, at the same time you crash the gates. We'll already be moving towards the house at 100 knots when you hit the gates. Your teams will be on the ground and ready to breach in a fraction of the time."

The rest of the command team in the MCV nodded in agreement. "Sounds like a much better approach to me," admitted Roberts. "I'm a little pissed that I didn't think of it earlier."

Tulley took the lead in notifying the chopper pilots and the designated breach team. Looking back at the others in the command post, he simply said, "Change of plan communicated and salutes all around. They're making the necessary adjustments now to make sure everyone is in place and ready to go at 2200. T-minus 10 minutes."

Ten minutes felt like an eternity. Kristyn could see the tension in JJ's face and movements and was growing concerned. Rolling her chair closer to her, she whispered, "Are you okay? You look like you're ready to either burst into tears or throw that workstation through the wall. Maybe both. What's wrong?"

JJ dabbed at her eyes, the tears flowing uncharacteristically for her. "I'm just scared that we're putting these teams seriously in harm's way. I know they're tough and experienced and willing to put their asses on the line, but if anything happens to them because we've put too much trust in Woodstra, I'll never forgive myself."

"I get it, but I don't know what more we could have done to get assurances about his truthfulness and cooperation. You would think that life in prison, in a supermax prison at that, would be enough to make anyone cooperative."

"Let's hope so. If I hear anything that raises a red flag once this op starts, we need to pull the plug. Or at least pull everybody back and regroup."

JJ looked at the clock. It was now down to T-minus four minutes.

81

Saturday, November 29th

JJ slipped the headset back on and adjusted it. She looked at the video conference screen and saw Woodstra seated at the dining room table of the safe house where he'd been held since his arrest. He was one of nine people and locations visible on the video screen, which was arranged in a 'Hollywood Squares' configuration. "Woodstra, are you ready for this?"

"I am. Just do what I tell you when I tell you to do it, and stay clear of the locations we talked about, and everything will be okay."

"Do you expect we'll take heavy fire when we breach?"

"Honestly, I don't know. That's one of the big, scary question marks. I know that Brother Jacobs has security, but I think it's less than a dozen guys at any given time. They don't walk around kitted out like they're ready for war, but they carry sidearms. I can't say what kinds of weapons they may have stashed in the house and other buildings around the property, but based on his virtually unlimited money and resources, I would expect some heavy shit."

"You think his security team is prepared to shoot it out with the feds for him, or maybe even willing to die for him? You know how crazy a bunch of cult-following zealots can be."

"That's true, but after spending a few days there, it's my opinion that his security team is a bunch of highly trained, highly compensated, and highly professional operators. They have a great reputation in the personal and corporate security industry, so I'd say there's almost zero chance they've been involved in his activities. Most likely, they aren't even aware that he's anything more than what he appears to be to the public: a media star that uses Jesus as a prop."

Tulley spoke. We're at T-minus one minute: Choppers 1 and 2, you're cleared to begin your approach. Drone operators 1, 2, 3, and 4, you're cleared to move to your assigned sectors; I want to see your camera feeds on monitor one. Ground assault teams, we breach the front and rear gates on my count. Body cameras active, no exceptions. Standby."

"Chopper 1 approaching, front entrance of house in sight."

"Chopper 2 approaching, rear entrance of house in sight."

Tulley was calm, the consummate professional. He checked all monitors one last time to make sure there were no last-minute gotchas before the assault. "Commencing countdown. Ten... Nine... Eight..."

JJ felt the growing tension, her stomach in knots.

"Seven... Six... Five... Four..."

Kristyn's eyes were closed, her lips moving in silent prayer.

"Three... Two... One..."

"Breach, breach, breach!"

82

Saturday, November 29th

Small explosive charges blew the front gate entirely off its hinges, and multiple assault vehicles rushed through. A similar scene played out at the rear property gate, with those vehicles rushing to secure the areas and buildings adjacent to the helipad and airstrip. The two helicopters were landing on each side of the house within seconds, the assault teams rushing to their assigned spots and the choppers lifting off to focus on the next part of their mission. Their spotlights lit up the area.

As JJ watched it unfold on the video monitors, it brought to mind scenes from the movie '*Apocalypse Now*' except, thankfully, she wasn't hearing a lot of gunfire and explosions. It was almost like watching the movie and seeing it scroll across the screen but with the sound muted.

The breach teams at the front and back doors of the main house used heavy two-man battering rams weighing nearly 60 pounds to crash through the heavy oak doors, and even with that it took several strikes before the doors gave way. As they entered and spread out to clear each room, they were shocked, but thankful, not to be taking fire.

"Command, this is Team One Leader. We have three bodies down in the kitchen. Adult female, two children. One male and one female. All deceased."

"Acknowledged. Assign two agents to remove those bodies ASAP. The medical team will meet you outside."

"You don't want the medical team or coroner's team to go in and retrieve them? Let the assault teams keep focusing on clearing the house?" Reasonable questions from the Dallas PD commander.

Tulley responded. "Normally, yes, but I don't want to put anyone else at risk, just in case. Just because our team hasn't taken any fire yet doesn't mean they're not going to."

"Woodstra, how long will it take Brother Jacob to get to the tunnels? Any way for us to intercept him before he gets there?" Isaksen was on his game but was definitely feeling the tension.

"It depends on where he and his mother are in the house when we breached, assuming they're in the house at all rather than one of the other outbuildings. But assuming they're on the first floor, like the kitchen or main living area, they could probably reach the tunnels in 60-90 seconds if she doesn't slow them down too much. If they're on the top floor, add another minute. There are two different stairwells down to the basement, one near the kitchen and one at the other end of the house. It's anyone's guess which one they'll use."

"Will he be armed?" asked Kristyn.

"He's not normally armed, in my experience, but in this situation I would expect him to be."

"Command, this is Team Two Leader. We just entered a room and were hailed by the leader of his security detail. He and three other men are in the study and have placed their weapons on a table and voluntarily gotten down on the floor with their hands behind their heads. They do not appear to be a threat. I repeat: not a threat. We informed them we will secure them for our mutual safety and will remove them from the house, and they have agreed and are being cooperative."

Roberts shook his head. "That's not something you see every day, but thank the Lord for it. Major Tulley, I'll be happy to proceed to the house and take control of those gentlemen for now, see if they have any information that may be helpful."

"Agreed," said Tulley in response. "Team Leaders One and Two, expect SAC Roberts to approach the house to speak with the security detail. He'll meet your men outside."

"Affirmative," came the reply.

"Still no sign of the suspects? Have you made your way to the basement yet?" Tulley worried about an ambush and signaled one of the drone operators to do a flyover of the house with the infrared cameras active to see if they could spot anyone.

"No sign yet, sir. We're just reaching the basement now. Luckily, we've not encountered any resistance, but we still used caution in case there were booby traps."

As the assault team entered the basement, shots rang out, sending them scurrying for cover. There were two shooters, each firing a semi-automatic pistol. Better than large automatic weapons, but bullets from a 9mm flying around in tight quarters can still ruin your day.

"Command, we're taking fire. Two shooters. Preparing to engage."

Before they could raise their weapons, they heard the clang of a heavy metal door shutting and what sounded like a heavy seal lock, similar to a ship's watertight door, being spun in place.

"Command, shooters have made it into the tunnel system. Door is locked and sealed in place."

"JJ, get your people out of the house. Now!" screamed Woodstra.

83

Saturday, November 29ᵗʰ

"Mother, the barbarians are at the gate, as they say. We're under attack. We have to hurry. Let's grab your bag and head straight to the basement." The sound of the helicopters, the assault vehicles, and dozens of men yelling as they approached was clear even with the house's thick walls and well-insulated windows. He regretted now not having opted for bulletproof windows. Too late for such regrets.

"Bastards. They'll rue the day that they set their sights on us, that I can promise you."

"We'll talk about that later, Mother. For now, we need to get the hell out of here and into the tunnels. Once we get there, we'll have several options for escape depending on what our enemies are throwing at us."

"Brother Jacob, we need to take the stairs on the east side of the house to reach the basement. We have assault teams approaching from the front and rear of the house." Harris grabbed Ashley Beckett's duffel bag and started leading them away from danger.

"Scott, can we count on the security team to engage with the assault teams to slow them down and give us more time to escape?"

"I wouldn't count on it, sir. Shooting it out with the FBI and God knows who else is beyond the scope of their engagement, especially if the authorities have valid search and/or arrest warrants. Which I'm sure they do if they're conducting a raid of this magnitude."

"Has my family been removed from the equation?" He directed the question to Scott, not being nearly as coy and cryptic as he believed.

"Yes, as you instructed. The assault teams will find them in short order, which should slow them down for a moment or two as they reach out to their onsite commanders to decide how to handle it."

"Excellent."

As the three of them reached the basement, Harris moved directly to the tunnel entrance and pulled the heavy door open. Made of steel and nearly three inches thick, it required some effort. Once opened, he hit the light switch inside the tunnel to illuminate the way. Nearly eight feet in circumference, it was large enough to make travel via the Kawasaki KX450 dirt bikes stored there almost as easy as traveling on a paved road.

Harris heard the assault teams approaching the stairs. "Get your mother into the tunnel, and take this gun," he said as he handed him a Glock 19 semi-automatic pistol. "We just need to slow them down so we can get the door closed and sealed. No need to aim, just a few quick shots to make them take cover. By the time they can react, we'll be gone."

Seconds later, seven shots rang out, fortunately none of them coming close to the assault teams. But as Harris had predicted, enough to make them take cover and delay their approach to the tunnel entrance.

With the tunnel door now closed, Brother Jacob took a minute to plan their route. "It's about a quarter mile to where the tunnel intersects with the other branches, and when we reach that intersection we'll take the tunnel to the right that leads to the barn and helipad."

"And I assume, sir, that when we get to the control center, you'd like me to set the timer to destroy the residence and provide cover for our escape?"

"Exactly. And we don't have time to dawdle. Set the timer for a few seconds, not a few minutes."

8 4

Saturday, November 29th

"Everybody out, now!" Tulley practically yelled into the microphone. "Clear the residence now!"

The assault team didn't have to be told twice. They were aware of the explosives in the house, having been briefed on that important aspect of the raid by JJ. They wasted no time in getting all members of their teams, as well as Brother Jacob's security contractors, out safely. Fortunately, the bodies of Karoline, Brett, and Angela Bernard had already been removed and were now in the hands of the onsite medical and coroner teams.

JJ's adrenaline was spiking to where she couldn't sit still. "Woodstra, what the fuck?"

"You've probably got less than 45-60 seconds before Brother Jacob blows that house to hell and back. When he hits the first tunnel intersection, there's a small communications and network center where he can activate any of the explosives anywhere on the property. You can bet your ass that he's going to set off the C4 packages spread around the house. You won't be able to recover anything bigger than a splinter when it's done."

"And you're just telling us about this secondary location where he can set off these explosives *now*?"

"Whoops."

"Whoops, my ass! I ought to have them throw your ass in jail right now, you son of a bitch."

"Well, you can, but I wouldn't advise that." Seeing that JJ was practically crawling through the video screen to get to him, he smirked and continued. "I'm telling you now because I don't want to see any of your people get killed or injured. If I wanted retribution against law enforcement, there wouldn't be enough left of your team to even identify the bodies once that house goes up. I'm trying to protect you."

"How magnanimous of you, but that still doesn't explain why I shouldn't have them drag your ass out of there right now."

"I think that will become clear shortly, my dear. But let's take a moment and appreciate the beautiful sight you're about to see."

Moments later, almost exactly as Woodstra had predicted, the house exploded in a fireball that could be seen for miles. Debris spread hundreds of yards in every direction, and homes several miles away felt the shockwave. A few homes within half a mile even had some windows shattered from the force of the explosion.

Inside the MCV, the explosion hit almost like an earthquake, even though it was parked a considerable distance away. As JJ looked at the live feed on the monitor, she realized that Woodstra's words about the level of destruction were eerily prescient. It looked almost as if a house had never existed on the site.

After confirming that everyone was safe and accounted for, the leadership team was back at it. Kristyn had been looking over the pictures that the GPR drone had taken and compared them to the ranch's site plans. She had drawn the tunnels on the original site plan to be a visual aid in understanding where things connected and eventually ended.

Kristyn addressed the larger group. "They've reached this intersection, which is about a quarter mile from the house, or what's left of it. The tunnel they were in branches off in three directions, as you can see here," pointing to the site plan. While we can't be 100% certain which branch they'll take, we've always assumed that their first choice would be to head towards the barn because it's closest to the helipad. And we assumed the second choice was the building where he houses his exotic car collection. I don't think he'll try to cram three people into a McLaren or Bugatti to make his escape, but it's not inconceivable that he could have a large SUV or truck capable of going offroad."

Isaksen thought through what she'd said. "The helipad isn't really doing him any good. He's got to know that we control the skies at this point, so there's no way he's getting out via chopper or his private airstrip."

"I guess he could have some other vehicle stashed at the barn that he could use to escape, but it's basically the same challenge as he has from the car garage, just on the other side of the ranch." JJ was studying the site plan and the maps of the surrounding areas beyond the thousands of acres he owned.

"I wonder...is it possible that we're not seeing all the tunnels?" Kristyn had that look that she gets when she's thinking out loud. Anyone who's worked with her knows it's better to let her go with it.

"Why wouldn't we see them all?" Isaksen was confused. "We used the same GPR-equipped drone for the entire survey, and we had it make multiple passes."

"True," Kristyn said almost like she was half-listening, "but it's my understanding that GPR penetrates to different depths depending on things like soil material, density, ambient temperature and water content, and more. What if Brother Jacob has some tunnels dug to different depths or that traverse some other materials that are keeping them hidden? Maybe they don't end up in one of his many buildings like the others; maybe they end in the middle of a field, or somewhere beyond his property line? Maybe he just opens the door and walks away without a trace."

85

❦

Saturday, November 29th

Woodstra smiled ear to ear and slowly started clapping. "Bravo, Kristyn, bravo. Absolutely brilliant!" Everybody on the video call looked at him, wondering if another shoe was about to drop.

"Care to expound on that?" asked JJ.

"Kristyn is absolutely correct, and for the very reasons she speculated. For every tunnel heading to one of the main buildings that you've identified, each has at least a single sub-branch that goes off in whatever direction. I was told that some of them are simply dead ends and nothing more than diversions or false flags should anyone ever pursue them. Others run a mile or two and then a ladder leads to a heavily secured door—camouflaged, as you'd expect—out in the woods, or in the middle of a hayfield. Think of it as a 'belt and suspenders' kind of security in case their primary exfil locations are compromised or inaccessible."

"Once again, I have to ask, what the actual fuck? Why are we just hearing about this now? You realize we can have your ass thrown in ADX Florence at this point."

"There was absolutely no reason to delve into the many what-ifs regarding the tunnels. It was totally reasonable to expect him to head either for the helipad or the exotic car garage. I didn't want to confuse you with too many variables." His smirk made her want to reach through the screen and choke the life out of him.

No one in the MCV or on the video call was the least bit amused. Isaksen, usually the one most likely to stay under control, was so red in the face with anger that JJ feared he was having a stroke or heart attack.

Isaksen tried to keep his voice calm and under control, a monumental task at the moment. "As if we didn't already have a considerable challenge in closing out this operation without unnecessary bloodshed, now we have to contend with considerably more routes for them to use for their escape. What were relatively few tunnels has now grown damn near exponentially, and we have no way of knowing which tunnel they're in and where they might be heading."

"Well, I wouldn't necessarily say that..." Woodstra said. All eyes turned to him.

"I'm going to kill him. I swear I'm going to fucking kill him," JJ said under her breath, though barely. Most people on the call could tell by the look on her face that she wasn't offering prayers or platitudes.

"Enlighten us, please," said Isaksen, once again barely under control.

"When Brother Jacob hired me to create the explosives plan for the ranch, I took it upon myself to add a few extras that I thought might prove useful somewhere down the road. Maybe not for him, but possibly for me or for someone aligned against him."

"So much for honor among thieves," said Kristyn with a scowl.

"Quite true. But I never liked Brother Jacob, and I sure as hell never trusted him. I was more than happy to take his money, and he was quite generous, admittedly, but I always covered my ass. I do that with all my clients, but especially with him. He's basically a snake oil salesman, at best."

"Back to enlightening us, if you please. Time is wasting." Isaksen was growing impatient and considering JJ's threat to have his ass thrown straight into jail.

"I installed passive listening devices throughout the tunnels, so it's a simple matter of accessing them and identifying exactly where they are. If you like, I can do that from right here and have them pinpointed in seconds."

JJ muted the microphone as Woodstra worked at his PC nearly 1,000 miles away. "This son of a bitch has played us from the beginning. If it were up to me, I'd cancel his entire immunity agreement and have him rot in prison."

"I don't disagree, JJ. I plan to have that very conversation with the California Attorney General the second this is over."

86

Saturday, November 29th

"Mother, how are you holding up? I know riding on the back of this motorcycle isn't exactly the travel you're used to."

"My back may never be the same, but if this hellish mode of travel gets us away from here safely, all will eventually be forgiven."

"Scott, I've been thinking. Back at the house, I heard at least three helicopters and saw at least one drone; I'm guessing they may have brought even more. That rules out being able to get a chopper here to pick us up, and not just at the helipad. Anywhere. I think our best bet is to take a different tunnel that leads to one of the stashed SUVs, then we'll try to put some distance between us and Fort Worth."

"And then have the jet you left down in Mexico pick us up there and head out of the country?"

"Actually, we'll probably need to charter using our fake passports until we get clear of the US, then we'll pick up the jet down in Monterrey."

"The most direct tunnel is the one that leads west for about a half mile and exits near the outbuilding where we keep the hay baler. There's an old Ford Explorer stored there that should work to get us out of there. It's not as new and plush as the Suburbans we're used to, but it runs. That's all that matters." Scott didn't mind the less-than-glamorous transportation. Survival was the name of the game.

Brother Jacob nodded. Let's head in that direction then. You lead the way, and let's keep it slow so it's not any harder on Mother than it has to be."

***

"Got 'em." Woodstra smiled, proud as a peacock. Based on the look on everyone else's faces, he was the only one impressed. The rest were beyond pissed at this point.

"Show us on the plans," directed Isaksen.

"They're in this tunnel right here," he said, highlighting the tunnel that he could hear audibly but had not been visible to the GPR. "It runs west for maybe half a mile and comes up here," he said as he pointed to the outbuilding that was seemingly in the middle of nowhere.

"If they make it there, do they have access to any kind of vehicle, or will they have to be on foot? There doesn't appear to be much around there for miles. That's some rough terrain for anyone to traverse in the dark, much less his 70-something year old mother." JJ's mind was going a mile a minute, practically stream of consciousness, but she was trying hard to control it.

"I suspect they might have vehicles stashed there and at other spots around the ranch, but I can't say for certain. What I will say is that he's not stupid; I don't think he'd head for an exit that didn't have access to some type of transportation. Especially with his mother in tow. He's not planning on walking his way to freedom." Woodstra was right, of course, but nobody appreciated his condescending tone.

"How long until they reach the end of the tunnel? Do we have enough time to get a team there to greet them when they emerge?" Isaksen was trying hard to control his fury as he asked.

Woodstra looked at his computer again. "They're moving slowly, barely faster than walking speed. I would guess 5-7 minutes before they reach the end."

"Major Tulley, can you transport Assault Teams 1 and 2 to these coordinates and be ready to apprehend them when they emerge from the tunnel?"

"Absolutely, let me get them moving."

Woodstra interrupted. "Actually, Major, I have a better idea." With that, he entered a quick command sequence into his computer, and less than three seconds later everyone was shocked to hear the sounds of a distant explosion as it came through the speakers that Woodstra had been monitoring.

The drone flying over that part of the ranch caught the moment of the explosion as the whole ground seemed to erupt like a giant worm reaching for the surface. Flames and debris flew high into the air along a path that stretched nearly a quarter mile. The wooden outbuilding that housed farm machinery was obliterated as well.

Everyone in the MCV, and everyone on the call, sat in silence, staring at their monitors. Everyone except Dave Woodstra. He had a smile from ear to ear, and as he leaned back in his chair, he slowly clapped his hands, applauding himself.

"Goodbye, all," he said as he blew them a kiss before disconnecting his remote end.

87

Saturday, November 29*th*

Roberts came rushing through the door of the MCV, totally out of breath after running all the way from the primary residence—or what was left of it—back to the offsite staging area where the large trailer sat. "What the hell was that explosion? It nearly knocked us off our feet from a quarter mile away!"

Isaksen was seething. "Woodstra double-crossed us. He detonated explosives remotely and blew the tunnel that Brother Jacob, his mother, and his bodyguard were using to escape."

Now Roberts looked as confused as everyone else. "I don't get it. We gave him the deal of a lifetime — signed, sealed, and delivered. Now he just walks away knowing that he'll get life in prison? In a supermax?"

"What the hell happened to our connection with the safe house in California? Why isn't Woodstra still on here?" screamed Tulley.

"He dropped the video conferencing connection from his end. There's nothing we can do to get him back; we need someone in that room to reestablish the link," Kristyn explained.

Isaksen addressed Roberts. "Isn't Assistant SAC Hurd overseeing Woodstra's security? Call her and tell her to get his ass back in that chair and in front of that screen right this minute! If she has to get the guards to drag him there by the goddamn throat and cuff him to the chair, I don't care. Just do it!" He rarely raised his voice, much less uttered any curse words, so to hear him do both was a sure sign of the rage he was experiencing.

It had been almost 10 minutes since the explosion, and it was still pandemonium on the ranch. Fire and rescue teams had swarmed towards the site of the explosion. Fortunately, they had not come upon any other injuries or fatalities, but the fire department was struggling to get the flames under control.

JJ turned to Kristyn and spoke to her privately. "What a complete and utter clusterfuck this turned out to be. Six dead, including two children, and a scene that looks like it's right out of a Hollywood disaster movie."

Kristyn nodded in agreement. "The only saving grace is that there were no injuries or fatalities from our teams. After seeing the carnage here, that's a miracle."

Roberts loudly announced that Hurd was rejoining the video conference now, and seconds later she appeared on the screen. To say that she looked pale and completely shellshocked would be an understatement.

"Where's Woodstra?" demanded Isaksen. "I want his ass in that seat right this minute, and if he resists, have your men do whatever it takes to get him compliant. Anything."

Hurd hesitated for a moment, trying to figure out how to explain the seemingly unexplainable. She took a deep breath to relax, but it didn't help. "He's gone, sir."

Everyone in the MCV and on the video bridge practically exploded all at once.

"What the fuck does that mean, 'he's gone?'" Roberts practically screamed at his second in command. "How the hell could he have escaped?"

"He didn't escape, sir. He was taken away by agents with CIA and DHS credentials, and they were backed by almost a dozen heavily armed men that had to be CIA black ops. They all looked like former SEALs or Delta operators."

Isaksen was apoplectic. "Under whose authority are they able to bust in there and take our prisoner, a prisoner with state charges against him, and spirit him away? I'm going to reach out to Director Ferguson and Acting Attorney General Hruska right now and get this fixed. Heads are going to roll when I find out who's behind this."

"Sir, before you make that call, I can tell you under whose authority this was done." She held up the paperwork the government agents had presented. "It was signed by Acting Attorney General Joseph Foster and initialed by the President. And before you ask, when I asked the agents who the hell this Joseph Foster is, I was informed that the President had just appointed him to the position via Executive Order and had fired Hruska and Director Ferguson and had them both taken into custody."

Hurd continued. "I also have a signed document from the White House, with the President's signature, showing that he has granted Woodstra a full and unconditional pardon for all crimes, even for crimes for which he has yet to be charged."

They were all shocked, totally unable to grasp how something like this could transpire. Arresting Hruska and Ferguson? Granting a mass murderer like Woodstra a presidential pardon and an escort from CIA and DHS contractors? Seeing their three suspects, including the man that had led a violent insurrection and murderous bombing campaign, killed by the bomber's duplicity rather than arresting them and seeing them stand trial, and then rewarding the bomber with a get out of jail free card? What the hell is happening?

The arguing, recriminations, threats and speculation went on for another few hours. It only ended when everyone was too exhausted, too emotionally drained, to continue.

Isaksen looked at the clock, seeing that it was nearly 2am. "I don't know what's left to say, to be honest. Despite this latest shot to the heart from forces beyond our control, you all did great work here tonight. Don't forget that. Any time we can leave an op of this magnitude and every single cop gets to go home to their families—no injuries, no casualties—it's a win. Please extend my sincere thanks and appreciation to your people for their outstanding work. Now I think it's time that I head home for the night, and I'd suggest the rest of you head back to the hotel and get some rest."

"Should we set up a time to debrief and update everyone tomorrow morning before we fly out of here? Kristyn, SAC Roberts, and I are all on the same American Airlines flight from DFW to San Jose at 3:15pm."

Major Tulley acknowledged the suggestion and said that he was available for the call.

"Alright, then. How about 10am, and I'll send out the Zoom logistics to everyone first thing in the morning. Get some rest. You've all earned it."

"Somehow this doesn't feel like the end, like things are incomplete." Kristyn expressed what they were all feeling.

Isaksen nodded. "You're not wrong, Kristyn. Things definitely feel incomplete. Unfortunately, I think it's how things *are* ending on this one." He looked around at all of them one last time, a look of shame, failure, and regret on his face. "Case closed."

Epilogue

Friday, December 12th

As much as JJ and Kristyn loved their rental home and the time they spent in Carmel, it was nice to be back at their place in Santa Monica. After connecting with their realtor, they told her to proceed full speed ahead in helping them complete the purchase. They knew that their shared wanderlust might one day rear its ugly head and make them want to consider living somewhere else, but for now this was definitely 'home' and they couldn't be happier.

They were kicking off a three-day 'girls' weekend' with their good friend Shelly Blackburn, who had taken a few days off from her job as Napa Chief of Police, to visit. They were having lunch out on the balcony overlooking the beautiful Pacific, a view that never got old. It was a gorgeous December day, the kind of day you take for granted if you're lucky enough to live in Southern California. Clear skies, 72 degrees, low humidity, and a gentle breeze wafting that luscious salt air in from the ocean. If this wasn't heaven, it was pretty damn close.

As they dined on delicious fish tacos, ceviche, poke, authentic Hawaiian side dishes, and lemonade from a nearby restaurant, JJ and Kristyn were praising the efforts of Beth Hinshaw for keeping the movie on track and on budget during their extended absence. The consensus was that Beth was a godsend. There was also a consensus that Beth would be bumped up to an executive producer role with commensurate compensation.

"Beth sent us some of the dailies and the results from the test groups she brought in to get an early glimpse of the film, and people raved about it. They love your story, your character, and how smart and resourceful you are." JJ was thrilled that things were testing so well.

"Well, that's a Hollywood version of me, not the real me," Shelly giggled. "You guys can use your moviemaking magic to make anyone look and sound good."

"Bullshit," laughed Kristyn. "You know we didn't have to build you up much for this story. If not for you, that dreaded Alyssa LaCroix might still be out there terrorizing wine country."

"That's right," added JJ. "Our hardest part was casting someone that could pull off your brains and your bravery. And while beautiful women are a dime a dozen here in Tinseltown, there are damn few that have your beauty and the brains and balls to go with it."

The three of them had spent weeks trying to nail down the right actress to play Shelly when they were first crafting the script, finally deciding on Ana de Armas. Beautiful, smart, talented, and rough and tumble enough to do almost all her own stunts. There was a huge celebration when they sent her the script, and she immediately agreed to do the picture.

"Barring any unforeseen delays, we're planning for a Memorial Day weekend release," JJ said enthusiastically. "I'm crossing my fingers that it becomes one of the biggest hits of the summer season."

"I'll toast to that," said Shelly as they all reached out to clink glasses.

***

After doing a quick cleanup of their lunch dishes, they returned to the balcony to enjoy a lazy and relaxing afternoon. All three stretched out on lounge chairs, wearing bathing suits to maintain their perpetual California glow.

It was Shelly who broke the silence. "I wanted to thank you guys again for helping me with the Napa Custom Crush case. If not for your involvement, I probably never could have tied it to the whole Brother Jacob debacle."

"We're glad you called us in, and I was excited to read that their insurance company is going after Brother Jacob's estate and Sacred Waters Church to recover the cost of rebuilding. I hope they take them for every penny they have." JJ didn't mince words.

"One thing that's never been reported—in fact, it feels like it's kind of been swept under the rug—is what happened to Dave Woodstra. Is that something you guys can tell me about or is it some kind of state secret?"

"You joke," said Kristyn, "but you're not that far off. It took some serious digging from SACs Isaksen and Roberts, at great personal risk to their careers, I should add, before they found anything. The bottom line is this: the President recruited Woodstra, whether directly or via his minions, because they'd caught wind of Brother Jacob's plan to destroy the current administration and force the President to resign."

"To what end? I don't quite follow."

JJ picked up the explanation. "Over the past few months, it had become increasingly clear to the current administration that Brother Jacob had used the funds, resources, and followers he'd amassed to create anarchy that was starting to spiral out of control. It became clear that his goal was to push the country to the brink of civil war and then claim that only he, and a return to God, could save us from the evils of secular humanism and woke culture. Simply put, he wanted to create an America that mirrored Iran, the only difference being that we would be a purely Christian nation instead of a Muslim nation. That's when they decided it was time to eliminate him before his movement gained any more momentum or followers."

"But back to your question about Woodstra," Kristyn said, "from what we understand, he was coerced, maybe even forced, to be a double-agent. He carried out his bombings on behalf of Brother Jacob, including in your backyard, but provided evidence to implicate him at the same time. Once the administration decided that Brother Jacob was becoming too much of a threat, that's when Woodstra moved from double-agent to executioner."

"Sick..." Shelly said with a disgusted look on her face.

"My God, is this even still America?" Had she heard this from any other source, Shelly wouldn't have believed it.

"We wonder the same thing some days," said JJ. "Actually, most days."

"And do we know what became of Woodstra?"

"Let me put it like this," JJ answered somewhat sheepishly. "And you can't repeat this to anyone. *Ever.* This is the sort of thing that could land you in hot water in the current environment. Maybe even disappeared."

Shelly had to suppress a shiver when she realized JJ was not being dramatic. She was completely serious. "I got it."

"As far as the world is concerned, Dave Woodstra no longer exists. In fact, there's no longer any record of his ever having existed. No birth certificate, no high school or military records, not even his criminal convictions and prison records. The man is a ghost. I'm sure you can read between the lines. From the little we've been able to uncover from a few friendly sources, he's now part of a highly secretive paramilitary unit working on off-the-books covert ops. Ostensibly, the unit is tied to the CIA's Special Activities Center (SAD), but our sources believe that's really just a cover. They think the team is controlled by, and answers only to, the President himself."

"Holy shit..." Shelly responded, shocked and almost disbelieving.

Kristyn shook her head. "It's like you asked, Shelly, is this still America? It sure doesn't feel that way."

The afternoon grew quiet as they all looked deep inside themselves, fighting back anger, fear, and even tears. It was not the way they'd hoped to kick off the weekend celebration, but if they were honest, it more accurately captured the prevailing mood of the country. And that was perhaps the saddest part of all.

THE END

Divine Deception

Divine Deception

HUDSON